DAUGHTERS OF THE LAMP

DAUGHTERS
OF
THE LAMP

Nedda Lewers

putnam

G. P. Putnam's Sons

G. P. Putnam's Sons
An imprint of Penguin Random House LLC, New York

First published in the United States of America by G. P. Putnam's Sons,
an imprint of Penguin Random House LLC, 2024

Visit us online at PenguinRandomHouse.com.

Library of Congress Cataloging-in-Publication Data
Names: Lewers, Nedda, author.
Title: Daughters of the lamp / Nedda Lewers.
Description: New York: G. P. Putnam's Sons, 2024. | Series: Daughters of the lamp; book 1 |
Summary: Twelve-year-old Sahara prefers logic and science over magic, but when she travels
to Cairo for a family wedding, her resistance to magic fades when she discovers that she is
next in a line of women tasked with guarding Ali Baba's treasure.
Identifiers: LCCN 2023017843 (print) | LCCN 2023017844 (ebook) |
ISBN 9780593619308 (hardcover) | ISBN 9780593619315 (epub)
Subjects: CYAC: Magic—Fiction. | Family life—Fiction. | Egyptian Americans—Egypt—
Cairo—Fiction. | Fantasy. | LCGFT: Fantasy fiction. | Novels.
Classification: LCC PZ7.1.L4957 Dau 2024 (print) | LCC PZ7.1.L4957 (ebook) |
DDC [Fic]—dc23
LC record available at https://lccn.loc.gov/2023017843
LC ebook record available at https://lccn.loc.gov/2023017844

Printed in the United States of America

ISBN 9780593619308

1st Printing

LSCH

Design by Eileen Savage | Text set in Arno Pro | Hamsa image courtesy of Shutterstock

◇—○—◇

For my daughters, Lucy and Violet, and the daughters who came before: Fatma, Mahassin, and Intisar.

CONTENTS

ONE: FLIGHT

1. Pop! 3
2. Secret Preparations 14
3. Good News 21
4. Don't Forget 27
5. A Final Vow 37

TWO: NEW LANDS

6. Welcome to Egypt 47
7. Sacred Calls 54
8. It Is Time 64
9. At the Inn 71
10. A Break-in 76
11. Kitmeer 83
12. El Ghoula 91
13. The Tea 100
14. Bimbos 104
15. The Journal 111
16. The Winds of Fate 123

Three: The Wedding

17. Umm Zalabya 129
18. Crash! 135
19. Medusa's Army 141
20. Catching a Witch 150
21. The Sacrificial Apple 157
22. Beautiful Mess 160
23. All Good Here 167
24. Mustafa Fouad 175
25. Jinx 182
26. The Magical Trio 188
27. Witness 193
28. A Gift 203
29. The Spyglass 207
30. Forget the Scrunchie! 211
31. I See You 213
32. It Feels Like Love 218
33. I Knew It! 224
34. Through the Talaga 229

Four: The Chamber

35. Why Me? 241
36. Ancient Secrets 246
37. 911 255
38. The Lamp 260
39. Hope 269
40. The Amulet of the Four 276

41. Scared and Ready 282

42. The Curio 288

43. One Amazing Ride 292

44. El Borg 299

45. Good Catch 304

FIVE: HOME

46. To Cairo 317

47. Noora's Story 321

48. Wake Up 326

49. Wedding: Take Two 331

50. The Sahara 335

PART ONE
Flight

Pop!

Sahara Rashad did not bet on luck. Her money—her dollar, to be exact—was on logic. For years, she'd been outsmarted by the Balloon Dart Throw. But today, her seventh and final fair at Horace Harding Elementary, she'd defeat it. It was now or never.

Sahara's gaze flitted across the board of pastel-colored balloons. *More translucent equals more air inside and easier to pop,* she reminded herself, settling on a yellow one—three rows down, second from the end.

Closing one eye, she aimed her dart at the center of the balloon. But just as she let go—

"Sa-Sa-Sahara Ra-*shad*!" Corey walked by and pretended to sneeze her name the way he always did when their sixth-grade teacher called it for attendance. The dart flew to the right, missing the board entirely.

"Dah! You messed me up, Corey Burke." Too bad his name didn't sting with the same alienness as her own.

Her best friend, Vicky, stood beside her. She stopped

munching on her popcorn long enough to shoot Corey a scathing look that sent him and his bonehead friends snickering away.

Shake it off. Sahara picked up another dart. She still had two more chances. Throws, *not* chances. She wasn't leaving this up to chance. She peered at the board. "Okay, yellow balloon. Your seconds are numbered."

"Pretend the balloon's Corey's face," Vicky blurted.

"Kinda violent, Vic." Corey might've been the biggest jerk in all of Queens—scratch that, all of New York—but that didn't mean Sahara wanted to make his face explode. At least not right now.

On the plus side, Sahara's second dart *did* hit the balloon. It just didn't pierce it, bouncing off upon contact. Sahara pressed her finger against the tips of the remaining darts in the basket, but it was as she suspected. All of them were dull.

It was time for *Operation Pop That Sucker.*

She turned to Vicky and gave her *the* look. A twinge of guilt poked at her conscience, but Sahara prodded it back. It wasn't cheating when the game was rigged. After all, the guidance counselor had said, "Life isn't always fair, but it's our job to make it so." Underinflated balloons and dull darts weren't fair, so Sahara was *making* it so.

Vicky nodded her understanding, knocking over the basket onto the blacktop. She slapped her head at the PTA volunteer behind the booth. "Ugh. I'm such a klutz. I'm so very

sorry. My friend and I will have this mess cleaned up in a jiffy."
Vicky tended to lay it on thick, *too* thick.

"Rein it in," Sahara whispered as she bent down, pretending to help pick up the darts while sneaking a rogue one out of her backpack. Vicky had stolen it from her brother's dartboard set.

After returning the basket to the counter, Sahara yanked a scrunchie off her wrist—she never left home without the hair band, tie-dyed in galaxy colors—and pulled back her mess of dark curls. The last thing she needed was to miss because her hair had gotten in the way. She reached for the dart she'd strategically placed at the top and hurled it at the balloon. *Pop!* That noise usually made her jump. But not today. Today it was the sound of victory and the reward for a well-planned, smoothly executed scheme.

Vicky broke into her happy dance, a spirited mash-up of the moonwalk and the robot. Long brown braids bouncing, she bopped Sahara with her hip. "Winner winner—"

"Chicken dinner!" Sahara bumped her back as a bunch of kindergarteners swept past, their parents yelling for them to wait up.

Overnight, the recess field had been transformed into the annual end-of-the-year fair. Fast-food stands and snack and ice cream carts lined the entrance. Since it had been a half day, the girls feasted on corn dogs and cheese fries for lunch, then shared a bag of sweet fried zeppole for dessert.

Beyond the refreshment station loomed rides like the spinning Round-Up, which had made Vicky throw up last year—they were steering clear of it today—while game booths covered the back of the field.

This year, the PTA had hired a palm reader. Vicky insisted they visit her tent before leaving, but why would Sahara waste her time and money on all that "your secret admirer will be revealed" nonsense? It was about as plausible as a magic carpet whizzing past the brick apartment buildings towering above.

Sahara scanned the CONGRATULATIONS, SENIORS! banners hanging along the chain-link fence she'd climbed to the top of many times for secret meetings with Vicky. A feeling of loss crept in, pushing aside her balloon-popping victory. She knew how to win games *here*, but she wasn't sure she could win them in junior high. Did they even have them *there*?

"Which will it be?" The volunteer pointed to the giant stuffed animals dangling above the balloons.

Sahara's prize had been beating the fixed game. But she knew someone who'd love the ginormous penguin with the ridiculous pink feet.

With the stuffed animal in her arms, Sahara waddled to the picnic table where her friend waited for her. "For you."

Vicky's gray eyes widened. "Are you sure?"

"I am. Besides, you love penguins." While Vicky hugged the stuffed animal, Sahara grabbed two packs of M&M'S from her backpack, then shook them into their popcorn box.

The girls loved this salty-sweet combination of M&M'S corn, as they called it, and two of the individual-sized packages ensured they got more than one chocolate candy with each handful of popcorn.

"You're coming with me to camp," Vicky cooed at her new pink-footed friend, then turned to Sahara. "Are you sure you can't come too?"

Tomorrow, Vicky would be leaving for sleepaway camp. As much as Sahara would miss her friend, she wasn't sure she'd want to spend six weeks in the woods of Upstate New York. Even if she did, her father would never let her go.

Sahara shook her head. "My dad said, 'Young Egyptian girls don't spend summers in the woods away from their families.'"

They both giggled at Sahara's imitation of her father's Arabic accent.

"I have something for you too." Vicky rummaged through her backpack and pulled out a neon-green rabbit's foot key chain.

Sahara flinched at the intense color. "Wow. It's . . ." She racked her brain for the right words, but all that came to mind was *bright*.

"Awesome, right?"

She'd go with that. "*So* awesome."

"It's from that knickknack shop at the mall."

"I love it." That wasn't a lie. Sahara *did* love it. Its color might take getting used to, but her friend had taken the time to buy it for her. That's what mattered.

Vicky beamed, her smile nearly outshining the neon green. "Make a wish."

Though Sahara wasn't one for superstition, Vicky's rabbit's foot had come at the right time. She wanted something so badly she'd even wish on a silly rabbit's foot to get it. Closing her eyes, she rubbed its soft fur between her fingers and made a wish.

"Don't tell me. Merlin's again." Vicky snorted.

For years, Sahara had longed to visit Merlin's Crossing, a massive theme park in northern New Hampshire named after the famous fictional wizard. All the kids in her class had gone at least once. When they were learning about graphing, Mrs. Hoffman had made a bar graph based on the number of times they'd visited. Sahara's answer was responsible for the short bar representing "never." And if that wasn't bad enough, Corey suggested everyone wear their MERLIN'S MAGIC FIVE: MYSTERY, ADVENTURE, GALLANTRY, IMAGINATION, AND CURIOSITY pins the next day, knowing full well Sahara didn't have one. *Yet*, that is. In the past, whenever she had asked her father if they could go, he'd nod and say, "Insha Allah." "God willing" was his way of saying "Probably not." But *this* year would be different.

"I think my dad's finally gonna buy us tickets. After the *Ten Reasons the Rashad Family Should Go to Merlin's Crossing* list I gave him, he's gotta say yes."

Vicky rolled her eyes. "You included sciencey stuff, didn't you?"

"Yup." Sahara grinned.

Last Sunday, she'd spent the afternoon at the library researching and loading her list with attractions that would appeal to her engineer father. Mainly ones from the park's new Futureville Center, which President Reagan had declared open last month at the ribbon-cutting ceremony, and the long-standing Behind Merlin's Magic tour. Truthfully, there wasn't a thing on the list that didn't excite Sahara too. She'd inherited her passion for "sciencey stuff" from her dad. She was way more interested in seeing the futuristic robots and computers and meeting the engineers responsible for fabricating the "magic" at the park than taking photos with some dude dressed up as Merlin.

Sahara reached for the popcorn box. "I have a feeling this summer will be—"

"The summer of magic," Vicky interjected.

"How'd you know I was gonna say that?" she mumbled through a mouthful of M&M'S corn.

"Because you've been saying it for the last five years."

Sahara clipped the rabbit's foot to the belt loop of her jean shorts. "I know going isn't a big deal for you. You've been there three times already. But it *is* for me. I've *never* been."

From sleepaway camp to family trips to Merlin's Crossing, there were experiences Sahara yearned to have that seemed to just drop into her friend's lap.

Vicky squeezed her shoulder. "I hope you get to go. Really."

Sahara knew she meant it. It wasn't Vicky's fault their

lives were so different. As close as they were, she still viewed Victoria Miller's life as a world away from her own. Vicky had a mom, and siblings, and a name that didn't make everyone ask where she was from even though she'd been born here in Queens. Sahara didn't think her friend's life was better, just easier.

Once they'd finished their snack, the girls spent the next hour riding the Ferris wheel, the Scrambler, and the Sky Flyer. Seven years of annual fairs, and they still hadn't learned to go on the rides *before* eating. At least Vicky didn't throw up in the garbage can this time.

After a quick drink at the water fountain, Sahara scampered past the palm reader's tent, hoping Vicky wouldn't see it. But she did.

"I saved the best for last!" Vicky dragged Sahara toward the tent.

This was far from Sahara's idea of "the best," but she still let Vicky pull her in. Why not? She'd already wished on a rabbit's foot. Might as well see what the palm reader had to say, even if it was a bunch of mumbo jumbo.

Inside, Sahara's eyes expanded, adjusting to the darkness. Would it have killed the PTA to wire in some lighting? At least there were candles, though she'd never seen any with silver flames before. They had to be trick ones.

"Hello, my dears." The palm reader glided into a seat at a small round table. Between her long, billowy gown and waist-length hair, she looked like she belonged at a renaissance fair, *not* a school fair. She'd dressed for the psychic part. Sahara had to give her that.

After watching Vicky go cuckoo for Cocoa Puffs over the absurd prediction that she'd experience great fame in her future, it was Sahara's turn. She plopped into the folding chair and extended her hand. "Go for it."

The moment the reader pressed her thumb to Sahara's palm, a tingling warmth rushed from her fingers to the rest of her body. Sahara leaned back, a nervous laugh escaping her mouth. It appeared she'd underestimated Woo-Woo Rapunzel.

"Your fate line runs deep, child." The palm reader traced her finger across the line that went from Sahara's wrist to the base of her middle finger. If Sahara hadn't known better, she'd have sworn the woman's thumb was glowing and lighting up her hand along with it.

"Whoa," Vicky marveled from behind.

She was so easily fooled. Clearly, the woman had a mini-flashlight hidden up her sleeve.

"The winds of fate approach. You must turn to them."

Sahara twisted her head around. The only thing she saw was Vicky leaning in close, hanging on every word.

The reader smiled, her deep blue gaze gleaming. "Not with your eyes, my dear." She let go of Sahara's palm, then brought her hand to her chest. "But with your heart. You must trust what you cannot see."

Give me a break. What Sahara saw through her eyes—the

organs of the body's visual system . . . *duh*—was a fake. And now, thanks to Vicky, she'd wasted her last two dollars.

THE SECOND SAHARA entered her apartment, the familiar aroma of stuffed grape leaves—or wara ainab, as Amitu called them—greeted her. Inhaling the savory scent of buttery rice coupled with the freshness of dill and lemon, she followed the hissing sound of the pressure cooker into the kitchen, where her aunt beamed through a cloud of steam.

"Susu, you're home!"

"I smell grape leaves!" Sahara sang.

"Wara ainab to celebrate your last day of school and the start of summer break."

Sahara flung her arms around Amitu. Even though she referred to her father as "Dad," she'd always called her aunt Malak "Amitu." Maybe it was because there were two words for aunt in Arabic—*amitu* for an aunt on your father's side and *khaltu* for one on your mother's. Sahara had never even met her mother's sister, who lived in Egypt. But Amitu was different. She'd lived with Sahara since the day she was born. And though Amitu didn't have a husband or kids of her own, she said she didn't need them. Sahara and her father were her family.

For as long as Sahara could remember, her aunt had always made wara ainab for her last day of school. They were her second favorite thing to eat, behind pizza, which was in its own league.

"Thank you, Amitu. I can't wait for dinner!"

"You won't have to wait long. Your father will be home soon."

Sahara's eyes darted to her watch—3:30 p.m. Her father came home every weekday at six, give or take ten minutes, depending on the subway.

"Coming home early? Why?"

"Ma rafsh." Amitu shrugged. "He called five minutes ago and said he has good news to tell you."

Sahara could count on one hand the number of times her dad had left work early, and one of them included the day his boss sent him home for coming in with a fever.

What if his news wasn't *just* good news but good news for *her*? She tried to dismiss the excitement flooding her body as she rushed to her room, but it was too late.

"Merlin's!" Her list *had* worked, turning her dad's "God willing/Probably not" into "Absolutely yes, we're going to Merlin's Crossing!"

Secret Preparations

985 CE

Tonight's dinner needed to be perfect. It wasn't every day that a prince and princess came to visit. Morgana had promised her master that nothing would go wrong. She couldn't go back on her word. It was the one thing she owned outright.

As the late-afternoon sun cast a glow on the courtyard, Morgana stretched up and plucked another fig from the tree. She would share some with Cook for his lamb stew and serve the rest with the watermelon she'd bought for dessert. Mama had taught her how to select the sweetest melon at the market. "Give it a tap. The hollower the sound, the riper the fruit."

Morgana smiled at the memory of her mother's advice when a bulbul in the branches above caught her attention. "Ahlan, ya bulbul. It's a beautiful day, isn't it?" she cooed to the bird, who sang back as if to answer that it was indeed.

Just then, Ali Baba emerged from the house, dressed in his robe of honor, his graying hair neatly combed to one side. Her master only wore the gold-embroidered khil'a for special occasions. Two years ago, the emir had awarded it to him for uncovering the chamber of stolen riches.

"I've just come from the reception room." He tapped her head softly. "You have outdone yourself."

"Shokrun, my mawlay," Morgana thanked him, beaming as she bowed. Ali Baba had only gotten word a few days ago that the royal couple was on their way to Baghdad, leaving him and his servants little time to prepare. Morgana had worked hard to make sure everything in the reception room, where they would be hosting tonight's dinner, was in order.

Ali Baba's voice turned serious. "Have you remembered to give Abu Hamid the night off once he's done preparing dinner? Whatever brings Prince Ala el-Din and Princess Badr here in such a hurry demands discretion. *Our* discretion."

Morgana tightened her headscarf. "Yes, my mawlay." A question crept into her mind. The same nagging question that had kept her up last night. She thought she'd shooed it away by reminding herself it was an honor to host royalty. But here it was again, buzzing in her ear like an annoying mosquito— *why the urgent visit?*

"Do you . . . do you have any idea what they may be bringing with them?" Morgana plunked another fig in the basket by her feet.

"I've heard rumors of a jinni lamp in His Royal Highness's possession." Ali Baba grinned. "We will soon see. In the meantime, I am headed to town to run a few last-minute errands."

Morgana nodded as he walked, practically bounced, out

the arched portico. She could tell he was excited about tonight. She wouldn't let him down. Her mawlay was a good man. And she wasn't the only one who thought so. The emir had been so impressed by Ali Baba's honesty when he'd reported the stolen gold and gems he found in the thieves' chamber that he entrusted him with their guarding.

Ever since, news of her mawlay's trustworthiness had spread beyond the city. Wealthy people with fancy titles, near and far, requested his presence in their homes. He frequently returned from his travels with more riches for safekeeping in the chamber. Once, after a visit with the princes of India, he'd come back carrying a sack of *enchanted* treasures, including a carpet that could fly anywhere in the world at the fastest of speeds.

But tonight was different. The prince and princess were coming *here*. And they might be bringing a magical lamp with them!

Morgana shook her head in disbelief. Reaching for another fig, she urged herself to remain calm. She couldn't let her nerves get in the way of her work.

Shortly, the tap of footsteps came from behind.

"Deena," Morgana squealed. "What are you doing here? Your father didn't mention you'd be visiting."

"Then I shall go," Ali Baba's daughter teased, pretending to leave.

"Come back." Morgana giggled.

She started to bow, but Deena stopped her, pulling her

into a soft embrace. She'd never treated her like a servant. Sometimes, she'd even referred to her as "sister." Morgana was proud Deena had wed one of the emir's top officers, but she missed the days when her mawlay's daughter lived here.

She hugged Deena tightly, breathing in her expensive perfume. Though only fifteen, two years older than Morgana, Deena was now a lady with kohl-lined eyes and fancy silk dresses—not a child anymore like Morgana.

"Ya Allah. You look so grown-up." Morgana marveled.

"They're just clothes. And not comfortable ones at that." Deena wiggled her shoulders. Her eyes fell to the basket. "Cook's making his lamb stew, isn't he?"

There was nothing more delicious than Abu Hamid's stew. Morgana wished Deena could stay for dinner. They would have so much fun after, comparing notes about what Princess Badr wore. But the royal couple's visit was a secret, even from Ali Baba's daughter.

Just because Deena couldn't enjoy the stew tonight didn't mean she couldn't have it later. Morgana promised to save her enough to send over for lunch tomorrow.

"You always know what I need." Deena squeezed her shoulder. "Are you sure you won't come live with me?"

Morgana was supposed to join Deena in her husband's home when she married, as Mama had done when Deena's mother wed Ali Baba. But even the firmest of plans must yield to the winds of change. Last winter, a terrible fever had spread through Baghdad. Ali Baba's wife caught it first, and though the doctor warned she was contagious, Mama insisted on taking care of her. By the end of the season, both women had passed. Now with Deena married, it was just Ali Baba, Morgana, and Cook at home.

"You know your father needs me here."

"I know," Deena groaned. "I hope he knows how lucky he is to have you tending to his house."

Morgana wished she could tell Deena the *real* reason she hadn't moved in with her. It had *nothing* to do with chores. A few months ago, Ali Baba had requested she help him protect the chamber's riches. Imagine that—a thirteen-year-old servant trusted to look after such valuable treasures. She was honored that her mawlay had so much faith in her. She couldn't say no, though it meant swearing not to tell anyone, especially not Deena. If word ever got out about what they were guarding, who knew who might come after them? The last thing Morgana wanted was to put Ali Baba's daughter in danger.

"I have something for you." Deena peeked her head out of the portico and called to her new servant. A skinny girl hurried into the courtyard, handed something to Deena, then scampered back out.

"Kol sana winty tayiba. I know your birthday was a few days ago, but I didn't want to come until I could give you this." Deena held out a small box made of carved ivory.

Morgana's mind searched for the right words as she took hold of it. But all she could come up with was "How?"

She'd thought Deena was too busy being an officer's wife to remember her birthday. She should never have doubted her. "Ya Allah! It's so pretty." Morgana traced the box's chiseled patterns.

Deena broke into laughter. "The present's inside, you silly girl."

Morgana's cheeks turned red. She *was* a silly girl—a silly servant girl not used to getting fancy gifts. She unfastened the latch. A sparkling silver necklace gleamed back at her. Morgana slowly removed it, studying the round pendant hanging from its chain. An open palm facing down was engraved on it, each of the five fingers adorned with intricate scrollwork.

"The hand of Fatima. I had it made for you by the best silversmith in all of Baghdad. May it protect you from evil."

Morgana's mouth fell open. The necklace was beautiful. Deena must have traded several gold dinars for it.

"I love it. But I can't accept it. It's too much."

"I insist. You wouldn't refuse your sister, would you?"

Morgana shook her head.

"Good." Deena took the chain and clasped it around Morgana's neck.

"How ... how does it look?"

Deena stared at her and sighed. "Meant to be."

"I'll never take it off." Morgana smiled, a tear falling down her cheek. As Deena wiped it with her shawl, the late-afternoon call to prayer echoed from the nearby mosque.

"Asr already. I'd better head back before my husband returns and wonders where I've gone. He's been out hunting with the emir all day."

"And I should get the figs to Cook."

Deena kissed her cheeks, then started for home, her skinny servant trailing closely behind.

Morgana had a strong urge to run after Deena and tell her about tonight. But she had promised her mawlay she'd keep his secret. Secrets were like that. They bound you to one person, all the while distancing you from another. Morgana thumbed the pendant as Deena disappeared into the soft afternoon light, taking a part of Morgana's heart with her.

Good News

Sahara plunked down between her father and aunt at the kitchen table. She was glad Amitu had decided to set up their early dinner here and not at the black marble dining room relic, which screamed *not for everyday use*. Sahara preferred the clunky wooden table, where she didn't have to worry about spilling anything on its dark vinyl cushions or adding another scratch to its already nicked surface.

Here, she awaited the "good news" that had brought her dad home early. If she were one of the balloons from the fair, she'd have been the most inflated for sure. *Play it cool.* She picked up her fork, but it was hard to eat with her stomach doing backflips. She took a bite for Amitu's sake.

"That's it, khalas, sixth grade has ended?" Her dad sliced through a heartily stuffed grape leaf on his dish. He often asked questions he knew the answer to when making conversation.

Sahara kept it short and sweet. "Mmm-hmm." This was no time for small talk. She wanted to get to the main event.

He put down his fork, then grinned. "So, Sahara, would

you like to hear some wonderful news?" His normally steady voice vibrated with excitement.

Duh! "Uh-huh." She blew bubbles into her fruit punch.

"Your mom's brother, Omar, is getting married!" Her father clapped his hands, causing her to jump and spill some punch.

Amitu wiped it up as she gushed over the news in a free-for-all of languages. "Ya Allah! C'est magnifique! That's wonderful!"

Her aunt's over-the-top celebration made it hard for Sahara to think. "Err. It's great." There had to be a part two. Getting married was nice for her uncle, but what did it have to do with Merlin's?

"It all happened very fast," her father continued. "Your grandmother called from Egypt this morning to invite us to the wedding. It takes place next week."

He opened his mouth to speak again, but Amitu interjected with how disappointed she was that summer classes would prevent her from attending. She'd enrolled in Queens College last fall at the age of thirty-two and wasn't wasting any time getting her degree.

Sahara's dad assured her that his brother-in-law would understand, then turned back to his daughter. "I bought the tickets today. We leave tomorrow!" he announced like a game show host presenting the grand prize to the winning contestant.

Only Sahara didn't feel like the big winner. It was dawning

on her that there was no *other* part to her father's news. This *was* the good news.

"Wait, what? Tomorrow, as in the day after today?" Great, now she was the one asking the ridiculous questions. Tears burned in her eyes. She tried to hold them back, but one managed to escape.

"Susu, you're crying." Amitu moved her chair closer. "You're not happy to be going to Egypt?"

Sahara swiped her cheek with the back of her hand, willing her tears to stop. She hated crying. It made her feel out of control. And it wasn't that she didn't want to go to Egypt. She'd always wanted to see the Pyramids. "No, it's not that. It's just . . . it's just I was expecting something else."

"What *else*?" Her father's head swung back and forth between his sister and Sahara, searching for answers.

Had he forgotten the list? She'd worked so hard on it. Anger and disappointment swelled in Sahara's chest, threatening to explode. "Not this." The tears fell fiercely now.

"I don't believe it." His voice got louder. "I buy tickets to our country to surprise my daughter, and she cries. What's happening?"

Why was *he* angry? Shouldn't *she* be angry? She was the one who'd have to face Corey Burke and his "let's all wear our matching pins" crap.

"The news is still fresh. That's all, my brother." Amitu squeezed his hand. "Give her a moment to think it over."

But Sahara didn't need a moment. She narrowed her eyes at her dad and raised her voice too. "You didn't even ask me. You just went ahead and bought the tickets."

"I didn't ask because I wanted to surprise you. I thought you'd be happy!"

Sahara shoved the table and leaped out of her chair. Its legs screeched against the kitchen tiles. And just like that, she'd burst—*pop!*

"I'm *so* happy. Can't you tell?" she yelled.

"If you don't want to go, stay with Amitu!" he shouted back.

"Fine!" She bolted to her room.

"Sahara, you didn't finish eating." Her aunt's plea was the last thing Sahara heard before she slammed the door.

SAHARA THREW HERSELF onto the bed. "It's so unfair," she repeated over and over, her angry tears soaking the pillow.

Why hadn't her father asked her before buying the tickets? If he had, she wouldn't have spent the afternoon thinking she was going somewhere else. She wouldn't have wished on a silly rabbit's foot. The rabbit's foot—that's what was poking her in the stomach! Had it not been a gift from her best friend, she'd have flung it across the room. Instead, she unclipped it from her shorts and attached it to her backpack.

But not before casting a forlorn glance at an envelope taped to her closet. A GOAL WITHOUT A PLAN IS JUST A WISH, it read in bold letters, along with the logo of the retirement company that had sent it. A few years ago, she'd snagged it from her dad's junk mail pile. She'd looked at it every day since.

Why hadn't she reached her goal? She'd *had* a plan. She'd *made* the list. This wasn't like that time in second grade when her class had visited Central Park and her teacher passed around pennies to throw into some famous fountain. "Whisper your wish to the Angel of Waters. If you're lucky, it might come true," she'd said. But Sahara hadn't been lucky. She'd been foolish. Foolish to think that a wish—even one she wanted with all her heart—could bring her mother back to life.

Sahara slid down to the floor and turned to her most prized possession, an electronic robot her dad had given her for her twelfth birthday. Now *that* had been a great surprise. They'd spent hours programming Omni together so he could do awesome things like carry a soda from the kitchen to her bedroom.

She hugged the robot's dome-shaped head, eyeing the objects behind him on her desk. The motorized fan, the mini-catapult, the hydraulic car—just some of the science fair projects her father had helped her with over the years. They'd always been a team. Guilt twisted in her stomach. Today was the first time they'd ever yelled at each other.

She returned to bed, her eyes heavy. Crying stunk. Not only was it impossible to control, but it also made her super tired. She lifted the covers over her head and, before she knew it, drifted off into a dream.

In front of her stood a woman with a sheer scarf draped

over her dark hair. She smiled softly at Sahara. *How do I know you?* The woman nodded as if she could hear Sahara's thoughts and held out her hand. Sahara tried to reach out and take it but couldn't. As much as she willed her hand forward, it wouldn't budge.

"I can't, Mom!" It wasn't until Sahara had said her name aloud that she understood this was her mother.

"Not yet," her mom replied softly. "But you will."

Don't Forget

As Sahara resurfaced from beneath the covers, a faint light snuck through the window blinds. She glanced at her alarm clock—7:48 p.m.

Mom. The memory of her mother rushed back. Sahara told herself it was just a dream, even though Amitu would say it was a sign since she'd never dreamed of her before. What Sahara needed was an answer, *not* a sign. Should she go to Egypt or stay here with her aunt?

Not going might hurt her dad's feelings, and the last thing she wanted to do was upset him further. But going would mean she'd have to finally meet her mom's family. Why would her uncle want her at his wedding after the way his sister had died? She could always pretend to be sick—that had gotten her out of the last four Mother's Day school picnics.

Amitu peeked her head through the door. "You didn't finish your wara ainab." She entered, carrying a plate of reheated grape leaves.

The warm smell made Sahara's stomach grumble. She

propped herself up and took hold of the dish. Amitu sat beside her, the fabric of her dark teal galabeya tucked in between her crossed legs. She liked to wear these traditional long tunics at home.

Within minutes, Sahara had emptied her plate. Crying made her not only tired but hungry. "Thank you for making the wara ainab." Now that her anger had subsided, she couldn't believe she'd run out on dinner.

"Of course." Amitu tucked back the curls that dangled in Sahara's face. "You got your beautiful hair from your mother. In Egypt, women would iron their hair to straighten it, but Amani wasn't interested in any of that." Amitu chuckled. "She used to say to me, 'The Pyramids were built in the time you spend at the coiffeur.'"

Sahara giggled, imagining her mom teasing her aunt about all the time she spent at the hair salon. Amitu's eyes turned glassy. They always did when she talked about Sahara's mother.

"Where's Dad?" Sahara looked down at her lap. *Is he still mad at me?*

"He went for a walk. And he's not mad." Amitu had a knack for answering her unasked questions. "He just wants you to be happy."

"I know. It's just when you said he had good news, I . . . I thought it was Merlin's Crossing. I've been asking to go forever. But it doesn't matter. We're not going!"

"Seems you've also inherited your mom's temper. Your

father hasn't been back to Egypt since he moved here with your mother." Her aunt hesitated. "After your mom—Allah yarhamha—passed, he couldn't bear to go back." Amitu frequently added "God rest her soul" when referring to Sahara's mother. "It's taken an event like your uncle's wedding to get him to return. I'm sure he rushed to buy the tickets before he could change his mind."

All those times Amitu had gone to Cairo, and her father had come up with a reason they couldn't join her—he hadn't been *busy*. He'd been too *sad* to return to the place where he'd met and married her mom. A low, dark whisper sounded in Sahara's ears. *If you hadn't been born, she'd still be here.* She shook her head, trying to rid herself of its message. "I could stay here with you."

Amitu caressed her cheek. "I don't think that's a good idea. I know it's not what you'd hoped for, but it *is* good news. Your mom was very close with her brother. She'd want you to attend his wedding. It's time for your father to return to Egypt and for *you* to see it with your own eyes. It's time for your world to get bigger."

How could her world get bigger? The earth was one size. But maybe Amitu was right about the other part. She'd always said that when she arrived in New York all those years ago, she was clutching two suitcases: one filled with her belongings and the other with stories from home. Everything Sahara knew about Egypt had come from her father's and aunt's memories. Maybe it *was* time to see it for herself.

"I wish you were going."

"Me too. But you can call anytime you need—day or night. Besides, you will only be gone for two weeks. They'll fly by, Susu. You'll see."

What she *saw* was Amitu's lip tremble as she slid her hand into the pocket of her galabeya. "I have something for you." She removed a small ivory jewelry box.

"Is there anything inside?"

Amitu gestured for her to wait, then stared straight ahead, both at everything and nothing all at once. She always did that when she reached into her suitcase of stories, deeply tucked away in her memory, and dug one out from her youth when her best friend had been Amani Abdel Aziz—Sahara's mom. Sahara leaned in closer, ready to catch a glimpse of the mother she never knew.

WE WERE SIXTEEN. *Amani insisted we go to El Fishawy, a coffeehouse in Khan el Khalili, Cairo's oldest and largest market. There are hundreds of shops selling anything you can imagine.*

Amani had heard from a classmate that the famous writer Naguib Mahfouz drank his coffee and wrote there every Wednesday afternoon at four. And this week, it was rumored he'd be doing a public reading of one of his short stories.

"I have to go, Malak. Please come with me," she pleaded.

When your mother got something in her head, you couldn't talk her out of it. Better to just go along. So after school, we took two buses to the marketplace, arriving at El Fishawy a few minutes before four. It was packed with men sipping coffee and smoking sheesha. I followed Amani as she walked around the tables and water pipes, but there was no sign of the writer. We sat outside and ordered tea while we waited for him to show.

And then—from where, I don't know—a small woman appeared. She wore a black niqab, which covered her hair and most of her face. Only her dark eyes showed. She stood in front of us, carrying a tiny cup in her hand. I immediately recognized the strong scent of Turkish coffee as she lowered the cup to your mom and said, "Ishrabi."

My heart pounded in my chest. I'd heard stories about fortune tellers who told people's futures by reading the patterns in the coffee grounds. Some said they were witches whose seeing abilities came from a dark place. I ordered the woman to go away, but she pointed to the cup again and repeated, "Drink."

Till today I don't know why Amani listened. I stared, frozen, as your mother finished the coffee in seconds. She slid the empty cup to the fortune teller, who closely examined the remaining grounds, whispering words I didn't understand.

After a few minutes, the woman reached into her pocket and pulled out a small jewelry box. Then she grabbed your mother's hand.

"Ashan bitnik," she told Amani as she placed it in her palm.

"For your daughter," I repeated to myself as the woman picked up the cup and wandered back into the sea of people.

"*Ma tinseesh. Don't forget,*" *she called back, smiling.*

When she was finally out of sight, Amani packed the books she'd brought for the writer to sign.

"*What are you doing? What about Naguib Mahfouz?*" *I asked.*

"*Forget him now. Allah sent us here today for this,*" *she said, placing the box inside her school bag.*

She didn't speak on the bus ride home. But I had to know. "Why did that woman say the box was for your daughter? You don't have *a daughter."*

She looked out the window and grinned. "Not yet, but she saw it in the grounds. One day, insha Allah, I will."

AMITU'S GAZE RETURNED to the room. Sixteen years later and a world away from El Fishawy she held out that very jewelry box. Sahara thought about her mother's words to Amitu, so similar to the ones she'd said in her dream. *Not yet, but you will* echoed in her head. Unlike in the dream, Sahara *could* reach out her hand. She clasped the box, tracing its carved patterns.

"*Now* can you tell me what's inside?"

Amitu shrugged. "The truth is I don't know. Amani believed it was meant for her daughter, for *you*, to open, and no one else."

"Where'd you find it?"

"In your mother's dresser after she passed away. You were just a baby, Susu."

After she passed away, Sahara repeated in her head, trying to make sense of it. Her mom had died twelve years ago. "You had all this time to give it to me. Why didn't you?"

"I was scared. I didn't know what was inside." Amitu's voice turned to a whisper. "What if it was black magic?"

"Black magic! You know that's not real, right? And if whatever's in here is evil, *why* are you giving it to me?"

Amitu shook her head. "I know it's not evil now. Yesterday when I was eating lunch under one of the trees at school, something fluttered above me and spoke. It was a female voice, telling me, 'Ma tinseesh,' just as the fortune teller had all those years ago."

A talking bird. Her aunt was making zero sense. Sahara placed her palm on Amitu's forehead. "Are you sure you're feeling okay?" But then again, she was the one who'd just dreamed of her deceased mother. Strange fortune tellers, weird dreams, talking birds—what the heck was going on today?

Amitu nodded toward the jewelry box. "For so long, I've held on to it. Not sure when would be the right moment for you to have it. But the voice I heard yesterday and your father's news today . . . they're signs. We can't ignore them. For whatever reason—only Allah knows—the time has come for you to discover whatever's in this box and whatever awaits you in Egypt."

Sahara considered telling Amitu about her dream but decided to keep it to herself. Like Cairo, everything she knew about her mother had been borrowed from someone else. It was nice to have something that *only* belonged to her. And now whatever was inside would belong to her too. Though her aunt had gone off the "it's all a sign" deep end, she did have a point about the timing. What if everything that had happened today wasn't a sign but *evidence*? Evidence proving that she *should* go to Egypt and learn more about her mother. She could think of it as a fact-finding mission.

Sahara took a deep breath and reached inside the box, removing a silver necklace. Dangling from the chain was a round pendant engraved with a hand, of all things.

"It's a hamsa. Some call it the hand of Fatima," Amitu explained. "A symbol believed to ward off the evil eye . . . but I've never seen one like this."

Sahara knew what she meant. Not the evil eye nonsense, but the pendant itself. She couldn't take her eyes off the round sapphire sparkling in the center. It wasn't huge, but it glimmered like it was. "Is it real?"

"I think so." Amitu's gaze was also fixed on the stone.

Sahara rubbed her thumb across it. She'd expected it to be smooth, not *warm*. *Whoa. Did it just pulse?* Just then, the hamsa flashed a blue light and quivered in her hand. If she'd blinked, she would have missed it. She shut her fingers and looked at her aunt, who didn't appear to have noticed.

Maybe *Sahara* was the one making zero sense.

In twelve years, Sahara's father had never let a night pass without saying good night—until today, that is. "Time to face the music," Sahara huffed to her robot as she left her room for the first time since this afternoon.

Her dad was kneeling on his prayer rug in the living room, palms resting on his thighs. His caramel eyes were softly open, a million miles away. Praying had always been a part of her father and their home. He looked so tranquil, even as he moved through the various postures. His body rippled like the surface of the ocean while his heart and mind held still like the quiet in its depths.

Sahara lingered in between the kitchen and living room. Affection filled her, thawing any coldness that remained from this afternoon's argument. The hand of grace reaching from him to her.

Slowly, her dad's eyes focused, and his attention shifted. "Hi, habibi." He spoke quietly, greeting her as he often did, using the Arabic equivalent for "darling" or "sweetheart."

She waved, inching closer.

He stood and rolled up his rug. "Are you feeling better?"

"Yeah. I'm sorry about before. I was just shocked. But now, I'm kinda excited to go to Egypt. I wanna see where you and Amitu grew up. And, of course, the Pyramids." Vicky would be *so* jealous when she found out.

He raised his eyebrows. "Really?"

"Yes, really."

"You know, you're not the only one who's *shocked* to be going. It's been a long time since I've been back home."

Sahara bit her lip. "Isn't this your home?"

He hesitated for a few seconds. "*You* are my home." As he knelt in front of her and enveloped her in his arms, she rested her cheek in the cozy spot between his shoulder and neck. She'd take this over arguing any day.

"What did you think I was going to tell you this afternoon?" Sahara whispered in his ear, "Merlin's Crossing."

"Yes, of course. The list." He paused for a few seconds. "I'll make you a deal. After we return from Cairo, we can think about going to New Hampshire."

Score! If Sahara weren't so comfortable, she would've jumped out of her father's arms. *Thinking* about going may have been a small step for someone else's dad, but it was a giant leap for hers. She'd take it. She couldn't wait to shove her I MET MERLIN THE MAGICIAN pin in front of Corey's smug face.

"Deal!" Sahara nestled deeper into her father's embrace.

A Final Vow

985 CE

When they were young girls, Morgana and Deena liked to hang upside down from the oldest fig tree in the courtyard and stare at the sky. The world seemed so vast, and Morgana wondered if she'd ever get to see more than her corner of it. Tonight, that big, elusive world came to her.

The prince and princess didn't reach Baghdad until well after the last prayers of the day, when there were scarcely more than a few lights twinkling in the city. As their carriage rolled to a stop before her mawlay's house, Morgana rushed to Deena's old room on the second floor—it had the best view of the courtyard. Her heart pounding in her chest, she peeked through the lattice window in time to catch Ali Baba bowing before the royal couple's crimson robes. The jewels on the princess's golden crown shimmered in the moonlight like stars atop her raven hair. Morgana threw her hands up to her mouth, stifling the excited squeal on the edge of her tongue. She'd better hurry downstairs to the kitchen before they came inside.

Despite its late start, dinner couldn't have gone better. If

Mama were still alive, she'd have smiled her toothy grin and said, "Everything was twenty-four karats perfect." The guests devoured Cook's lamb stew, the prince even asking for a second helping. The princess complimented Ali Baba's home, the word *exquisite* dripping from her red lips more than once.

Ever humble, Morgana's mawlay credited her for its fine state. "After the loss of my beloved wife, this house would've become a drab shell of walls and floors if not for Morgana. Alhamdulillah. She has preserved and protected its sparkle." Ali Baba's appreciation filled Morgana with pride, nearly lifting her off her feet.

Polite conversation stretched into the middle of the night, with Prince Ala el-Din requesting that Morgana prepare a drink he'd brought from the palace. "Tea," he called it, instructing her to whisk the green powder in hot water until it turned into a milky froth. Though Morgana had never heard of tea before, her mawlay had, begging the couple's pardon for not partaking in any tonight. In one of his voyages east, he'd consumed a cup late at night, keeping him up until dawn. He promised to enjoy some in the morning, when his sleep was not in peril. Tonight, it would be hot water and lemon for him again.

As Morgana placed a steaming bowl in front of Princess Badr, she couldn't help but stare at the indigo borders of the princess's silk dress. She memorized the intricate stitches of the embroidered golden birds, just in case one day she'd be able to tell Deena about tonight and how the princess's beauty had rivaled the moon at its fullest. Not to mention her poise and the way she spun intelligent words together. Those came with high status, something Morgana would never have. But surely, the princess was rattled sometimes. Wasn't it time to find out why she and her prince had left their palace in such a hurry?

Ali Baba was of the same mind, for when everyone had taken their first sips, he cleared his throat. "Your Royal Highnesses, while I am most honored to have your company in my home, I must ask. What matter has brought you so urgently to Baghdad?"

Morgana restrained herself from blurting, *Are you here because of the jinni lamp?* That would've gotten her thrown out of the reception room, especially since she shouldn't have been privy to their conversation in the first place. If she was going to linger, she'd better look busy. She searched for something, anything, that needed tidying, thanking Allah when her eyes met with the cushions that had fallen off the settee.

As she made her way over, the prince answered. "We have come all this way, without anyone save our carriage driver, to make a hefty request of your honor. Your reputation for guarding riches, as well as treasures of the *enchanted variety*"—he whispered the last two words—"has reached our land. We have it on good word that you and your trusted servant are the only people who can help us."

Morgana froze. She mustn't have heard correctly. Good word had led the royal couple to seek Ali's assistance, *not* that of a young servant girl.

"It's no secret that I am the owner of a magnificent jinni lamp." The prince reached into the jade satchel hanging from his belt, sliding a brass lamp onto the table. Morgana would never gripe again at the time it took to remove the tarnish from the table's silver top, for tonight it held an enchanted lamp! Her gaze darted to Ali Baba, whose wide eyes reflected the gleaming brass.

Ala el-Din pointed a gold-ringed finger at the lamp. "The magic of the great jinni inside has brought me much good fortune for which I will be eternally grateful. Without it, I wouldn't have my beautiful bride." At that, Princess Badr wrapped her hands around his.

"However, it has also robbed me of peace. Ever since I discovered the lamp, a sorcerer from North Africa has claimed to be its rightful owner. For months, he's attempted to break into the palace to steal it. I know not if the lamp originated with him. Nonetheless, his hunger for it has driven him mad, making it imperative its powerful magic never falls into his hands. For we fear—" The prince coughed, taking a sip of his tea. His luminous face had grown pale.

"We fear," the princess went on for her husband, "that the wretched sorcerer would use the jinni magic to advance his interests, giving no regard to the consequences. Unlike you and my dear husband, he has no restraint or moral compass. He's already slain several of our guards in pursuit of it." Badr's eyes darkened. "We turn it over to you and beg you to relieve us of the burden of its protection."

Ali Baba nodded. Morgana had no doubt that, after everything her dutiful mawlay had just heard, he'd guard the lamp, but she couldn't help but worry about the cost. What if this awful sorcerer came after Ali Baba?

The princess's voice shook. "Will you protect the lamp? Will you ensure it never touches the sorcerer's greedy hands?"

Why was Princess Badr looking at her? Morgana dropped her head and hurried into the kitchen. Her eyes flitted to the watermelon she hadn't yet served. Swiftly grabbing a large knife, she cut through the rind. But even the fruit's sweet fragrance wasn't enough to make her forget the plea in the princess's eyes. Of course Morgana would help Ali Baba keep the lamp safe, as she'd done with all of the chamber's valuables, but this duty had been bestowed on him, *not* her.

"Not one step closer, sorcerer!" The blare of her mawlay's voice broke through her thoughts.

Morgana shot into the reception room. Her eyes darted, trying to make sense of the chaos. The prince and princess on the ground, gasping for their final sips of air. Her mawlay clutching the lamp to his chest. A gray-cloaked figure pouncing toward him, sword drawn.

"Look out!" Morgana screamed, but it was too late.

MORGANA CLUTCHED THE knife, still trembling in her hand. Minutes before, she'd been using it to slice watermelon, and now—

What have I done?

The question drummed in her head as she lifted her gaze to the front window. A light breeze rustled through the trees of the dark courtyard, cooling her flushed cheeks. No flickering candles or signs of movement. The city was still asleep, unaware of the horrors the rising sun would bring to light.

"Mor . . . Morgana."

She jumped at the sound of her name. *Ali Baba.* The knife fell from her hand, clanging onto the stone floor as she scrambled to her mawlay's side.

"You're alive!" Morgana knelt beside him on the ground. How had he survived the sword's sharp jab to his abdomen?

There was no time to waste. Morgana untied the sash around her tunic and pressed it to his stomach. He coughed, struggling to breathe. Moments ago, her mawlay was strong and full of life, but he now lay helpless on the ground, his prized robe soaked in blood. A knot climbed up her throat. She swallowed it back. He had wanted tonight to go well, and she'd promised it would. She had broken her word. How would she explain to Deena that she hadn't been able to protect her father? If only she could go back in time and follow her home.

"Sw . . . swear." Ali Baba's eyes drifted to the enchanted lamp, lying on its side next to the lifeless body of the wretched sorcerer whose sword—an emerald glinting in its pommel— and fine silk cloak suggested he'd been as wealthy as he'd been malicious.

Morgana's stomach lurched. *I didn't have a choice,* she told herself, eyeing an odd gold circle on the sorcerer's head, peeking out under his hood. If she hadn't used the knife, she wouldn't be alive, and the lamp would be gone. The prince and princess would've died in vain.

"Swear you will take it far away." Her mawlay struggled to speak. "Take all of the magical treasures . . . far away."

"The apple!" Morgana remembered one of the enchanted objects her mawlay had brought home from India. He'd told her that its scent could heal any malady short of death. She had to act fast.

"No. Promise me . . . no." Ali Baba's voice may have been weak, but his eyes were firm with conviction. He'd always maintained that their duty was to protect the treasures, not employ them for their advantage. Though the apple might save his life, it would cost him his integrity. Morgana knew he valued that above all else.

"I swear, my mawlay. Now rest. All will be well," she assured him even though all would *not* be well. She'd been there for her mother's last breaths and knew it was only a matter of time.

As Ali Baba closed his eyes, she took hold of his hand and pledged once more to do what he'd asked. She didn't know where she'd take the treasures or how she'd protect them without him, but she had to try. She would not go back on her word *again.*

Perhaps she should go to Deena and confess everything.

But that would only put her in danger. Morgana couldn't bear that. The less Deena knew, the safer she'd be. Tears spilled down Morgana's cheeks as she hoped beyond hope that Deena would realize she wasn't responsible for what had happened tonight. "They will always blame the servant when catastrophe strikes," Mama had warned her. "Even if she was halfway around the world when it struck."

An idea sprang into Morgana's head. She ran to Ali Baba's study and grabbed a sheet of parchment and a quill from the chest where he kept his old correspondences. Though she wasn't very good at writing, Morgana thanked Allah that she could manage a sentence or two. None of the other servants knew how to read or write, but Deena had insisted on teaching her so they could send messages to each other when she married.

Morgana's hand quivered as she scribbled, *Believe me, sister. I did not do this—*

"Morgana, where are you?"

She dropped the quill and ran to her mawlay's side.

He opened his eyes wide and squeezed her hand with what life he had left, giving his final order.

"Run now!"

PART TWO
New Lands

Welcome to Egypt

"Sahara Kareem Hassan Fareed Rashad," the customs offi-cer declared as he scanned their passport. Sahara bit her lip, eyeing his stiff white uniform and black beret. A cloud of refreshing steam wafted from his cup of mint tea.

Unlike Sahara's American passport, she shared her Egyptian one with her dad. Until yesterday, Sahara hadn't even known she *had* an Egyptian passport.

"You're a citizen of America *and* Egypt," her father had said proudly as he organized their travel documents.

It felt odd to be a citizen of a place she'd never been before.

She watched as her dad opened the passport to a page with a younger photo of herself and pointed to a line of Arabic writing. "You're listed as my daughter—Sahara, your name; Kareem, my name; Hassan, my father's name; Fareed, his father's name; and Rashad, our family name. Sahara Kareem Hassan Fareed Rashad."

"Whoa! That's a lot of names." She never knew she had so

many. *Try sneezing* that, *Corey Burke!* "How come all these names aren't on my American passport?"

"Because they do it differently in Egypt. Your name links you to the people who came before you. A lot of names for a lot of history."

"But they're all names of men. What about the *women* who came before me?"

Her father chuckled. "Oh, Sahara. You're reminding me more and more of your mother."

She smiled. The mention of her mom had always made her stomach tighten. But since dreaming of her and finding out about the necklace, Sahara couldn't help but want to learn more about her. "My mom? Why?"

"Because she would've said the same thing in the same way. 'Why always men? What about the women? The world would be lost without them.'"

"Was she wrong?"

"No, she *wasn't* wrong."

One day after learning she was an Egyptian citizen, Sahara now stood speechless in front of the officer, inspecting her from under his glasses like he might an exotic animal at the zoo.

"Ahem, are you Sahara Kareem Hassan Fareed Rashad?"

Her father nudged her shoulder. "Sahara, you must answer."

She tried to say yes but was momentarily incapable of speech. She nodded instead.

The officer peered at her a little longer, then announced, "Okay. Welcome to Egypt, family of Rashad." He waved them on, flashing a set of stained teeth.

Phew! Sahara hurried, following her father and their luggage cart to the Arrivals terminal. A sweet, woody aroma shrouded the hall. It reminded her of the incense sticks Amitu sometimes burned in their apartment. All around her, people spoke Arabic. It was as if somewhere between New York and Egypt, the English switch had been flicked off and they'd traveled through a time machine. One that transported them from Saturday in Queens to Sunday in Cairo.

The terminal was as crowded as Rockefeller Center at Christmas. Sahara had never been anywhere where so many people looked like her. Well, not exactly like her, but with brown-toned skin and dark hair too. Even so, plenty still eyed her as she walked alongside her father in her T-shirt and leggings.

Many of the women wore hijab—long sleeves covering their arms and headscarves over their hair. Although Amitu didn't cover her hair with a tarha, Sahara's mom had. And she'd seen plenty of photos of other relatives who did too. It wasn't the hijabed women themselves who surprised Sahara. It was the way she *felt* in their presence that did. Like she was doing something wrong, strutting along with her arms bare and hair out for everyone to see.

Through the crowd, a man hurried toward them. A wide

smile was plastered across his face, and he appeared to be limping, but Sahara couldn't be sure because he moved so fast. She inched closer to her dad.

"Kareem!" the man yelled.

"My God! Gamal, is that you?" Her father saluted the mustached man. The buttons of the man's sky-blue shirt were working hard to stay fastened against his plumpish belly, which stood out amid his lean frame.

Amitu had mentioned that Sahara had an uncle who'd been a colonel in the army and retired after injuring his leg. This had to be him.

"Mohandis Kareem Rashad." Uncle Gamal bowed his head. "The engineer's finally back in Cairo." He kissed her father on each cheek, then wrapped him in a bear hug.

What in the world?

"And this must be Sahara." He bounded toward her.

No sooner had Sahara held up her hand to wave than she found herself being hoisted up in his sturdy arms. Her backpack dangled off her shoulders. Her face must've given away her horror, because her father mouthed, "It's okay." To top it off, Uncle Gamal planted a kiss on both of her cheeks.

"Yeesh," she mumbled when he lowered her to the ground. What a big show of affection from someone she'd just met!

He slapped her father's back and bellowed, "Yalla, let's go. Egypt awaits!"

NOTHING COULD'VE PREPARED Sahara for the drive from the airport to her grandmother's house in Uncle Gamal's blue Fiat. As a New Yorker, she was no stranger to high-pressure car trips. However, her uncle's driving defied all laws of physics—squeezing through razor-thin gaps between vehicles and pedestrians, remarkably without hitting either.

Even her father seemed nervous. He flinched and squeezed his armrest as Sahara slid from the passenger to the driver's side of the back seat during one of many sharp turns. Uncle Gamal treated red lights like stop signs—braking, checking that the coast was clear, then stepping on the gas. If Sahara hadn't known better, she'd have mistaken him for James Bond chasing some spy gone rogue.

As they turned onto the 6th of October Bridge—an elevated highway connecting the eastern and western parts of the city—the car slowed into a sea of red brake lights and blaring horns.

"Why is everybody honking? It's not like they can go anywhere."

Sahara's father shook his head. "It's to express their displeasure. Get used to it," he quipped.

Uncle Gamal roared with laughter, making Sahara jump. Her dad didn't seem to mind, though.

She rolled her eyes, spotting a cylindrical tower in the distance. A needlelike point at its top shot up into the navy sky. She had no idea that Egypt had such tall buildings. "What's that?" She pointed.

"*That* is el Borg." Her dad explained that the Cairo Tower was the tallest building in all of Egypt. There was even a restaurant on the highest floor that spun.

Sahara's stomach—already topsy-turvy from her uncle's car acrobatics—flip-flopped as she remembered the spinning rides at the fair. "Wouldn't you get dizzy?" *Or worse, throw up?*

Her father chuckled. "No, it moves too slowly. One full rotation takes about seventy minutes."

Sahara stretched up out of her seat to get a better view. The tower might not have been as tall as the 1,454-foot Empire State Building, but it was still impressive. She hoped they'd have time to visit because she couldn't wait to find out what made the restaurant spin.

"It reminds me of the skyscrapers in Manhattan."

"Yes, like the Empire State, but no King Kong on top." Her dad loved that scene from the movie.

Uncle Gamal burst into laughter again at his corny joke.

Her father smiled and slapped him five. "I've missed you, Gamal."

"Me too, wallahi. Welcome home."

There was that word again. *Home.* How could a person have two homes? And since when did her dad give high fives? He had friends in New York, though she'd never seen him this comfortable or carefree with any of them. Part of Sahara was happy for her dad. But then there was that other part—guilt.

Was *she* the reason he hadn't been here for so long? Here, where people he loved and missed lived.

Maybe she was making too much out of one high five. Sahara rested her head against the window and closed her eyes, feeling the car gain speed. Finally, they were moving.

7

Sacred Calls

Fifteen minutes later, Uncle Gamal's Fiat rolled into Shobra, the town where both Sahara's parents had grown up and her mother's family still lived. The street outside her window bustled with pedestrians, motorcycles, and cars. It pulsed with Arabic music, emanating from nearly every shop and café they passed. Sahara was surprised to see so many open on a Sunday night, though Amitu had told her that people did everything later in Egypt. "They wake up later, go to work later, and stay up later."

Sahara unzipped the front pocket of her backpack and peeked at her *Everything I Need to Know for the Next Two Weeks* list. Yesterday morning—at least she thought it was yesterday—she'd fired away any question she could think of about the trip as her aunt rushed to fold the clothes Sahara had thrown in her suitcase. She scribbled down Amitu's answers in her planet pad, a black memo pad with the planets on its cover.

Sahara squinted in the dark car, trying to make out what she'd written under the *Relatives I'll Meet* section. Uncle

Gamal—check. Sittu, Khaltu Layla, Ahmed, Naima, Khalu Omar, and Magda—still so many people left to meet.

She glanced at her watch as the car slowed—2:15 p.m., well, 9:15 p.m. here. Something about being seven hours ahead of New York made her feel farther away from home, from Amitu.

"Ready?" Her dad opened the door while Uncle Gamal unloaded their suitcases. The layered scent of coffee, tobacco, and warm spices entered the car. *Where have I smelled this before?* It made no sense to ask that in a new place, but that was the thing—Cairo didn't exactly *feel* new. Ever since Sahara had arrived, an old tune hummed in her ear. One she was sure she'd heard before but couldn't name.

She slid toward the door, freezing when her uncle's voice echoed into the night. "All of Shobra, the Rashads are here!"

All of Shobra was an understatement. She was sure the Pyramids back in Giza had heard too. It was nice that her uncle was excited they were here. She'd just never met anyone this dramatic, not even Vicky, and that was saying a lot.

As Sahara crossed the street to her family's building, the same one her mom must've crossed countless times, a rush of uncertainty took hold.

No one, not her father, not Amitu, had ever told Sahara she was the reason for her mother's death. But it was the only logical conclusion. Her mom had gone to the hospital to give birth and hadn't returned. Instead, a newborn Sahara had.

What if her mother's family blamed her for taking away their Amani? Sure, Uncle Gamal seemed glad to meet her, but he'd only known her mother since he married into the family. *He* hadn't grown up with her. *He* wasn't related by blood.

"Ahmed!" Uncle Gamal shouted, jarring Sahara out of her thoughts. He poked his head into the storefront of a small shop on the street level of the building.

"Here I am, Baba." A dark-haired boy with wavy bangs hanging over a white bandana stepped out. Muffled music emanated from the headphones around his neck.

Her dad drew the boy into his arms. "My God, Ahmed. The last time I saw you, you were barely crawling. Your father tells me you're now thirteen and excellent at karate."

As her dad let go, Ahmed reached into the pocket of his athletic pants. *Click.* His headphones went silent. He stood taller, beaming as he explained how close he was to earning his black belt. Sahara was wondering if he was as good as Bruce Lee when he moved toward her. She quickly stuck out her hand, hoping to deter another kiss-on-both-cheeks greeting. He shook it. *Yes!*

"Hello, Sahara. I'm very happy to meet you."

She was blown away by his polished English—British-sounding with a hint of Arabic influence underneath—and thrilled she wouldn't have to use her rusty Arabic to communicate with him. She'd grown up hearing Amitu and her dad speak it all the time, but it felt awkward coming out of her mouth, like it wasn't even her voice.

"Your English is great!" Her New York accent suddenly sounded casual and gruff compared to his proper tea-with-the-queen one.

"Tab'an. He goes to school at the British Academy." Uncle Gamal tousled his son's hair, leaving the bandana askew on his head. "If he listened more to his teachers than those *boom ticka boom* songs, he'd get better grades."

Ahmed swiped his father's hand away. "It's called pop dance music. Everyone in America listens to it," he huffed. "And *this*"—he adjusted his bandana—"is the style there. Like *The Karate Kid*. Please tell him, Sahara."

Not only did her cousin speak English, but he'd also seen American movies and listened to American music. Maybe they would have more in common than she'd thought. Even though karate bandanas weren't the rage back home, she could tell it was important for her cousin to *believe* they were. "I guess they're kinda popular."

Ahmed shot a look at his father that had "I told you so" written all over it.

"Okay, my son. I'll leave your headband alone."

"Baba, it's a hachimaki." Ahmed groaned. "The courageous samurai warriors used to wear them."

But his father wasn't paying attention. Instead, he asked Ahmed to call his mother to watch the shop while they brought up the luggage.

Sahara's cousin nodded, immediately cupping his hands and yelling, "Mama, come down."

Sahara winced. She thought "call your mother" meant go inside the shop and call her on the telephone, not scream her name like you were on fire. Was everyone here this loud?

Ahmed grinned at Sahara. "You can call me Fanta. All my friends do since I always bring an orange soda with me to school."

"That's cool." Sahara's favorite drink was Cherry Coke, but she was definitely not a Cherry.

"*Not* cool," Uncle Gamal countered. "Such a silly name when you have a beautiful one like Ahmed."

"It's not silly. There are five other Ahmeds in my class. At least I know who they're talking to when they say 'Fanta.'"

Good point, Sahara thought as a click-clacking sound came from inside the building. It grew more and more pronounced until a female figure burst out the entrance, the tail of her maroon headscarf flapping behind her. Not until she slowed down did Sahara recognize her as Khaltu Layla. She'd seen photos of her mother's sister in Amitu's album. All these places and people she'd grown up hearing about—here they were.

Despite having rushed out the building, Khaltu's button-down shirt remained neatly tucked into a pencil skirt, which fit like it had been tailor-made. The skinny strap of a black leather purse hung off her shoulder. She stared at both Sahara and her dad, not saying a word.

Sahara looked down. What if she'd been right and her aunt *wasn't* happy to see her?

Seconds later, Khaltu cried, "Kareem . . . Sahara . . . you're here! It's been too many years. Too, too many."

Sahara's dad stepped toward her. "I know." A tear spilled down his cheek. "But we're here now."

Sahara had never seen her father cry. Part of her wanted to yell, "Stop," while the other wanted to throw her arms around him and tell him it was okay. Instead, she reached into his shirt pocket—he always kept a handkerchief there—and handed it to him. He mouthed, "Thank you," then dabbed his eyes, returning to the father she knew.

"And you . . . look at you," Khaltu Layla said. She smiled and pulled Sahara close. It had been silly to worry. A wave of relief fluttered through Sahara as she stood entangled in her aunt's embrace—a cocoon of soft silk and sweet floral perfume. She couldn't help but wonder if this was what it would've felt like in her mother's arms. Her aunt let go just enough to kiss Sahara's cheeks over and over. It was nice, but when would it end?

"For God's sake, woman. Let the child breathe."

Khaltu glared at her husband. "It's the first time I'm meeting my sister's daughter. I have twelve years to make up for."

"I think she made up for it." Fanta snorted as his father hauled one of their suitcases toward the building's entrance.

Sahara's dad hurried over, insisting he help because of her uncle's injured leg.

"I've got it! Kareem, please," Uncle Gamal blasted, making her father step back.

An awkward pause choked the air until her uncle teased, "Oof, what's in your luggage? Don't tell me you brought your amitu Malak with you from New York." He roared his signature laugh and staggered into the building, Fanta following with their second suitcase.

Sahara would note later in her planet pad *not* to ask her uncle about his injury. It was clear he didn't want to talk about it.

Before heading into the shop, Khaltu bent down in front of Sahara. "Your cousin Naima and your sittu are waiting upstairs. The two of them are dying to meet you. They wanted to come downstairs, but I thought it might be too much for you to meet everybody at once, especially after a long day of travel."

Sahara smiled. They'd only just met, and Khaltu was already thinking about what might be *too* much for her.

Her aunt snuck in one more kiss. "I'll see you upstairs after I close up the shop." She pulled a set of keys out of her purse and jingled them. "This is the most beautiful day!"

Amid all the unknowns of being in this new place, Sahara glimpsed a familiarity, a certainty in Khaltu Layla's honey-colored eyes. Sahara may have been exhausted, but she was *ready* to meet the rest of her mother's family.

AFTER TRUDGING UP four *long* flights of steps to her grandmother's apartment, Sahara was winded. She hadn't thought to ask Amitu if the building had an elevator—bad call.

In front of the open apartment door, a girl rocked back and forth on her heels. Judging by her height, she was around the same age. Sahara mentally went through her list. This had to be her cousin. "Naima, right?" Sahara's dad asked.

The girl nodded excitedly. Sahara's eyes flitted from her zipped-up sweatshirt and jeans to the tarha covering her hair. She'd seen photos of Naima, but she wasn't wearing a head-scarf in any of those. Sahara hadn't realized girls covered their hair at the age of twelve. She adjusted her ponytail, suddenly feeling self-conscious about her visible tresses.

As Sahara was about to say hello, Naima jumped forward and hugged her. She kissed Sahara's cheeks—after Khaltu's storm of kisses, two felt like nothing—and whispered in her ear in the same buttoned-up accent as her brother's, "We are going to have so much fun." Then, Naima pointed downstairs and beamed. "I live on the third floor, which means we can have as many sleepovers as you want."

Sahara smiled, psyched to have gone from zero siblings to two cool cousins in a matter of minutes.

Fanta now appeared by his sister's side. "Are you going to let them into Sittu's, or have they come from America to stand at the door?"

Naima took Sahara's hand and led her inside the apart-ment, but not before side-eyeing her brother.

There was no sign of their grandmother as she steered Sahara around the large mahogany table in the entry room. Doubt crept back in. Sittu *wasn't* "dying" to meet her.

Sahara froze at the sound of footsteps coming from one of the bedrooms. Within seconds, Uncle Gamal strode out, urging his children to get drinks from the shop to serve their guests. Sahara wasn't sure if she was relieved or disappointed that it hadn't been her grandmother as Naima started for the door, doubling back to retrieve her brother.

"Where's Fayrouz tonight, anyway?" Fanta groaned. "Shouldn't *she* be helping with our guests?"

Sahara didn't know who this Fayrouz was, but before she could find out, her father turned to her uncle. "Where is she?"

Uncle Gamal gestured toward a room on the left. "She's been waiting on the balcony all night. And now that you're here, she doesn't know what to do with herself."

Sahara rubbed the back of her neck. She didn't know what to do with herself either. Maybe she should turn around and head home. What was another fifteen hours?

"Let's go meet your sittu."

Too late. Sahara followed her father into the room. She couldn't decide whether it was a bedroom or a living room. There was a twin bed on one side and a couch and small television on the other. Too bad she had to share Sittu's room while she was here. This would be a great place to crash. She'd have her very own TV, even if its antenna hung off the top with a piece of duct tape. She and her dad could easily fix that.

Out of nowhere, a man's voice thundered through the open shutters, penetrating the apartment. It stopped Sahara in her tracks. The words *Allahu Akbar* echoed around her. Sahara stared straight ahead, spotting the mosque across the street. That had to be where the call to prayer was coming from.

She was no stranger to the adhan. Back home, a small

golden mosque on one of the shelves in the living room played the five daily calls to prayer, each corresponding to the sun's current position in the sky. But as the final adhan of the day engulfed the home her mother had grown up in, Sahara experienced something she couldn't explain. It was as if the call had pierced through her and was drawing her forward from *within*.

She let it lead her past her father and onto the terrace, where an older woman sat to the right, gazing at her cupped hands like they held an invisible book. Although the white headscarf draped over her hair hid the side of her face, Sahara unmistakably knew she was her sittu. Why else would her heart feel like it was about to catapult out of her chest?

When the adhan ended, Zainab Salem lifted her head and turned to Sahara. Their eyes met for the first time. Grandparent and grandchild—separated by miles and oceans, but somehow still connected by the love and grief for the *one's* daughter and the *other's* mother. While Sittu remained quiet, her round honey-brown eyes glistened with a message: *Welcome home.*

Sahara could worry about the technicalities of a person only being able to have one home later. All that mattered now was being on this starlit terrace with her grandmother. Sittu reached for Sahara's hands and intertwined them with her own.

"Sahara," she said. Her name reverberated in the air like its very own sacred call.

It Is Time

I t would be an understatement to say that Sahara was drop-
dead tired tonight. Nevertheless, sleep didn't come easily.
She'd always had a hard time falling asleep away from home,
even when she'd spend the night at Vicky's. And that had only
been across the street, not across the Atlantic Ocean. Plus, the
loud snoring coming from Sittu in the bed next to her wasn't
making it any easier. Sahara plugged her ears with her fingers,
but it wasn't enough to block out her grandmother's endless
opera of grunts and snorts.

Ugh. There was no use trying anymore. She slipped out of
bed and headed for the door. It creaked, but fortunately, Sittu
appeared unfazed. Sahara didn't dare open the door more,
though, sliding through the slim gap to the dining room.

"Dad," she whispered, peeking into the room where her
father had gone to bed.

No answer. He'd told her she could wake him if needed, but
she felt bad doing that after such a long day. Instead, Sahara

pivoted away, coming face-to-face with the door to the third bedroom in the apartment. She carefully turned the knob, her palms sweating, and tiptoed into the darkness. Why was she so nervous? It wasn't like she was doing anything wrong. Squinting, she spotted a table lamp across the room. On her way to it, she stubbed her toe on something hard.

"Ow!" She immediately covered her mouth with her hands, praying no one had heard. She hopped on one foot to the lamp, fumbling around until she found the switch. It produced a soft light, illuminating a fancy bronze-framed sofa and matching gold-tufted armchairs that looked like they belonged in a museum. In the middle of them sat a white marble coffee table, the likely culprit of her throbbing toe.

This was definitely the largest room in the apartment. Sahara wandered over to the other side, where a gallery of photos hung on the wall. She recognized one of the few color images—her parents on their wedding day. A similar one sat on a bookshelf in her living room back home. To the left of her parents' photo, another wedding picture—this one of Khaltu Layla and Uncle Gamal dressed in his military uniform, several medals decorating his jacket.

And farther along the wall, a large black-and-white close-up of her late grandfather, who'd been a professor of something; Sahara couldn't remember what. She'd have to check the planet pad. He wore a regal-looking brimless cap, a silk tassel dangling from its top. *Tarboosh.* That's what Amitu had called it when she'd shown Sahara a wallet-sized version of the same photo. "Your giddu passed away when your mother was fifteen, but she never got over his death."

Standing in the dim light now, Sahara wondered if anyone "got over" death. She scanned the rest of the photos, pausing at another black-and-white one. This time two girls holding hands and dressed in matching pleated skirts and V-neck sweaters beamed back at her. One stood taller than the other, her hair tied neatly in braids, while the second wore a head-band over a mane of wild curls.

"Layla and your mother on their first day of school."

Sahara spun around. Standing before her in a long night-gown was her grandmother.

"Sittu, you scared me to death!"

Her grandmother brought her hands to her chest. "God forbid."

"I . . . I woke up and couldn't go back to sleep."

"It's been a long day, habibti." Sittu tucked a strand of Sahara's hair behind her ears. Her scrunchie must've fallen out in bed. "Your hair is just like your mother's." Apparently, Amitu wasn't the only one who thought so. "Layla would sometimes tease her and call her Medusa."

"Medusa!" Sahara was shocked to hear that Khaltu Layla, who radiated floral affection, had once compared her mom's hair to that of a mythical snake-haired monster, even if it had been when they were younger.

"Sisters." Sittu sighed. "One minute, best friends; the next, enemies."

Sahara pointed to the photo. "How old was my mom here?"

"About six, and Layla, around eleven. It was Amani's first day of school. She couldn't wait to learn how to read." Sittu's voice shook.

Great, not only had she woken her grandmother, but she'd made her cry too. "Does it make you sad to talk about my mom?" Sahara's eyes fell to her feet. "Do *I* make you sad?"

"No, of course not. I'm not crying because I'm sad. Remembering Amani is a joy. Alhamdulillah for those memories." She lifted Sahara's chin and gazed into her eyes.

Everything about Sittu—minus her snoring—was soft and warm. From the way her eyes smiled to the velvet feel of her hands. Sahara was surprised by how smooth her grandmother's skin was. Even though Amitu had told her she was sixty, which was young for a grandmother, Sahara still imagined she'd have wrinkles like Vicky's nana. Didn't all grandmothers?

"And thank God for you. *You* are her gift to me, to all the world. Do you understand?"

"Uh. I think so." But Sahara *didn't* understand. Not only did Sittu *not* blame her for her mom's death, but she also saw her as a present her mom had gifted the world before she left it. How was that possible?

Sittu kissed Sahara's head, then started for the doorway. "Yalla, let's go back to bed."

WHEN SAHARA FINALLY fell asleep, she dreamed of an outstretched hand.

"Ma tinseesh." A female voice reminded her not to forget.

"Amitu, is that you?"

No answer came. Sahara looked back at the extended hand. It was too small to be her aunt's. Suddenly, a silver necklace materialized inside it, identical to the one Amitu had given her a few days ago.

Sahara lifted her eyes, discovering her mother in front of her, six years old in her school uniform. Sunlight cast auburn ribbons through her dark curls.

Young Amani smiled as she took hold of her hand. She pressed the pendant into her palm.

"It is time, Sahara."

The sapphire at the center of the hamsa glimmered, casting an indigo halo around her mom. Her form grew lighter by the second. She was disappearing.

Please don't leave.

"Time . . . what time is it?" Sahara cried out.

"Yours." Her mom nodded toward the necklace.

Sahara stared in disbelief as the engraved hamsa slowly spun inside the pendant, stopping with an echoing click when the hand pointed upward.

"Now wake up," Amani commanded, becoming part of the light around her.

A flash of blue jolted Sahara awake. It was still dark outside, and somehow Sittu's snoring had managed to grow louder. She'd had another dream of her mother. *Two dreams in the last two days,* she thought as a loud bark echoed through the window. Why was a dog barking in the middle of the night? Was she still dreaming? Sahara lifted her hand to her face. It was empty, but she could still feel the weight of her mother's hamsa.

Through her fingers, she spotted a blue glow emanating from the corner. It was coming from her backpack.

What the heck? Sahara crept over. She had to be hallucinating from exhaustion. The light was shining *through* the front pocket. She unzipped it and pulled out the jewelry box. She'd packed the necklace to wear at the wedding. *Maybe that was a bad idea.* As the blue glow illuminated her face and hands, she flipped open the lid. The gleaming sapphire overtook the bedroom, reminding Sahara of how young Amani had glimmered in her dream.

"It is time . . . Yours," her mom had said. Sahara didn't understand. Maybe it was just exhaustion getting the best of her, like when she'd dreamed she had taken a bath overflowing with all thirty-one flavors of Baskin-Robbins ice cream. Dreams didn't have to make sense.

No sooner had Sahara thought this than the pendant started to vibrate. She shut her hand to keep it from falling out, but that only seemed to make it shake more feverishly. Quickly, she unfurled her fingers, groping around in case she'd missed the switch to turn the dang thing off. She hadn't. The indigo light burned fiercely, forcing her to squeeze her eyes closed. She braced herself for the worst, but instead, the shaking eased until the necklace was perfectly still again.

"Phew," she muttered, daring to peek through one eye. The light was gone. Sahara didn't hesitate. She stashed the necklace inside her backpack and slid into bed, not risking anything else absurd happening tonight.

One night down, thirteen more to go.

At the Inn

985 CE

Home grew farther away with every hoofbeat. Morgana rode west, taking advantage of every hour of daylight to forge as much distance between her and Baghdad as possible. It had been three days since she'd fled with the enchanted treasures. She'd promised her mawlay she would take them far away. Though that had meant disappearing in the middle of the night and leaving the only home she'd ever known, she wouldn't let him down.

Had Ali Baba foreseen this day? After all, he'd been the one to teach her to ride—a skill most female servants lacked. "There may come a time when you need to run faster than your feet can take you," he'd told her.

And when he'd returned from India with the enchanted apple, the flying carpet, and a mysterious ivory spyglass, he insisted on keeping them at home where he could guard them day and night instead of in the chamber. "The magic in these treasures must be closely protected from the evil shadows lurking in the darkness, waiting to strike. If given a chance to possess the enchanted objects, they will exploit them for their own greed, with no regard for the costs."

The prince and princess had feared the same for the lamp. And they'd been right. An evil shadow *had* struck, and there *had* been costs, irrevocable ones. Nevertheless, Ali Baba's foresight to hide the three magical treasures under the stone floor of his bedroom in a woven sack had given Morgana the chance to grab it, stick the lamp inside, and flee with all four treasures before any other shadows came out of the darkness.

She threw a glance at the sack, now tightly tied to the horse's saddle. Pressing the hamsa to her chest, she prayed Deena could forgive her for leaving without saying goodbye and that she'd found her letter. Otherwise, it was only a matter of time before the emir sent his officers to hunt her down. That's if he hadn't already.

Shortly after the late-afternoon adhan, Morgana reached Jericho, where she stopped at a caravanserai. As much as she wanted to keep moving, her body demanded rest—her muscles aching from sitting upright on the saddle for so long. She could only imagine how the horse was feeling.

Morgana dismounted the colt, tucking a loose strand of hair under the wool shawl wrapped around her head. The scarf not only protected her from the blistering sun but concealed the fact that she was a girl traveling alone. Back in Baghdad, the market was filled with stories of merchants who'd been attacked and had their wares stolen by roadside bandits. If they could rob grown men, they'd have no trouble stealing from a servant girl.

"Staying overnight, sir?" asked the bearded porter situated in front of the inn's tall wooden gates. Two armed guards stood at attention at his side.

Morgana nodded, deepening her voice the way she used to when she and Deena imitated the many suitors who had asked Ali Baba for Deena's hand. But that had been pretend. *This* was real. Her palms sweat as she answered, "Insha Allah."

The porter slowly circled Morgana and her horse, stroking his beard. "That's a fine colt you've got there."

Morgana chided herself for the split-second decision to flee on Ali Baba's Arabian. He was the fastest of her mawlay's horses—an asset on the run—but also the finest, attracting undue attention from the porter who stopped in front of the sack. He swept his hand over the rolled-up carpet sticking out of the top. Morgana prayed that the enchanted rug wouldn't use this opportunity to show off its flying prowess. "How much for the carpet?"

Her breathing eased. She'd had plenty of hours on the road to devise an answer to questions about the partially exposed rug. "I apologize, sir." She bowed. "But this one's not for sale. A gift for my sister on her wedding day." If Deena were here, she'd have fallen down laughing at Morgana's feeble manly impersonation.

The porter hesitated, looking annoyed. "Very well." He turned to his guards, signaling them to open the gates.

All her life, Morgana had held doors for others. This was the first time anything had been held open for *her*. She should've savored the moment, but given the precariousness of her current situation, she hurried through, pulling her poor horse along with her.

The courtyard brimmed with caravans of travelers— camels, horses, and mules loaded with their packs. After being on her own for days, it felt good to be in the company of others, even if she had to keep to herself. She scanned the expansive courtyard. Ten of the ones back home could fit in here.

Home. Her throat tightened. *Will I ever see it again?* she lamented, eyeing the scattered merchants' stalls. Her stomach grumbled at the warm, nutty smell coming from a nearby pistachio stand. For days, she'd been living off the figs left over from Cook's stew. It seemed like ages ago since she'd picked them and even longer since she'd had a proper meal.

Unable to stave off hunger any longer, Morgana quickly steered her horse to the stables. She undid the sack and heaved it over her shoulder, then headed straight for the dining hall. A servant girl about her age brought over a plate of roasted hen that made Morgana's mouth water. She restrained herself from jumping up and showering the girl with grateful kisses—a move that would've earned her male facade a slap.

Just as she was about to take her first bite, a rowdy group of uniformed officers entered the hall. Morgana froze, recognizing the gold insignia embroidered on their coats. *The emir's officers!* Her heart thumped, making the necklace quiver against her chest. She'd been found.

A Break-in

It was past noon in Cairo—but before sunrise back home—
when Sahara rubbed her eyes open. Her first thoughts were
of the necklace and how it had shaken and burst with light
like a creepy poltergeist had possessed it. *Oh crap!* She was
starting to sound like Vicky. There had to be a logical reason
for the necklace's behavior. She just hadn't figured it out yet.

As she turned away from the wall to check on her backpack, her eyes met with a tall woman standing at the edge of
the bed. A tattered dress shrouded her figure, frayed threads
dangling loosely over her tan hands. Sahara gasped, springing
up on her elbows and inching back. "Who . . . who are you?"

The stranger didn't answer, only furrowed her brow. Sahara
had no idea if she was confused or scowling. She racked her
brain for the words in Arabic. At last, they poured out into the
space between them.

"Inty meen?"

"Mat khafeesh, Anissa Sahara." The woman asked her not
to be afraid—too late for that—then introduced herself as

Fayrouz, her grandmother's maid. "I was sent to wake you." She opened the shutters.

As sunlight drenched the room, Sahara wondered why her name sounded familiar. And then it hit her. Fanta had mentioned a Fayrouz last night. Sahara's breathing began to settle. She returned her attention to her backpack. After the scare she'd just had, she was relieved to find it lying on the floor where she'd left it, no sign of monkey business.

Her gaze shifted back to Fayrouz, whose dark brown eyes stared back at her. "Where's Sittu?"

"Madame Zainab's down at the shop." Fayrouz swung the loose scarf that covered her hair over one shoulder, then began to make Sittu's bed.

As she popped the sheets above her head, a voice called Sahara's name.

Dad. Thank God!

"Good morning, or should I say good afternoon." He flashed Fayrouz a polite smile as he entered. "I see you've met Sittu's maid."

She sure had. Sahara frowned, recalling *how* they'd met.

Fayrouz started for the door. She paused momentarily, turning to face Sahara and her father. "Nawartoona, Ustaz Kareem." She bowed her head. "You and your daughter have lit up the house with your presence."

"Shokrun." He thanked her as she hurried out.

"*That* was weird. Why does Sittu have a maid, anyway? Is she rich?"

Her father narrowed his eyes. "Don't be rude. You're not used to Fayrouz's way. She's trying to be respectful."

"I'm not trying to be rude. I'm just not used to people being *sent* to wake me or bowing and calling us *sir* and *miss*."

"It's different than what you're used to, but different doesn't have to be *weird*. And no, Sittu's *not* rich. All classes of people hire servants here."

Sahara winced. "Servant! Yeesh. What are we in—the Middle Ages?"

"Servant, maid, or whatever. Fayrouz takes pride in her work. And if your grandmother hadn't hired her, she might not have enough money to eat. She isn't educated, and her choices are limited."

"I guess. *Servant* just sounds so belittling."

"There's nothing *little* about earning money to provide for yourself and your family."

She'd better change the subject. Her father could go on all day about the virtues of work. "So, where is everyone, anyway?"

"Down at the shop. It seems someone tried to break in last night."

"Wait, what? A break-in!" Sahara jumped out of bed.

Her dad quickly assured her that nothing had been stolen, thanks to some stray dog managing to scare the thief away.

She had thought she'd been dreaming, but could this have been the same dog she'd heard barking in the middle of the night?

Her father peeked his head out the door. "Looks like everyone's back. You get changed, and I'll see if there's any more news."

First the crazed necklace, now the attempted break-in. What could possibly happen next?

EVERYONE—BUT NAIMA, that is—was huddled at the dining table when Sahara left Sittu's room. The pungent smells of garlic and cumin reminded her of Amitu's cooking.

Amitu. A hollowness pulsed deep within Sahara's stomach. It had been less than a day and a half, but she already missed her aunt.

Nobody noticed Sahara's arrival until she dragged out the chair next to her father's. In unison, heads swung in her direction, and a fanfare of greetings commenced.

Sahara pulled her scrunchie tight as Fanta—dressed in his full karate uniform today—announced her arrival into an imaginary microphone while his father impersonated a royal trumpeter. "*Too-too-too-toom.* Welcome, Princess Sahara." Uncle Gamal was barely done blowing his last note when Khaltu Layla nearly yanked his arm out of its socket and forced him to sit.

How could they joke at a time like this? Sahara turned to her grandmother and asked about the shop.

"Alhamdulillah, all is good." But the nervous glance Sittu cast at Khaltu Layla said otherwise.

"It'll be okay." Khaltu drummed her fingers on the table. "We'll keep the shop closed for a few more hours to give things a chance to settle."

"That won't be necessary. It was probably just a poor scoundrel in need of food or money," Uncle Gamal huffed, turning to Sahara's dad. "Egypt has changed since you left for America. The rich are richer than ever while the poor struggle to eat. We do what we can to help those who are hungry, but some still resort to stealing."

Stealing was definitely not right, but neither was going hungry. Amitu would say it was one of those complicated situations that didn't have a right or wrong answer. Those situations kept Sahara up at night.

Last winter, after watching a news report about homelessness, she'd persuaded Vicky and Amitu to help her with *Operation One Hundred Cookies*. They baked as many chocolate chip cookies as they could in one afternoon, ending up with ninety-six. Sahara threw in four Chips Ahoy! to get them to their goal. Afterward, Vicky's father, a police officer, took them around in his car to distribute them to some of the homeless people in Manhattan. *That* had been a great day.

Speaking of the police, what did they have to say about the break-in?

Fanta waved his hand when Sahara asked. "Pfft. We didn't call them. Instead, Baba gave his army friend Morsy fifty pounds to snoop around. If anyone can find out who did this, it's him."

"Things work a little differently here," her father explained. "It's not as easy as dialing 911 when a crime occurs."

That was different, all right. Sahara had assumed that everyone in the world called the police in an emergency.

"The good news is that the thief failed," her dad added. "Luckily, the gate had two locks and—"

Uncle Gamal interjected with how it had been *his* brilliant idea to get two locks while Fanta threw a karate chop in the air and claimed the thief ran away because he realized it was *his* family's shop.

Sahara wasn't used to so many people talking at the same time. She jerked her head back and forth, trying to keep up, as Sittu slid a plate in front of her. Sahara lifted one of the pita pockets, trying to figure out what was inside.

"Don't tell me my granddaughter has never had fool and tameya sandwiches before?"

"She has—" her father started before Sahara cut in.

"Fool are the brown fava beans Amitu sometimes cooks for breakfast on weekends, and tameya is the falafel my dad orders from the Astoria Diner," Sahara said proudly. Luckily, both had made the *Foods I'm Likely to Eat* section of her list.

"Your mother adored fool and tameya," Sittu told her. "Almost every day after school, she and Malak stopped by Ismail's stand down the street for sandwiches."

Though Sahara could've gone for a slice of pizza from Avelino's, she enjoyed thinking about her mom and Amitu buying sandwiches together as kids, the way she and Vicky sometimes grabbed hot dogs after school from the cart at the park.

"What's the matter, Layla?" Uncle Gamal asked. "There's no need to worry. The thief won't return."

Khaltu's eyes darted from Sittu to the door. "It's not just the shop. What's taking Naima so long?"

"She's fine," Fanta groaned. "You know how she loses herself with Kitmeer."

"Who's Kitmeer?" Sahara asked.

Khaltu shook a finger at her son and husband. "Kitmeer is the real hero. He's the one that saved the shop *and* us."

11

Kitmeer

Filled with curiosity about last night's "real hero"—and needing a breather from the family chatter—Sahara insisted she help Fanta fetch his sister.

"'Go get Naima.' 'Where is Naima?' My whole life, I've been responsible for that girl." Fanta slipped on his headphones and hurried downstairs.

"Wait up." Sahara marched after him, not sure he'd heard her over the music blasting in his ears. As she stepped out of the building, the afternoon sun delivered a scorching slap. "Yeesh, it's hot!"

"Come under here."

Sahara swung her head to the left to find Naima waving her over. She sat cross-legged in the small oasis of shade created by the shop's awning and the terrace of the apartment above. Next to her lay a large dog covered in short gray-and-tan fur.

"Naima, khalas with that dog already! Mama wants you upstairs."

"His name's *Kitmeer*!" she snapped at her brother. "And

after last night, he deserves more respect from you, from everyone. If it weren't for him, the thief would've gotten into the shop, and our family's business would be ruined."

Fanta pointed to his headphones. "I can't hear you," he yelled back, but Sahara doubted that because she could barely make out the music now. He must've lowered the volume or turned it off when they'd gotten outside.

As she approached Naima, Kitmeer stood up, his tail swishing from side to side. His nose wiggled over Sahara's legs. She held her breath, unsure what he'd do next, until he swept his long tongue over her hand. Sahara giggled at the wet sensation, her fear dissolving.

"You've got some bark, buddy." It had been loud enough to scare away the thief *and* outmatch Sittu's snores.

"He likes you. He can tell when someone's kind." Naima stuck her tongue out at her brother.

"Watch it, or I'll tell Mama and Baba that you've been sneaking food from home to feed him."

Sahara stroked the dog's pointy ears, which bent to her touch before springing back up. "He looks like he has eyebrows." She smiled, running her thumb over the folds of fur above Kitmeer's eyes, then turned her attention to the pedestrians walking by.

People spilled off the sidewalk onto the road, seemingly unfazed by their proximity to the moving vehicles. Not one but two donkeys passed by lugging carts carrying both their owners and crates of goods. The sweet aroma of ripe mango emanated from one, while the warm smell of freshly baked bread wafted out of the other. Sahara's mouth fell open as she watched a woman sliding between traffic, supporting a basket on her head with one hand and holding a young child's hand with the other—all the while not breaking a sweat.

Naima stood up and dusted dog hair from her pants. Gold and gray wisps flew everywhere.

Sahara blew them away from her face. "So, how did you and Kitmeer meet?"

Fanta rolled his eyes, sliding his headphones down and around his neck. "A few years ago, *this* silly girl got lost for a whole night and—"

"I wouldn't have gotten lost if you hadn't left me behind! *I'll* tell Sahara what happened." Naima waved her brother off. "One evening, we went into town for bread. It was our first time going alone. Mr. Speedy here"—she glared at her brother—"was moving so fast to that loud music in his ears I couldn't keep up. One minute he was in front of me, and the next, he was gone."

"Naima, you weren't paying attention. You were too busy daydreaming like you always do."

"That's not true, and you know it!"

Boy, these two could bicker. They were worse than Vicky and her brothers. "What does any of this gotta do with Kitmeer?"

"*He's* the reason I found my way home." Naima rubbed the dog's head. "I was walking around for hours before I noticed a dog following me. When I sat on the sidewalk to rest, he lay down by my side. I was scared. I'd never been that close to a dog. But the more time I spent with him, the more I trusted him. I started walking, and he followed me again. I don't know who was leading—me, the dog, or Allah—but I finally made it home. After I told everyone how he'd helped me, Sittu gave him water and leftover lamb, Mama named him Kitmeer after the faithful guard dog from the Koran, and she and Baba agreed he could hang out in front of the shop. He's come by every day since."

"Every day," Fanta groaned. "If it were up to you, he'd sleep in our house!"

"And what would be wrong with that?"

"You know what's wrong with that. It's a sin to have a dirty dog in the home, especially one people pray in."

Sahara's dad had told her the same thing the *one* time she'd asked for a dog. At least she had her robot, Omni. Her stomach clenched, thinking about him back home in her room. Why did being somewhere new have to mean leaving so much behind? She needed a distraction. She pointed to the Arabic letters embossed on the sign under the awning. "Is that the name of the shop?"

"Yes. Ali's," Fanta answered.

"Hmm. Is it named after someone in your family?"

"*Our* family." Naima beamed, drawing a circle in the air with her finger that encompassed Sahara, her brother, and herself.

Sahara smiled back. "Okay, who in *our* family is the shop named after?"

"No one knows," Fanta said. "Sittu doesn't remember meeting or hearing about a relative named Ali."

That was odd since it was a common Arabic name. Maybe it had belonged to a family member from a long time ago. Amitu had said the shop had been in Sahara's mom's family for generations.

Fanta signaled to Kitmeer. "Time to say bye-bye. We have to head upstairs for lunch."

His sister plodded toward the corner, Kitmeer in tow.

Sahara followed, wondering what her cousin was doing. When Naima reached the end of the street, she stared down the intersecting alleyway and drew a tennis ball from the kangaroo-like pocket of her hoodie. Sahara watched as Kitmeer zeroed in on the ball.

"I'll see you in a little bit," Naima told him, hurling the ball deep into the alley. Kitmeer raced after it.

Her cousin had quite the arm.

"It's the only way he'll leave," Naima explained, making her way back to the shop. "The farther I throw it, the longer it takes him to come back. And by then, I've already gone upstairs."

"Clever!" Sahara appreciated good problem-solving at work when she saw it. She and Naima *would* have lots of fun together, she thought as she rushed to keep up. When they were back in front of the shop, Sahara realized she had no idea what her family sold. Amitu had only said it had been in the family for years.

"Do you want to see what's inside?" Fanta asked.

She *did*, but she also remembered the worry on Sittu's and Khaltu's faces as they tried to convince her everything was okay after the break-in. Besides, they'd been downstairs—she glanced at her watch—for fifteen minutes. "We told your mom we'd get Naima and head upstairs. We should stick to the plan."

"We can be quick. Open the gate before Kitmeer comes back," Naima directed her brother.

Fanta waved his hands at the store's entrance. "Open sesame."

"With the key, you clown," his sister railed.

As Fanta twisted a key into the steel padlock, Sahara remembered that the thief had broken the other one last night. This was a bad idea. "Are you sure it's okay to go in . . . you know, after what happened?"

"Tab'an." Fanta pulled the gate up. "It's like I said, now that the thief knows he messed with Fanta Saeed's family, he's not coming back."

Sahara resisted the urge to roll her eyes at her cousin's conceit while Naima shoved him down the two stairs that led into the shop. She turned to Sahara and pointed to the bottom step. "Be careful. It's a little loose."

Sahara lunged over it, entering the dark shop. When Naima flicked on the lights, delight ousted Sahara's hesitation. She must've looked like the cartoon characters whose eyes pop out of their heads.

"Whoa!" was all she could say. Everywhere she looked, there were stacks and shelves piled to the ceiling with boxes and bags of deliciousness. Sugar cookies, crinkle-cut potato chips, caramel chews, chocolate bars, candy-coated gum— you name it. Between the wooden counter at the front and all the goodies around her, Sahara could barely move. She ogled the treats, recognizing a few brands from home.

What should she try first? Wait, she didn't have any money. Would she have to pay in her family's shop? Her mind raced with excitement.

It *hadn't* been a mistake to visit the shop, Sahara thought, quickly eyeing some of the non-food items—cassette tapes, cigarettes, batteries, and small glass lanterns in various bright colors. Who cared about those?! Next to the Coca-Cola fridge lined with soda bottles was an old white refrigerator. A smaller lock hung off its handle. What did her family need to keep under lock and key?

There was no time to think. Was that what she thought it was? *Ice cream. Yes!*

"Wow, I can't believe all this is in here." The shop reminded Sahara of AJ's corner store, which she and Vicky visited at least once a week to stock up on essentials like Bazooka bubble gum and Red Hots candies. Her family's store was half the size but had triple the supply of treats. Before giving more thought to the volume of items in the shop relative to its dimensions, she came across a shelf with gummy bears.

"I think I've died and gone to heaven. How do you not *eat* all this amazing stuff?"

"We can't. Our family makes money selling it," Naima answered.

"And they'd kill us if we did." Fanta leaned his elbows on a stack of local newspapers behind the counter. "But since *you're* here and Sittu and Mama would find a way to give you the moon if you asked, we can take some Bimbos for dessert."

Sahara's mouth watered as Naima reached over to a nearby shelf and snagged a handful of chocolate-covered biscuits, crinkling their wrappers in her tight grip.

Out of nowhere, a high-pitched howl penetrated the shop, stopping Sahara in her tracks.

"She's coming." Naima quickly jammed the cookies into her pocket. "Kitmeer always gets upset when she's near."

"Who . . . who is coming?"

Naima cupped her hands and whispered into Sahara's ear, "El Ghoula."

El Ghoula

Two years ago, Amitu had returned from Egypt with a handful of children's books. They were all written in Arabic, so she had to read them to Sahara, usually at bedtime. One of the tales featured an el ghoula. And from what Sahara remembered, she wasn't one of the good guys.

As her cousins raced to lock up the shop, she spat out, "What's an el ghoula again?"

"A witch!" Naima pulled down the gate with her brother.

Even though Sahara knew witches weren't real, and Fanta had shaken his head at his sister's ridiculous response, the urgency with which he was moving made her breathing quicken. She hurried into the building after her cousins. "Why . . . why would a witch be coming here?"

"To meet you," Naima cried as they sprinted up the stairs.

When they arrived sweaty and sucking air, Fanta lied to Sittu and Khaltu—who were busy setting the table—and said they'd been racing to see who could reach the apartment first. Neither he nor his sister mentioned an el ghoula.

Khaltu might have bought Fanta's lie, but she demanded to know why they'd taken so long downstairs.

"We were just showing Sahara the shop," Fanta answered casually, but Sahara could tell from the sharp look Khaltu aimed, then shot at her kids, that this wasn't going to be good. Though Sahara had warned her cousins about unlocking the shop, they'd only done it so *she* could see what was inside.

"It's my fault we're late. *I* asked them to show me it. I'm sorry. I know I should've waited until later, but I was so excited." Sahara's eyes darted nervously from her aunt to her cousins, unsure how Khaltu would react.

Before Khaltu could respond, Sittu spoke up. "Don't worry, habibti. Everything is fine now. *Right*, Layla?"

Khaltu took a deep breath and smiled. "Tab'an." She squeezed Sahara's shoulder. "What did you think of our little shop?"

Phew! "It's awesome!" Sahara answered as her father and Uncle Gamal walked out of the Room of Photos—her new name for the room with all the pictures she'd come across last night. She was dying to tell her dad about the shop, but after narrowly missing getting into trouble with Khaltu and Sittu, it was better not to tempt the fates. Instead, she began to tell him about Kitmeer.

A knock came from behind. Sahara twisted around as a wavy-haired gentleman opened the door and strolled inside. *Khalu Omar.* Sahara would check his name off in the planet pad later, but for now, she craned her neck to see if there was anybody behind him.

"Dr. Omar!" Sahara's dad hurried over and congratulated her uncle on his engagement.

According to Amitu, Omar had recently graduated from medical school and was a neurologist. Sahara had loads of questions for him, like where the brain's planning center was located, and if dopey Corey Burke might be missing brain cells. But she couldn't think of any of that now. She was too busy checking the door for his bride-to-be's impending arrival.

"Thank you, Kareem bey. I'm honored that you're here for my wedding." Omar beamed, his entire face lit up like Times Square at night.

Khaltu Layla ran over and embraced her brother. She looked over his shoulder. "Where's your fiancée?"

"She's coming now." Omar glanced back at the stairs. "Yalla, habibit albi."

"Love of my heart, pfft!" Naima said in Sahara's ear.

Out of nowhere, a blast of hot air blew through the front door, leaving in its wake the bride-to-be—Magda.

"Hello, darlings." Magda waved her hand as if holding an invisible wand. "So sorry to keep you waiting. Those steps are not made for shoes très élégantes."

Rude. Her uncle's fiancée may have been smiling, but Sahara knew an insult when she heard one. She turned to her grandmother. Sittu's expression hardened, and she muttered a few choice words.

Meanwhile, Naima's body stiffened. Sahara didn't have to

wait for her cousin to whisper "El Ghoula" to figure out that the bride-to-be *was* the witch. The tension in the room had gone from that of a loose rubber band to one about to snap.

Her eyes flitted from Magda's tight navy dress, which contrasted with her ivory skin, to her strappy high heels, fiery-red polished toes peeking out. Magda removed a wide-brimmed hat, revealing golden-blond hair that cascaded past her shoulders. She might've been witchy on the inside, but she was dressed like a movie star.

When Khalu Omar introduced his fiancée to Sahara's father, Magda thrust her hand in front of his face. He awkwardly kissed the back of it. *Yuck!*

Sahara had been so busy ogling Magda that she didn't notice her uncle walk over. He smiled at her, his eyes bright with affection *and* wonder, like he was gazing at an enchanted unicorn. She stood up even taller, blooming in his light.

"Magnificent." He kissed both of Sahara's cheeks. They immediately turned hot.

"She *is* magnificent," her grandmother agreed before heading into the kitchen. Khaltu Layla followed.

"Sahara." Magda said her name as if she were calling her into the principal's office. She dropped her leather purse onto the table Sittu and Khaltu had carefully set minutes before, then click-clacked toward Sahara. "I wonder. Are you as grand as your name?"

Sahara had been asked many questions about her name

before, but never *this* one and never in *this* snide way. She had no idea how to answer.

"Grander." Naima gave Magda the side-eye she usually reserved for her brother, then left to join her mother and Sittu.

Naima for the awesome save. Sahara owed her one.

"Is that so?" Magda pursed her red lips. Thick black eyeliner extended past the outer corners of her amber eyes, giving them a catlike appearance. They blazed with the intensity of the sun, forcing Sahara to look away. Before she knew it, her uncle's fiancée had taken hold of her hands. Compared to Magda's neatly manicured nails, Sahara's looked grubby. She studied the gold cuff around Magda's wrist, visually tracing its engraved patterns.

And then, Magda leaned in and spoke so only Sahara could hear. "Omar has told me so much about your mother. Allah yarhamha. Such a pity, Amani didn't live to see her brother marry. At least you're here."

Sahara yanked her hands away. She clenched them by her sides and gave her uncle's fiancée a forced smile. She was used to people being sorry that her mom was no longer alive, but the fake way Magda had said "such a pity" made her burn inside. She felt bad enough about her mother's death. She didn't need anyone, especially not someone she'd known for a minute, pouring lava onto her already stinging guilt.

Sahara blew out a breath, trying to calm down, as Sittu and Khaltu walked in with lunch, plunking down two casserole dishes of macarona béchamel. Fayrouz scurried behind them, carrying a silver platter, upon which a mountain of breaded chicken cutlets balanced.

"All this for Omar and me." Everything that came out of Magda's mouth reeked of arrogance.

"It's not *all* for you and Omar. It's also for my granddaughter and son-in-law," Sittu told her.

Sahara snickered inside at her grandmother's swift comeback.

"Of course." Magda's eyes flamed. "Bless your hands for cooking such a délicieux meal."

Khaltu Layla twitched as she eyed her brother's fiancée. Sittu and Khaltu might not have thought Magda was a witch, but clearly, they didn't care for her either. Sahara could see why. Her uncle's fiancée could give Corey a run for his money in the jerk department.

When her cousins left to get spare chairs from the balcony, Sahara rushed after them and whispered to the back of Naima's head, "You were right. She *is* wicked."

SAHARA KEPT A close eye on El Ghoula—it was too good a nickname not to use—during lunch as Khalu Omar gushed about their new apartment and how his "darling" Magda would move in with him after the wedding.

"Only three more days until we live together as husband

and wife." Magda ran her fingers through his hair, causing Naima to kick Sahara's foot.

"A lot can happen in three days," Khaltu said. "Allah created the heavens and earth in six."

Magda waved a dismissive hand in the air, commenting on how the days were flying by as Khalu Omar gazed into her eyes. Witch or no witch, their uncle was very much under her spell. How had Magda charmed him in the first place?

"So, how did the two of you meet?" Sahara asked.

Magda's eyes flashed with fire. "Your daughter is quite curious, Kareem."

"She is." Her dad nodded. "But she does ask a good question."

Go, Dad!

Omar put his fork down and explained how he'd met Magda two months ago when she was volunteering at the hospital. "One look into her beautiful eyes, and I was in love."

Khaltu shook her head. "It's so soon. I've never seen such a quick engagement."

"We're certain of our love," Magda pressed. "I hope you don't doubt your brother's ability to choose a wife. After all, he's a doctor, and you're a . . . What is it you are again?"

Before Khaltu Layla could respond to El Ghoula's dig, Omar cut in. "We've already talked about this, my sister. The wedding's in a few days. Please be happy for us."

Sahara was sorry she'd asked her question. She didn't mean

to cause trouble between her aunt and uncle. Magda's pot-stirring wasn't helping either.

Khaltu looked toward her brother. "But it's—"

"Layla!" Sittu snapped. "Your brother's right. It's time to let it go. Nothing good comes from holding life tightly. We put our faith in Allah and wish them well. That's all we can do."

Khaltu nodded, mustering a smile. "I *am* happy for you. Wallahi," she swore to her brother.

"Sahara and I are also happy for you." Her dad raised his glass. "Here's to Omar and Magda. May God bless them with a long and happy life together."

Sahara felt the one-two punch of sadness and guilt in her gut as she watched her dad take a sip. She looked down at her plate. *He* hadn't gotten to live a long life of happiness with her mother. *And I'm the reason why.*

Sahara was still staring down when Naima grumbled, "He would've had a happier life with Noora."

"Noora?" Magda's voice shook with the question.

Who the heck was Naima talking about, and why had her name rattled Queen Pompous—

"Magda, you're bleeding!" Sittu exclaimed.

Sahara's head shot up. Blood surfaced underneath El Ghoula's gold cuff, trickling down her fair skin. But Magda said nothing. Maybe she was in shock. Her eyes glazed over, their amber blaze momentarily dimmed. That is until Khalu Omar reached for her arm.

"No! Don't touch it!" Magda tugged her hand away. Omar

jumped back. "I mean, it's . . . it's nothing, darling," she corrected herself, regaining her composure and the fire in her eyes. "I must've gotten a cut from my bracelet. Some of the engravings are sharp underneath."

"You should get that fix—" Sittu started as a loud crash came from the kitchen.

A forlorn Fayrouz emerged with a tray in her hands— empty except for the remnants of whatever it had held. "M-Madame Zainab. The konafa, the dessert. I . . . I dropped it," she howled.

Uncle Gamal, Naima, and Fanta gasped in unison. Sittu consoled her maid as Khaltu hurried into the kitchen.

Only Sahara noticed El Ghoula disappear into Sittu's bedroom.

13

The Tea

985 CE

Morgana's hands shook as the emir's officers took a seat nearby in the dining hall. Could there be a chance they were in Jericho on business unrelated to her? Morgana hoped it was so, but the dread seizing her stomach said otherwise. She should get up and head for the courtyard, though leaving without touching her dinner would arouse suspicion. Instead, she lowered her head and attended to her meal, keeping her ears open.

"Is the captain sure she's headed west?" one of the younger officers asked.

"You dare doubt his authority?" the eldest officer railed. "If he says her horse's tracks lead west, then who are you to think otherwise?"

"No . . . no, sir. I'm just anxious to find her and bring her back to Baghdad as our distinguished captain has ordered, that's all."

Morgana's heart stopped. They were here for *her*.

"We will bring her to justice." The eldest officer seethed.

"No one, especially not a filthy servant, gets away with such villainous acts on our watch." He slammed his fist on the table and grabbed the girl who'd served Morgana earlier. "These hens are cold!" He knocked down her tray of dirty dishes. Several broke as they hit the stone floor. "Get us hot ones before I crack something else."

"Right . . . right away, sir." The girl trembled as she bent down to clean up the mess—*his* mess.

The fear coursing through Morgana turned into contempt. Over her years of servitude, she'd met with her fair share of cruelty—none from her mawlay or his family, but from other gentlemen and ladies around town whose purses overflowed with gold but whose hearts lacked a shred of kindness. Having started as a woodcutter, Ali Baba didn't take his new station in life for granted, nor did he tolerate his servants being disrespected. Once, Morgana had returned from the market in tears after a scathing encounter with a nobleman she'd insulted by forgetting to bow when *he'd* bumped into her. "Don't cry, my dear Morgana," her mawlay had said softly. "All work is honorable. In the end, we are all in the service of Allah," he told her before leaving to give the man a piece of his mind.

Morgana wanted so badly to help the servant clean up but couldn't risk drawing attention to herself.

Another officer piped up. "I heard she murdered her mawlay, the honorable Ali Baba. May Allah have mercy on his soul."

Morgana's worst fear had come to fruition. She'd been worried that fleeing would implicate her. But what choice had she had? She couldn't turn her back on her promise to her mawlay. If these men only knew how wrong they were.

"Rumor has it she also slew his gentleman guest."

"Using a sikeena from the kitchen."

Ya Allah! They thought the sorcerer had been a *guest.* What about his bloody sword, or had they overlooked it because of his expensive robes? Mama had always said that innocence could be bought. Apparently, even after death.

"Is it true she poisoned Prince Ala el-Din and Princess Badr with their own tea?"

The older officer nodded. "When we find this . . . this wretched Morgana, we will drag her back to Baghdad and hang her in front of all its citizens."

Morgana's stomach lurched. Unlike her mawlay, the prince and princess hadn't suffered fatal wounds from a sword. They weren't even bleeding. She'd assumed the sorcerer had used some kind of dark magic against them, but she had no idea *she'd* been the one to serve it.

She couldn't listen any longer. She had to get far away from Jericho *now.* While the officers hunting for her dined, she could make headway on the road.

But there was one thing she had to see to first. As the servant girl returned shaking with a steaming platter in her hands, Morgana crouched down and tied the older officer's leather laces to each other. He was too busy stuffing his face to notice. As dire as her circumstances were, she couldn't help but smile on her way out, imagining him falling flat on his despicable face.

14

Bimbos

After the calamity of the dropped dessert, Sahara hurried downstairs with her cousins to their apartment. Living a floor away from Sittu came in handy—like when you had to get away from your uncle's wretched fiancée. Besides Amitu, Sahara didn't have relatives in the same country, let alone the same building.

The Saeeds' apartment was very much like Sittu's—one main room at the entrance, three bedrooms, and a hallway that led to the kitchen and bathroom. Their central room didn't hold a large dining table but was furnished with stuffy decor that reminded Sahara of Sittu's Room of Photos. Why her family insisted on having furniture that looked like it had come out of eighteenth-century France, she'd never know.

Fanta shut the front door. "What a disaster! All of that delicious konafa in the garbage."

"Total disaster," Sahara agreed, imagining the wasted flaky phyllo dough, creamy ricotta cheese, and sweet syrup.

Identical looks of surprise took over her cousins' faces. "What?"

"We thought you only ate American food," Naima explained. "You know, like hamburgers and french fries."

"I *do* eat those, but Amitu also cooks a lot of Egyptian stuff. There's no way she'd let me eat burgers and fries every day."

Sahara followed her cousins into one of the bedrooms, where the sun peeked through the half-open shutters, casting horizontal stripes across everything, even them. Fanta removed a cassette from the music player in his pocket and slid it into a boom box on the floor. It might've been on the smaller side, but the loud beat that blasted out of its speakers made Sahara jump.

Naima turned down the volume, glaring at her brother. "This is not a disco!"

Once she could hear again, Sahara smiled at Fanta, shuffling his feet to the song "Rhythm of the Night." It had been a big hit a few years ago when it was featured on the soundtrack of the martial arts movie *The Last Dragon*. Sahara had gotten sick of the song because Vicky's brothers played it so much. But today, she latched on to the reminder of home—a life preserver helping her stay afloat in a distant sea.

"You're pretty good," Sahara told him.

He spun on one foot. "Mama says I learned to dance—"

"Before I could walk," Naima cut in. "Different day, same story." She scoffed under her breath.

Sahara tried not to laugh. "Do you take lessons?"

Fanta shook his head. "No time with all my karate practice."

Judging by the multicolored display of karate belts hanging on the wall, her cousin must've practiced *a lot*. Sahara pointed to the twin bed underneath them. "Is this your room?"

"I sleep here, but our family eats in here too." He gestured toward a small square table in front of the balcony.

Naima pulled out a chair. "We used to share a room before I kicked him out."

"You didn't kick me out." Her brother plopped down across from her. "I'm the one who asked Baba to move my bed in here when I turned thirteen."

"Only after I told Mama I was too old to share my room with a smelly boy."

Sahara knew where this was going. She took a seat in between them and changed the subject. "How long have you been doing karate?"

"Since I was eight. Never missed a practice. And next year, insha Allah, I'll qualify for the International Junior Karate Tournament."

There was an unusual shakiness in Fanta's voice. Maybe he was worried about qualifying. Sahara knew what it felt like not to get something you longed for. "I hope you make it."

He nodded, his lips curling into a soft smile. He looked *humble*. That is, before he turned to his sister and said, "Of course I'll make it."

Naima rolled her eyes, dumping a bunch of golden wrappers onto the center of the table.

Sahara tapped her hands and sang, "Ba . . . Ba . . . Ba . . . Ba . . . Bimbos."

Her cousins chanted along as they unwrapped the round chocolate biscuits. They popped whole ones in their mouths while Sahara savored hers with small crunchy bites. *Delicious!*

"Do you believe me *now* about Magda?" Naima asked, melted chocolate covering her front teeth.

"Kinda." Sahara swallowed. She didn't buy that Magda was the type of witch who produced evil spells, but she'd seen for herself how wickedly rude Magda could be. "What does Khalu Omar even see in her?"

Naima shrugged. "We think she bewitched him."

"*You* think that. *My* problem is we don't know anything about her. Just that her parents died in a car accident, so she doesn't have any family." Fanta slipped his fingers under his bandana and scratched his head. "What about aunts or uncles or *cousins*? Everybody in Cairo is *someone's* cousin."

"If nobody in the family likes Magda, why is the wedding even happening?" Sahara wasn't one to butt into other people's business, but she had to know.

"Because he's in love with her. Sittu doesn't think we should get involved. 'It's Allah's will,' " he said, imitating his grandmother. "Didn't you hear her tell Mama she needs to accept it?"

How could Sahara forget? It had been super awkward.

Sahara was all for love, but she wasn't sure about this acceptance. When she didn't like something, she came up with a plan to fix it.

"Do witches bleed?" Naima spat out.

Sahara quickly recalled the stream of red trickling down Magda's wrist. "It definitely looked like blood from where I was sitting. But I don't understand why she pulled her hand away when Khalu Omar tried to help."

Naima stood up and paced around the table. After a few seconds, she muttered, "Because she didn't want him to see what had caused the bleeding."

Sahara wasn't sure what her cousin was getting at.

"Get to the point." Fanta groaned.

"Think," Naima pressed. "Who stopped the thief from breaking into the shop?"

"Kitmeer," Sahara answered.

Naima nodded. "What if it wasn't his bark that scared the thief away but his—"

"Bite." The word flew out of Sahara's mouth before she could stop it.

"And what if the thief wasn't a man?"

Fanta waved his hand at his sister. "Don't tell me you think it was a woman."

"Not an ordinary woman, but a witch," she answered.

Sahara's breathing quickened. "Er, I'm not sure. What proof do you have that it was Magda?"

"Thank you, cousin, for being the voice of reason. Allah

knows Naima has none. And she's just sour that Khalu Omar didn't marry Noora."

There was that name again—the one that had unsettled El Ghoula. "Who is this Noora?"

"Sittu's maid before Fayrouz," Naima told her. "A beautiful person—the complete opposite of Magda. Our uncle *should* have married her. He loved her, and she loved him."

"I can't believe you brought her up at lunch in front of his fiancée. Wait till Mama gets home. I've told you before—it wouldn't have been proper for him to marry a maid."

"So what!" his sister blasted. "What about the story of Prince Ahmed and Peri Banu? They *shouldn't* have married, but they did because they loved each other."

Fanta huffed. "You and your silly tales. Ahmed was a human, and Peri was a fairy. Total nonsense!"

Sahara was still hung up on Sittu's former maid. "What happened to Noora?"

"She disappeared," Fanta answered. "Two months ago, she left Sittu a note saying she was going back to Ismalaya to take care of her sick father."

"She didn't even say goodbye." Naima's voice shook. "She'd been with us for ten years. She was part of the family."

"Will she come back?"

"Maybe." Naima shrugged. "But then it'll be too late. El Ghoula will have already married our uncle."

Sahara didn't care for Magda either, but what could they possibly do?

The question lingered in Sahara's mind for the rest of the day and into the night. She didn't like *not* knowing. Before bed, Sahara pulled out her planet pad and checked off Magda's name. Next to it, she wrote, *El Ghoula*, then flipped to a clean page and scribbled, *How to prove your uncle's fiancée is a witch.*

15

The Journal

It was past noon again when Sahara stirred in bed. Luckily, Fayrouz hadn't been sent to wake her today. A symphony of voices from the street traveled through the shutters. While Queens hummed with the buzz of cars on the expressway, the clang of construction vehicles breaking ground, and the beeps of trucks in reverse, here, it was the people who made the music—the street merchants touting their wares, the children in the alley yelling "goal," and Uncle Gamal howling at someone's joke.

Sahara rubbed her eyes. It wasn't that she disliked any of these new sounds—she just missed the ones from home. She missed *so* many things. The big stuff like Amitu and her room, but the little stuff too. Like waking up to her robot's radio alarm, having Cap'n Crunch cereal for breakfast, watching her favorite cartoons—*Scooby-Doo* and *She-Ra*, of course— and all the other pieces that made New York home.

As Sahara flung the sheets off, a familiar scent wafted

through the gap in the door. She drew in a deep breath and sighed, "Wara ainab."

In a matter of minutes, she was at the dining room table, where Sittu sat hunched over a plate stacked with grape leaves and a large bowl filled with rice. "I'm working on the second batch." Sittu smiled, sliding a dish of cooked wara ainab toward Sahara. "I made some this morning so they'd be ready when you woke up."

Sahara took a bite. Even though it was technically lunchtime, she had to admit this was way better than cereal for breakfast. She also couldn't believe how much they tasted like her aunt's. "Exactly like Amitu's!"

"That's because I taught your mother and her how to make them." Sittu grabbed a veiny leaf, placing a tablespoon of rice in its center. "When preparing wara ainab, you must remember three things. One: Don't fill with too much rice. Two: Wrap tightly. And the most important, three: Don't think, *feel*. Let your hands guide you." She folded one side of the leaf over the rice, then the other, like she was wrapping a tiny present. After, she carefully placed each finished bundle into a deep pot.

Sahara had never seen Amitu make wara ainab before. She'd always been at school. "Can I try?" she asked when she'd finished eating.

Sittu coached her through the steps, but her first one ended up looking like it had been gnawed on by a mouse. Rice spilled out of the clumsy tears she'd made attempting to fold it. Sahara stared at it, defeated. "I don't think I'm very good at this."

"Don't worry. No one's good at making grape leaves right away. It takes a great deal of practice and patience." Sittu took Sahara's creation and placed it into the pot.

"You're not gonna fix it before you cook it?"

Sittu shook her head. "Tab'an la. Your mother asked me the same question after she'd wrapped her first leaf. I told her what *my* mother said when she taught me. 'Your first should look like your first. If it were perfect, why would you try again?' And Mama was right. I'm sixty and still trying to make every grape leaf better than that poor first one I made when I was your age."

Sahara couldn't help but smile at her grandmother's story.

"Keep going," Sittu encouraged, then headed back to the kitchen.

Sahara repeated Sittu's words to herself. *Don't think,* feel. She wasn't sure how *not* to think. Maybe closing her eyes would help. She squeezed them shut, letting her fingers take over. Feeling for the edges of the leaf, Sahara folded and rolled. She braced herself for another disaster, but the rice remained intact this time.

Knock, knock.

"Sahara, can you get the door?" Sittu called from the kitchen. "My hands are covered in flour. It's probably your father."

Sahara opened the door, not expecting to find Khalu Omar smiling at her, a tan-colored book at his hip.

"Just the person I've come to see." He stepped inside.

She tightened her scrunchie around her hair, wondering why he had come to see *her*.

He sat at the table and tapped on the seat next to him. Once Sahara joined him, he slid the book toward her. "I've been saving this for you."

"What is it?" Sahara wiped her hands, then rubbed the smooth leather cover with her thumb.

"Your mother's journal. Our baba—*your* giddu—was a professor of literature. Amani never took one of his classes, but she was his most prized student. Every night, Baba would tell us one of the stories he'd studied at work." Khalu's voice softened. "I can still see Amani leaning forward, hanging on his every word. She was so worried she'd forget an important detail from one of the night's tales that Baba bought her *this* journal to write them down."

First the necklace, now the journal—precious pieces of her mother. "Where'd you find it?"

"Your mother gave it to me before she left for America to remember our baba, since I was only nine when he passed away. You know, if it weren't for her encouragement, I wouldn't be where I am today. I'd always wanted to become a doctor, but the years of schooling intimidated me. I can still hear her say, 'Omar, you can't let fear get in the way of what you want. The scarier the dream, the faster you have to run toward it.' So that's what I did." He sighed. "She was always looking out for me."

Sahara dropped her head, guilt creeping in again. But Khalu Omar raised her chin and gave his golden smile.

"I'll never forget the day Amani called from New York to tell us she was pregnant. She was certain you were a girl and even more certain of your name. 'I know it's not traditional. But her life won't be. Greatness is on the horizon for my daughter,' she insisted, sounding like one of Baba's stories. 'She will experience wonders and adversity. And like the great desert that has braved millions of years of shifting winds, Sahara *will* persevere.'"

Sahara sat up taller. She'd always wanted an ordinary name like Vicky's. But after what Khalu had just told her, her heart swelled with pride. *Take that, Corey. Bet your name hasn't braved* millions *of years of wind.*

Khalu Omar peered at her, his expression warm and tender. "I'm so happy you're finally here, Sahara the Great." He was being completely genuine, unlike his phony fiancée. "And I know your mother would want you to have her journal."

Sahara nodded, bringing it to her chest. For years, she'd missed out on the chance to connect with her Cairo family and her mom. As she basked in her uncle's light, affection coursed through her, pushing away the murky guilt.

"I'm so happy to be here too."

AFTER KHALU OMAR left, Sahara returned to Sittu's room. She thumbed the gilded pages of the journal, then unraveled the leather cord around it. *The back of the book is the front in Egypt,* she reminded herself, flipping it over. Five letters had been scratched into the top right corner: aliph, meem, aliph, noon, and yi. *Amani.*

Sahara opened the journal and studied her mom's handwriting, imagining a young Amani scribbling down her father's stories before she forgot them. She wished she could read more. Unfortunately, the weekly Arabic lessons she'd taken in the fourth grade left her able to write little more than her name. At least she'd been able to make out her mother's.

She leafed through the book, gasping at one of the pages. A sketch of the hamsa pendant, the very one Amitu had given her a few days ago, filled it. Underneath, the words *The two that must not join become one, unlocking what has been hidden in the dark* were written in English.

Amitu had said they'd never opened the jewelry box after the day at the market, but clearly, her mother *had.* Sahara jumped at a knock at the door.

Naima peeked in. "Did I scare you?"

"No . . . no, come in. It's not that." Sahara set the journal down.

"Why do you look like you've seen an afreet?"

Sahara gestured for her to close the door. "I *have* seen a ghost. Only it's not the kind you think. The day before I left home, Amitu told me this crazy story of when she and my mom were younger, and they went to Khan el Khalili to meet some famous writer—"

"Which writer?" Naima asked, sitting beside her on the bed.

"I can't remember his name, and that's not the—"

"How can't you remember?"

Sahara blew out a breath. "You're missing the point."

"Sorry, I'm listening."

"Okay. So this mysterious fortune teller gave my mother a jewelry box and insisted it was for her daughter. But my mom was only sixteen. She didn't *have* a daughter yet. Isn't that nuts?"

Her cousin shook her head, her eyes glimmering. "It's *wonderful!*"

Of course Naima thought so. She also thought Magda flew on a broomstick. "But that's not all." Sahara picked up the book. "Khalu Omar just gave me my mom's old journal. It's filled with all these tales our giddu used to tell her when she was young." Before Naima lost focus again, Sahara jumped in with, "And I promise I'll let you see them once I get this out."

Naima nodded, restraining herself.

"In the middle of those stories was this." Sahara pointed to the sketch. "A picture of the *same* pendant hanging from the necklace that was in the old box. The shape of the sapphire and the patterns on the hamsa are identical. Let me show you."

" 'The two that must not join become one,' " Naima whispered as Sahara brought her backpack over. "What does it mean?"

"One thing at a time. Let me show you the necklace first. I packed it for the wedding, thinking it would be special to wear since my mom meant to give it to me before ..." She'd thought the words so many times. How come she couldn't say them?

"Before she died," Naima said softly.

Sahara nodded, lifting the lid. It was *empty*. She tore apart her backpack in case it had fallen out of the box. *Come on. Start glowing, start shaking. Do something, anything. Please!*

Her stomach twisted into a tight knot as the truth set in. "The necklace ... it's gone."

Naima grabbed the box and turned it upside down, shaking it. "Are you sure?"

Sahara was certain. She clearly remembered stuffing it into her backpack on her first night. Her lips trembled. Her mom had saved it for all those years so *she* could have it, and now ... now it was gone. *Don't cry*, she willed herself. "I put it in here after it started acting wacky. I know it."

Her cousin's eyes widened. "What do you mean, 'acting wacky'?"

"The night we arrived, I dreamed of my mom holding the necklace. When I woke up, I ran to my backpack." Sahara swallowed. "I know you won't believe this—actually, you might be the only person to believe it—but the sapphire at the center of the hamsa glowed, and the whole thing shook. Not a little, *a lot*."

"It's enchanted!" Naima pointed to the sketch and the words underneath. "Your mother must've drawn it for a reason and written this in English so you could understand."

"But I *don't* understand. How could she have drawn an

exact copy of something she'd supposedly never seen? And I have no idea what the words underneath are about."

Naima didn't answer. She walked around the room, talking to herself, eventually stopping, her eyes dancing with ideas.

"I knew El Ghoula was the one who broke into the shop!"

Sahara shook her head, unable to follow Naima's train of thought because it had completely gone off track. "What does that have to do with my necklace? And what would a witch"—Sahara was using the term only to prove her point—"want with our family's shop? Bimbos are delicious, but come on."

"Maybe it's *more* than a shop that sells Bimbos."

"What are you talking about?"

"I'm beginning to think Mama and Sittu are hiding something in the shop. One night after closing, I remembered I had forgotten to feed Kitmeer, so I snuck downstairs with some leftover chicken. That's when I saw them go inside and lock the gate behind them. A second later, I peeked in, but they'd disappeared."

"Are you sure you weren't dreaming?" Sahara balked, recalling how there was barely room to move in the shop. "Where could they have gone?"

Naima shrugged. "But there's something strange going on. I know it."

Sahara didn't have any more time for her cousin's wild imagination. She had to find her hamsa. "Can we please get back to my missing necklace?"

"That's what I've been trying to tell you," Naima huffed.

"It's not *missing*. El Ghoula *stole* it! The hand of Fatima is a symbol of protection. The night of the break-in, it was shaking and acting so ghareeb because it sensed her danger. It was trying to warn you. So she took it before it could do that again."

Sahara suddenly remembered Magda hurrying into Sittu's room after her wrist had bled. As far-fetched as Naima's theory sounded, she couldn't dismiss it altogether. "I should never have brought the necklace here, but Amitu was so sure it was time for me to have it. I've gotta get it back."

"You *will*. I swear." Naima squeezed her shoulder. "And you can't blame yourself. El Ghoula would've managed to get her sneaky hands on the hamsa no matter where it was. She's behind all the bad stuff happening lately."

It was hard not to believe her cousin when she spoke with such conviction. But they needed *more* than conviction. The wedding was in two days. If there was a morsel of truth to Naima's theory, Sahara couldn't just stand by and do nothing while El Ghoula stashed her necklace who knows where and plotted who knows what against her family. She had to look out for them—she owed them that much after taking away their beloved Amani.

Her mom would want her to protect the family, especially Khalu Omar. Maybe that's why she was coming to Sahara in her dreams. Naima thought the necklace was trying to alert her about the break-in. But what if all the shaking and glowing and "*the two that must not join* or something creepy happens" business were because of the upcoming union—the joining of husband and wife?

Sahara's heart raced. "We've gotta stop the wedding!"

"Yes, exactly!" Naima threw her arms around her.

Sahara hugged her back, then grabbed the planet pad. *Hypothesis: El Ghoula is responsible for breaking into the shop* and *stealing my necklace,* she scribbled at the top of a clean page. "I'm sticking to what I said before. We can't just accuse Magda. We need proof."

"Yes, but what's a hy-po-the-sis?"

"It's a theory, a hunch you have that you're trying to prove with scientific evidence. You gather that evidence by conducting an experiment." Sahara flipped to one of the first pages in her pad, where she'd taken notes for a school project. "See, here I wanted to prove that plants exposed to music grow faster. So for one month, I watered a bunch of begonia plants but only played songs for half of them, the variable group, but none for the other half, the control group."

"And did it work?"

"Yup. The variable group bloomed faster and grew taller." Sahara flipped back to El Ghoula's page. This situation didn't exactly lend itself to typical scientific method protocol. She'd need to improvise. "We may not have a control or variable group, but we still have to prove our hypothesis."

Naima snapped her fingers. "Laylat el henna is tomorrow!"

Why then? Sahara thought until she remembered that Amitu had insisted she pack a special outfit for Magda's henna night—a celebration of the bride where everyone gets henna art on their hands, feet, ankles, *and* wrists. Her cousin was onto something. She crossed out her earlier hypothesis and replaced it with, *If El Ghoula is responsible for the break-in and stealing my necklace, then she will have Kitmeer's bite on her wrist.*

"Better hypotamus." Naima smiled.

"Hypothesis," Sahara repeated, giggling. "And thanks, but we've still gotta figure out how to get her cuff off. It's not like she's gonna just volunteer to do it."

"Then we'll snatch it off!"

The idea of snatching anything off El Ghoula gave Sahara the creeps. "There has to be an easier way." Just then, the seed of an idea began to take root in her mind. "What if somehow we get Magda to take it off herself, not because she wants to, but because she *has* to." There was no time to waste. They had twenty-four hours to figure out a way to make this happen and expose the bride-to-be for who she really was—a no-good, necklace-stealing, shop-trespassing witch.

The Winds of Fate

985 CE

An hour after leaving the caravanserai and the emir's officers behind, Morgana traveled along the rugged and steep trail that cut through the desert canyons bordering the Wadi el Qelt valley. She'd felt horrible rushing the colt out of the stables when he'd barely rested or eaten, but what could she do—stick around while the officers plotted all the ways they'd skewer her when she was found?

"I promise when it's safe, you and I will feast like kings and queens," she told Nasser, as she'd decided to call the horse. After all he'd done for her, he deserved a proper name.

The hamsa bounced against her chest as she rode, a constant reminder of Deena and home. As much as Morgana yearned for both, she knew that keeping her mawlay's daughter out of this mess was the right decision. The sorcerer was dead, but what if someone else came looking for the lamp or the other treasures? She'd never be able to live with herself if something happened to Deena.

As the setting sun cast fiery hues in the sky and the howls

of nearby wolves echoed through the secluded canyons, worry grew in Morgana's chest like a stubborn weed. Her mind swirled with the officer's accusations. Surely, Deena had to know that Morgana would never hurt her father . . . would never hurt anyone. An insidious voice wormed its way into her ear. *But you* did *hurt someone,* it said.

And then something glimmered in the fading light. "Alhamdulillah," Morgana cried, making out a small stream. Her horse could drink and graze on the nearby sprouting grasses while she found a place to rest before it got too dark.

"Who needs the comforts of the inn when nature is so generous!" She kissed Nasser's head before hopping off the saddle and leading him toward the stream. As he lowered his head to drink, she asked, "Where shall we live, my Nasserini?"

Since returning to Baghdad wasn't an option, Morgana considered heading to Cairo, where her aunt worked as a lady's maid in the Fatimid palace. Having just lost her closest friend, her mawlay, and the only home she'd ever known, she could use the company. A few years ago, when Ali Baba had returned from a visit to Egypt, he'd told the girls, "There's no city more beautiful on the face of the earth than Cairo." Afterward, Deena had insisted she'd marry an Egyptian gentleman with a palace along the banks of the Nile and bring Morgana with her.

Back then, it had just been sweet talk between friends. Never had Morgana imagined *going,* and certainly not without Deena. Mama had once told her, "When the winds of fate blow, let them carry you, for they are the wise hand of Allah guiding you in the right direction."

Morgana raised her face to heaven and whispered, "I will try."

THE WINDS OF fate *had* blown. They blew through space and time, through the darkness and the light, calling forth all that is, was, and will be. For some, the winds gust, blowing their well-meaning plans to dust. For others, they sing like a breeze, warming their hearts with hope. However they come, they cannot be avoided.

Morgana wasn't prepared for what the winds had summoned, but she wasn't alone either. For allies, near and far, were coming. But first, an enemy.

PART THREE

The Wedding

Umm Zalabya

The following day, Sittu's apartment bustled with preparations for laylat el henna. It seemed like Sahara's grandmother, aunt, and Fayrouz hadn't left the kitchen since yesterday. Too bad they were going to all this trouble for El Ghoula.

As Sahara watched Sittu wipe the sweat off her forehead in the sweltering kitchen, she took comfort in her mission. Magda might be getting her precious henna night, but if everything went as she and Naima had planned, there'd be *no* wedding, and El Ghoula would be out of their lives for good. And maybe, just maybe, Sahara would get her necklace back.

Sure, the hamsa was sparkly and pretty. But it was her mom's faith that it had always been meant for Sahara, not to mention the care she'd taken to save it for so long, that made it invaluable.

Just as Sahara finished getting dressed, Naima was at the door, insisting they hurry to visit an old friend. "I know Mama. Once it gets closer to henna time, she'll be calling our names every second to get this or that. Now is our only chance to see

Umm Zalabya. And trust me, if anyone can help us get more proof against El Ghoula, it's her."

Sahara wasn't sure how Naima's friend would help, but she couldn't resist the possibility of acquiring more evidence. She'd have to ask her father for permission first. He was likely down at the shop reading the morning's paper over a cup of coffee or laughing like a schoolboy at something Uncle Gamal had said.

"Stay close to Naima," he urged, while Uncle Gamal made Naima promise not to let her cousin out of her sight.

With that, the girls set out on their excursion. Kitmeer began to follow, but Naima shook her head. "I'm not sure how you'll get along with my friend's cat," she said, tossing the ball deep into the alley.

After ten minutes of weaving through pedestrians, food carts, and honking cars, Sahara and Naima reached an old brick building. They sprinted up four flights of steps to a rooftop garden with the most vibrant white blooms Sahara had ever seen. Naima's "old friend" wasn't just someone she'd known for a while but an older woman with a silver widow's peak jutting down her lined forehead. Rather than greeting the lady with the customary two kisses, Naima embraced her tightly, then introduced her to Sahara as "Umm Zalabya, the greatest seer in all of Shobra."

Another fortune teller. It took everything Sahara had not to leave. They'd come for solid proof, not mystical nonsense.

Naima was wise not to mention they were heading to a seer, because if Sahara had known, she'd never have come.

"At last, the desert rose we have been waiting *ages* for." Umm Zalabya flashed a smile at Sahara, revealing a mouth of missing teeth. Her voice rose on the word *ages*, giving Sahara the impression that she was talking about way more than the twelve years she'd been alive.

Sahara looked away, turning her gaze to one of the many raised garden beds. It was constructed of steel panels reinforced with wooden beams at the corners and center, most likely to support the weight of the soil. Sahara couldn't wait to tell her father about them. Maybe they could fashion a small one to keep on their terrace back home. "Your flowers are lovely."

"Not only is Umm Zalabya a talented seer," Naima boasted, "but she grows the most beautiful yasmeen. Sittu asked her to create ful for the wedding."

Ful? As the seer reached into the basket of cut flowers behind her, Sahara mouthed, "What's that?" to her cousin.

"Yasmeen garlands for the guests to wear around their necks," Umm Zalabya explained.

Before Sahara could determine how she'd managed to read her lips with her back turned to them, the woman spun around, holding a handful of blooms. "I will spend the rest of the day carefully stringing these beauties together." She brought one to Sahara's nose. "Picked right before the Fajr prayer. Unlike most flowers, yasmeen open in the middle of the night."

A sweet scent rushed up Sahara's nose. It reminded her of Khaltu Layla's perfume. "What's the secret to your gardening success?" Sahara asked, trying to steer *far* away from any fortune-telling baloney.

"Rich soil from the Fayoum Oasis *and* magic," Umm Zalabya answered matter-of-factly.

Not fertilizer, or watering, or even playing them music. But *magic*. This visit was going to be a crap show.

"Almaz," Naima cooed, bending down to pet the cat that had slunk by her side. Despite the morning's warm glow, the animal's fur glimmered a distinct cool silver.

After a few seconds of nuzzling, Naima turned to the seer, her face serious. "Umm Zalabya, we have a problem. My cousin and I suspect someone of doing terrible things. We're hoping you could use your divination to tell us if we're right."

What was all this "we" business? Sahara didn't want any part of Umm Zalabya's "divination." But she could tell from the way Naima's eyes were doing that dancing thing again that it was too late to stop this train to Hocus Pocus Land.

Umm Zalabya nodded, then crouched down and grabbed a handful of soil from a nearby planter. "I was getting this ready for some new seedlings, but it will do."

She shut her eyes and tossed the dirt. A cloud of it hovered in the air for way longer than gravity should've allowed, then landed on one of the stone pavers that covered the roof's floor. Sahara's mouth hung open. The soil had fallen into perfect patterns of dots. She might not have believed any of this foretelling stuff, but she couldn't look away as Umm Zalabya opened her dark eyes and scanned the dot formations.

"You were right to come. There is a dangerous female presence nearby."

"I knew it," Naima whispered in Sahara's ear.

"One fueled by generations of yearning to possess what your family and its ancestors have held dear."

"All that from some dots in the dirt?" Sahara grumbled under her breath, but Umm Zalabya still heard.

"You doubt the wisdom of the earth?" Her eyes lasered in on Sahara's. "You are missing something . . . something extremely valuable."

The back of Sahara's neck prickled. Naima could've told her about the necklace, right?

"You must reclaim it." Umm Zalabya's voice boomed, scaring a few sparrows off the ledge. "And you can, if you open yourself to the love your fear has locked away—and if you remember who you truly are. For *there* lies a force stronger than the most insatiable hunger for power."

Sahara had no idea where El Ghoula was hiding her hamsa, but she was positive it would take much more than *love* to find it.

"This female presence. Is there anything *you* can do to help us stop her?" Naima asked.

Umm Zalabya stood up and dusted the dirt off her hands. "Unfortunately, I cannot vanquish dark magic once it has been cast." She hesitated, a smile spreading across her face.

"But I can provide a level of protection. When you return tomorrow, the wedding garlands will be complete with my most enchanted blooms. Ones that can diminish evil sorcery's most dire and permanent effects."

Enchanted blooms, psychic dirt, cryptic predictions—Umm Zalabya's divination show had been impressive, but nowhere near helpful. Sahara had heard enough. She twisted around and headed for the door.

And then the older woman said something that stopped Sahara in her tracks.

"My desert rose, I have a message for you from the spirit world—ma tinseesh."

Crash!

Sahara racked her brain as they walked back to Sittu's. How could Umm Zalabya have known the plea, "Ma tinseesh—Don't forget," uttered to Sahara's mom sixteen years ago? Although Sahara *had* shared the necklace's history with Naima, she *hadn't* mentioned those words. She shook her head, trying to rid it of confusion. *Focus on the probable.*

She crossed her arms and asked curtly, "So when did you tell Umm Zalabya about my necklace being stolen? I know she couldn't have just *seen* that in some dirt."

Naima's face dropped. "I didn't tell her. I'd never tell *any-one* your secrets." She turned away from Sahara.

For the next five *long* minutes, the girls walked silently— all the while, guilt churning within Sahara. She hadn't meant to hurt her cousin. As they passed the mosque across from Sittu's building, she tapped Naima's shoulder. "I'm sorry. I shouldn't have accused you of telling Umm Zalabya. It's just lately there's so much happening that I can't explain."

"I know," Naima said softly. "But why do you need to

explain everything? It's much easier to believe. To trust. I trust you."

"I trust you too."

Sahara *did* trust her cousin, even if she couldn't comprehend how and why Naima put her faith in things that couldn't possibly exist.

"I told you Magda's after something in the shop. Something Sittu, Mama, and our ancestors have 'held dear.'"

Sahara hated giving credence to the seer's ancient-sounding gibberish, but Sittu and Khaltu *had* made a point of concealing their worry after the attempted break-in. Were they hiding something, as Naima suspected? Sahara's stomach flipped. There was so much uncertainty. At least she had a solid strategy. After hours of brainstorming last night, they'd finally devised a scheme that would persuade El Ghoula to remove the bracelet herself.

"We just have to stick to the plan," Sahara reminded herself and Naima. "If we can prove that Magda tried to force her way into the shop, then maybe we can get her to tell us what she is after." *And what she's done with my necklace.*

ONCE THEY RETURNED to Sittu's, Sahara understood why her cousin had insisted they visit Umm Zalabya's before it got too late. Because for the next hour, they trudged up and down the steps to and from Khaltu's kitchen retrieving ingredients she and Sittu needed more of, like lemons, rice, and sugar.

As soon as they'd caught their breath, Khaltu Layla remembered she needed soda from the shop.

"Sahara, yalla!" Naima called from the room with the balcony.

Shouldn't we be headed downstairs? Sahara wondered as she followed her cousin onto the terrace, where the early-evening sky glowed a deep pink and orange.

Naima leaned over the rail. "Fanta! Mama needs soda for tonight!"

Within seconds, her brother emerged from the shop. "Lower the basket," he called.

"Watch this." Naima winked at Sahara, grabbing a large plastic basket from the floor and hooking it to a thick rope. It was attached to some sort of wheel contraption hanging from the terrace's ceiling. She pushed up on the rope, quickly switching the position of her hands to lower the basket farther and farther.

"It's a pulley," Sahara muttered, remembering when she'd created one to lift a bucket of water in science class.

By the time the basket reached the street, Fanta had returned. He loaded it with bottle after bottle of Coca-Cola, Sprite, and, of course, Fanta.

All those bottles must've weighed a ton. "Do you need help?" Sahara asked as Naima reached for the rope.

"It's not too heavy. Would you like to try?"

Sahara beamed, then crouched beside her and gripped the rough fibers of the rope.

"Whatever you do, don't let go." Her cousin released her hold.

"Okay." Sahara took a deep breath and yanked the rope down. *Clink, clink, clink.* The bottles knocked into each other as the basket shook wildly in the air.

"Don't pull so hard," Naima coached.

Sahara nodded, zeroing in on her hands. After several more pulls that were either too forceful or too feeble, she eventually found the right balance of firmness. She smiled, watching the basket climb past the second floor. "I'm doing it!"

Naima chuckled. "You're officially from Shobra now."

Then the click of heels, a momentary warning before an icy voice sounded from behind. "Hello, darlings."

Sahara shivered, a veil of cold sweat crawling over her skin as she looked over her shoulder. *Magda.*

El Ghoula loomed above her, a sinister smile across her face, eyes blazing with their trademark amber fire.

"Noooo!" Her cousin's voice sounded miles away. Naima leaped for the rope, but it was too late. Sahara had let go, sending the basket crashing onto the sidewalk. Glass shattered, and streams of soda spilled into the street.

Tut, tut, tut. Look what you've done. Magda's words played in a vicious loop in Sahara's head as she helped her cousins sweep up the broken glass. She felt sick. The *one* thing Naima had told her *not* to do was let go. *Ugh!* Why had she let El Ghoula get under her skin?

If Magda hadn't left to get changed for tonight, Sahara would've marched upstairs and told her where she could shove her *darlings*. But—who was she kidding? El Ghoula unnerved her in a way no one had before. She was surrounded by proof of her fear: the sidewalk covered in shards of glass and brown, clear, and orange soda bleeding into the street.

Sittu and Khaltu had insisted it had been an unfortunate accident and that if they were angry with anyone, it was Magda. "The nerve of her to show up—at the last minute, no less—with platters of fancy food from Allah knows what restaurant. And did you hear the way she said, 'Tonight calls for more than home cooking'?" Sittu railed.

Sahara had never seen her grandmother so fired up, her cheeks as red as a ripe tomato. She knew how she felt— Magda's hoity-toity audacity made her blood boil too—but how could Sittu not be mad at *her*? She'd destroyed an entire basket of sodas. Her dad offered to pay for them, but that had only insulted Sittu.

There's gotta be something I can do. Sahara swept up the remaining glass. Maybe tomorrow she'd ask her father to help her install a safety mechanism to the pulley. As for tonight, she was more resolved than ever to reveal Kitmeer's bite on Magda's wrist.

On his way to the coffeehouse—the men would celebrate

the groom there tonight—Sahara's dad stopped to check on her. "I don't have to go to the ahwa. I can stay if you need me to."

"No, go. I'll be fine."

"Are you sure?"

"Totally." She mustered a smile for his sake.

He kissed her head. "Okay. Try to have fun tonight."

"I will, promise."

Naima grasped Sahara's hand and led her toward the building. "We'd better get dressed."

Sahara hesitated at the entrance, looking back at her father. Her conscience twinged. She wasn't used to keeping secrets from him. But if she told him what they had planned, he might try to stop her. She couldn't take that risk. She turned around just as Sittu called from the balcony, "Naima, Sahara, come up. Laylat el henna begins in one hour."

19

Medusa's Army

Clothes flew out of Sahara's suitcase and onto the floor until a knock came from the door. Khaltu Layla peeked her head through before walking in. As she stepped over the mess, Sahara explained how she couldn't find the outfit she'd packed for tonight.

"Then I've come just in time." Khaltu held out a violet galabeya.

"Thank you. It's pretty." It wouldn't have been Sahara's first choice, but it *was* pretty. And she did prefer the BIV colors of the rainbow over the ROYG ones. As with the blue tunic Khaltu wore, gold embroidery that began around the collar and stretched down to the center also adorned the one in Sahara's hands. "It looks a lot like yours."

"You're right." Her aunt chuckled. "I bought the same one in different colors for all of us. Naima's is fuchsia, and Sittu's is turquoise."

"Did you buy one for . . . for . . ." Sahara couldn't get El Ghoula's name out.

Nevertheless, Khaltu knew whom she meant. "For Magda—no. I offered to, but she'd already picked out something else." Her lips tightened into a thin smile. "Anyway, I thought you might like to see a photo from your mother's laylat el henna." She pulled out an album from the armoire and brought it over.

Sahara plopped down on the bed next to her. She'd seen pictures from her parents' wedding but never any from her mom's henna night. Being in Cairo was like using one of those Magic Markers that turned blank pages into colorful pictures. The more time she spent here, the more clearly she could see her mother.

Sahara leaned in as Khaltu stopped at a photo of her mom standing between Amitu and her, their arms around each other.

"Look at my sister—how she's smiling brighter than the full moon. I've never seen anyone so happy."

Sahara peered at the picture, trying to make out every last detail. Her mom and aunts wore galabeyas too, and swirly designs were on their hands. "Is that the henna?" She pointed to her mother's hand. "It kinda looks like a tattoo."

Khaltu explained that it *was* henna, but unlike tattoos, the natural dye only lasted a few weeks. She went on to tell Sahara about the history of tonight's tradition. "It started thousands of years ago with the goddess Isis. The ancient Egyptians believed that after Isis's husband, Osiris, was killed and chopped into pieces by the evil god Set—"

"Chopped into pieces! Ew, gross!"

"Fa'lan, ew!" Khaltu scrunched her face. "After her beloved Osiris died, Isis went around gathering the pieces of his body. The more parts she found, the more red and stained with blood her hands became. Since then, brides have been staining their hands with henna to show their devotion to their future husbands."

Surely, there were better and less bloody ways to show loyalty. Had Isis ever heard of a friendship bracelet? "If I ever get married, and my husband gets chopped into pieces, I *won't* go looking for his parts!"

Khaltu laughed. "I don't blame you. Your mother thought Isis's story was romantic, but I agree with *you*."

Naima had told her another story about the history of henna, but Sahara didn't share it with Khaltu. She'd hear about it soon enough. Their plan depended on it.

"You need to get ready, and I need to check on the shop." Her aunt returned the album to the armoire.

"Sounds good." Sahara blew away the stray curls in her face. "Looks like I got Mom's Medusa hair."

Khaltu swung around. "Where did you hear that?"

Oh no. Why had she brought up the whole Medusa thing? Sahara looked down at her hands. "Sittu told me you used to call my mom that when you were younger."

Khaltu's eyes grew distant. "So silly, the stuff sisters say and do to each other. Amani used to make fun of how I always had to be tidy and perfect, and I teased her about her wild hair.

The truth is, I was jealous of how free she was with it, with everything. I cared *too* much about what others thought." Her gaze returned to the room. "Medusa may have had wild hair, but she was a force to be reckoned with, as was your mother. As are you." She kissed Sahara's head. "I rather prefer wildness to perfection these days, if you know what I mean, darling." She imitated El Ghoula's pretentious air.

"I do, Khal—I mean, I do, darling." Sahara giggled as her aunt left the room. She grabbed the violet galabeya. *Watch out, Magda darling. Medusa's army is coming for you!*

STARING AT HER reflection in the mirror, which she'd spotted inside the armoire when Khaltu returned the album, Sahara wondered how often her mom had done the same. For so much of Sahara's life, her mother had been elusive. But standing in her childhood home surrounded by shadows of her past, her mom felt closer than ever—still not within reach, but closer.

She shifted her weight to one leg and continued to eye herself in the violet galabeya. What would Vicky think? Knowing her friend, she'd probably say it was awesome and beg to borrow it. There'd be so much to tell her when she returned from camp.

Naima called her name from the other side of the door.

"Come in."

Her cousin entered, twirling in her galabeya. "Matchy, matchy," she sang.

It wasn't *what* Naima was wearing that caught Sahara's eye, but what she *wasn't* that did. It was the first time she'd seen her without her headscarf.

"Why are you looking at me like that?"

"It's just I've never seen your *hair* before." Sahara ogled her cousin's shoulder-length dark-brown tresses.

"Do you like it?" Naima peeked at herself in the mirror, tucking some strands behind her ears.

"It looks great, but where's your tarha?"

"I need to borrow one of Sittu's." Naima reached into the armoire and pulled out a navy scarf adorned with pink flowers. The petals matched the color of her tunic.

Sahara knew that some Muslim women covered their hair for religious reasons. Except she wasn't sure if those were the *only* reasons why. Especially since Amitu didn't wear hijab but still believed in God and read the Koran. This was another one of those "no right or wrong" matters. Why were there so many of them? Maybe Naima could help her understand.

"When did you start covering your hair?"

"When I turned twelve," Naima answered, holding the scarf against her galabeya. "They go together, right?"

"Totally," Sahara responded. It wasn't the color of Naima's headscarf she was interested in. "I guess I'm wondering"—she spoke to her cousin through the mirror—"why you decided to cover your hair?" Sahara hesitated, remembering how out of place she felt amid all the women wearing hijab at the airport. "And if it's okay that I don't?"

"Tab'an." Naima nodded. "Is it okay that I *do*?"

"Yes. One hundred percent okay."

"Good." Naima smiled. "If Sittu were here, she would say, 'It's not about who wears hijab or who doesn't. Every girl or woman should choose that for herself.' That's what she told me before I decided."

"But *how* do you decide?"

Naima removed another scarf from one of the drawers. She draped it over Sahara's hair. "Look in the mirror."

Sahara giggled. "*So* weird. It doesn't even look like me."

"Exactly. From the first day I wore hijab, I felt like the way I looked on the *outside* matched who I was on the *inside*." Naima grasped some of her hair in her hand. "*This* feels weird to me."

The two girls stood in front of the armoire, silently studying each other's reflections. They remained that way until the sound of chatter and music coming from beyond the door grew too loud to ignore.

Sahara slid off the scarf. "The guests must be here." Her skin prickled. Any minute now, Magda would be here too.

It is time, her mother's voice rang in her head. Could her mom have somehow known what would happen? Even if it *were* possible, she'd have to think about it later. They had work to do.

Sahara rolled back her shoulders and breathed in deeply. "You remember what we rehearsed, right?"

"Tab'an. I never forget a story." Naima winked as she opened the door.

The apartment brimmed with women greeting each other with kisses, laughing, and dancing. Sahara's eyes flitted among them. There was no sign of Magda, but there *was* a dining table overflowing with food.

Hummus, and tameya, and konafa. Oh my! Sahara chuckled to herself as the savory aromas of sautéed onions and garlic—coupled with the freshness of lemon and parsley and the sweetness of vanilla and syrup—swirled around her. She grinned, spotting her clumsily stuffed grape leaf at the top of a tray of stacked wara ainab.

Naima slid a pita wedge out of the perfectly arranged circle of bread and plunged it into the cucumber yogurt dip. Meanwhile, Khaltu Layla stuck her head out of the room with the balcony. "Let's go, girls!" she yelled over the pulsating music.

Her cousin pranced in, but Sahara hesitated at the door. It had been a few years since Amitu had taught her to belly dance. What if she'd forgotten how? Her aunt had gone on and on about how sad she was to miss the belly dancer at the wedding, but she'd never mentioned that Sahara would have to do any dancing. A heads-up would've been nice.

"Yalla." Naima pulled her into the room.

Khaltu and Sittu wiggled over and joined their hands with the girls to make one circle. Intertwined in their clasps, Sahara's hands tingled with a warmth that traveled to her heart. She swayed her hips instinctively to the beat. Her brain might not have remembered the steps, but her body did.

Naima and Khaltu beamed at her as Sittu relished the moment. "I can't believe we're dancing with Amani's daughter."

Sahara smiled, her confidence bolstering with each movement. She shimmied her shoulders like Amitu had taught her.

Perhaps it was the loud music or her annoying habit of sneaking in, but Sahara hadn't heard Magda enter. Without warning, El Ghoula's nails dug into her wrist, breaking through her and Sittu's hands. She glanced back at Sahara. "Let me show you how it's done in Egypt."

Sahara cringed. Magda's sharp tongue stung as much as her claws.

El Ghoula danced in the center of the circle, dressed in a tightly fitting, cream-colored galabeya. Gold vertical stripes stretched down its bodice and sleeves. With every move, the belt of coins and beads around her waist shook and sparkled.

All of Magda gleamed tonight. Sahara couldn't take her eyes off El Ghoula and the way she tilted her head back and moved her red lips apart, releasing a reverberating cackle. She commanded the space at the heart of the circle, casting an invisible fortress around her that no one dared enter. She was both the most striking *and* grotesque woman Sahara had ever seen.

When the song ended, Sittu clapped her hands together. "This is laylat el henna, ladies! Let's start the henna!"

Sittu's declaration was met with cheers from everyone *but*

El Ghoula. Instead, she pursed her lips and charged out of the circle. Sahara and Naima scrambled out of her way.

Magda swung around in the doorway, her gold strands gliding past her shoulders. "Mais oui. But of course, we must do the henna now."

Naima rolled her eyes. "I think she speaks more French than Arabic."

"But of course." Sahara snorted, then whispered into her cousin's ear, "Let's catch a witch."

Catching a Witch

According to Amitu, the henna portion of the evening would begin with the bride-to-be. "The most time and care is given to adorn her with its beautiful designs," she'd explained. But tonight's bride-to-be was in no hurry to get her body "adorned."

"No, no. We must save the best for last," El Ghoula insisted in her signature fabricated tone.

Sittu pointed a rigid finger at her future daughter-in-law. "Tomorrow, I'm giving you my son. *Tonight*, you will go first." She stared Magda down from her golden tresses to her painted toenails. "Sometimes even the most *untraditional* must honor tradition."

Stick it to her, Sittu.

Naima smirked, also enjoying watching their grandmother stand up to El Ghoula. Sahara's gaze shifted back to Magda.

A flare of amber fire flashed in Magda's eyes, but it was promptly disguised with a tight smile. "But of course," El Ghoula said through gritted teeth as the henna artists, a mother-and-daughter team Sittu addressed as Mona and Samira, escorted her to the balcony room. "Only my ankles. Dye nothing else," El Ghoula hissed before she sat on the bed.

Yes! Sahara cheered in her head while watching from the doorway. Where Magda insisted on getting—and more important, *not* getting—the henna was critical for the girls' plan to work.

The two women hiked up the witch's galabeya, revealing a pair of shiny ivory legs. They were flawless—even her *knees*, which, for most people, were covered with scratches and scars from years of kneeling and falling on them. Then again, El Ghoula wasn't *most* people.

Aroosa. Sahara recalled the word for *bride* in Arabic. Interestingly, it was the same word used for a toy doll, which was fitting because Magda's eerie perfection reminded her of a life-sized Barbie. *What if she isn't a regular human?* The unexpected question sent shivers down Sahara's spine. She tried to dismiss it, but it was getting harder to deny.

Mona, holding a small cone-like contraption in her hand, knelt in front of El Ghoula. Her daughter held up one of the witch's ankles while she squeezed the cone, releasing a thin stream of dark-brown henna from its tip and onto Magda's pale skin. Within minutes, flowy leaves, flowers, and scrolls wrapped around Magda's ankle.

Sahara's eyes shifted to El Ghoula's face. It scrunched as the henna touched her skin. In fact, her entire body appeared to be squirming. She pressed her lips tightly—only a sliver of red lipstick remained—and gripped the bedsheets with her fists. Magda was in *pain*.

Sahara felt a pang of guilt seeing her nemesis suffer. "You didn't tell me henna hurt," she muttered to Naima.

"It's not supposed to."

"Then why does Magda look like she's in agony?"

Naima shrugged. "Henna is baraka. It's meant to bless the bride and keep away evil."

But Magda *was* the evil the henna was supposed to drive away. "What if she's in pain *because* of the henna?" As wild as this idea sounded, it made sense.

Before her cousin could answer, El Ghoula cleared her throat, having noticed the girls ogling her. Her distressed expression reverted to its usual mask of arrogance. Any sympathy Sahara felt for the witch disappeared when she opened her mouth.

"Be careful not to stare too close at the sun, darlings."

"Ha ha. You're so funny." Sahara gave an awkward laugh, then returned to Naima's ear. "Pain or no pain, we must stop her."

Naima nodded her understanding.

Sahara stood up taller. "Ahem. Tante Magda." She addressed her with the French word for *aunt* used in Egypt as a title of respect for an older female relative or close family friend.

Magda lifted her eyebrows curiously. The girls had guessed correctly—she took the pretentious title's bait. She was so predictable. "Hmm, what do you want, ya bint?"

It wasn't El Ghoula referring to her as "girl" that made Sahara see red, but *how* she'd said it, implying that she was *merely* a girl. Magda's cattiness only fed Sahara's hunger for vengeance.

It was time to test the validity of their hypothesis. After Naima called everyone in from the dining room, Sahara started to tell the story they'd rehearsed.

"Did you know that before Cleopatra married Marc Antony, she insisted on having her right wrist decorated with henna as a symbol of her love and devotion? I learned that at school."

She hadn't. They'd read it in one of her cousin's books last night. Well, Naima had read it and then told her what it said. Sahara channeled her inner drama queen for the next part— Vicky would be proud.

"Wouldn't it be amazing if Tante Magda did that too? Her beauty reminds me of the famous queen." *Barf!*

"That idea is just wonderful, cousin," Naima slapped on. "Khalu Omar likes to say that Magda is a vision, like Cleopatra."

They'd never actually heard him say that, but it sounded like something he'd say about his "lovely" bride.

Sittu kissed Sahara's head. "A wonderful idea indeed. Omar will love it."

Winner winner, chicken dinner. They were banking on Sittu's buy-in, and now they had it. The guests, too, nodded and chattered their agreement.

"I knew you'd think so." Sahara smiled at her grandmother.

"I . . . I don't think it's a good idea." El Ghoula was definitely hiding something. "This bracelet belonged to my mother. I must keep it on, especially for the wedding."

Sahara had expected resistance. A sound plan always accounts for potential pitfalls. She winked at Naima, who immediately cut in with, "Of course you should wear it to the wedding. How about switching the cuff to the other wrist?"

"Why? I can get the henna on the left—"

"No!" Sahara cried. "Um, it's just that Cleopatra's henna was on her *right* wrist." She turned to Sittu. "We should keep it the same. You know, tradition and all." They'd thought of everything.

"Yes, absolutely," Sittu agreed, but that was no surprise— she was a stickler for tradition. She stepped toward Magda. "Let me hold your bracelet."

El Ghoula slid her hand behind her back and glared at Sittu. "No one is touching my cuff, do you understand?"

"How dare you talk to Mama like that?" Khaltu blasted.

Sahara wrung her hands. They'd been certain Magda would eventually succumb to her future mother-in-law's insistence, if for no other reason than to keep the wedding charade going. Instead, World War III was about to erupt. Sahara had no choice but to do the unthinkable. As El Ghoula zeroed in on her aunt, preparing to say something scathing, Sahara yanked the bracelet off her wrist.

"Aha! Look, everyone. Do you see?"

But there was *nothing* to see. There was *no* evidence of a bite—Magda's wrist was as impeccable as the rest of her. Sahara's eyes shot over to Naima. She appeared just as confused. The rest of the women gaped at Sahara, some even shaking their heads disapprovingly.

El Ghoula rose from the bed and snatched the bracelet. She secured it to her wrist, then laid into Sahara. "What's the meaning of this, girl? Has no one taught you manners? I guess that's what happens when you grow up without a mother."

And just like that, Sahara was underwater, knocked over by the waves of humiliation. *Without a mother* crashing over her again and again. Driving her necklace farther and farther away.

Khaltu yelled at Magda to shut up. Sittu held up her hand, ready to strike the witch, but before she could swing it, Fayrouz grabbed it from behind.

"Madame Zainab, stop! Think of Ustaz Omar."

El Ghoula clutched her hand to her chest. "Merci, Fayrouz. Thank you for saving me from these . . . these mons—" She started to say "monsters" but thought better of it.

Sittu jerked her hand away from Fayrouz and glowered at her soon-to-be daughter-in-law. "Mention my daughter Amani in front of me again, and you'll see what a monster I can be."

The room was caving in. Sahara needed air. She ran,

charging past the guests and through the front door. She raced down the four flights of steps. *Crash!* Sahara didn't need to look up to know whom she'd collided with. Her head instinctively nestled into her father's snug middle.

"Dad," she cried. "Everything's ruined!"

21

The Sacrificial Apple

985 CE

The evening breeze drifted through the canyons, fluttering the blades of grass down by the stream. As Nasser finished drinking, Morgana undid the sack from his saddle and peeked at the treasures. The brass lamp gleamed amid its magical companions—the carpet, the apple, and the spyglass. All four enchanted items accounted for, it was time to make up the prayers she'd missed while riding. Morgana unwound the shawl wrapped around her hair, replacing it with a violet silk headscarf that had belonged to her mother. She'd managed to grab it, along with the ivory jewelry box, before she left home. *Home.*

Her breath quieted as she moved through prayer, anchoring to the ground beneath her with each familiar shift of her body and utterance of sacred words. She prayed for her mawlay. *May he be at peace.* She prayed for the royal couple whose hands had remained intertwined, even in death. *May they always be together.* Finally, she prayed for Deena, who'd lost her closest friend and her father in one night. *May Allah ease her grief.*

Though days of travel separated them, Morgana still whispered to her mawlay's daughter, "Please trust in my innocence." She pressed her hand to the pendant and took a deep breath, the warm and woody scent of sandalwood filling her nose.

"Bukhoor," Morgana sighed, relishing the familiar, soothing smell of incense. But as logic replaced instinct, her body froze. Someone else was here. How? She hadn't heard any foot—

An arm swiftly wrapped around Morgana's neck, and the cold, sharp bite of a blade jammed against it.

"The apple," a female voice demanded from behind. "Hand it over *now*."

Morgana's mind raced. Who was this woman, and how did she know about the apple? What about the other treasures? Did she know about those? As much as the prospect of relinquishing the healing apple pained Morgana, she would have to let it go. If she didn't, the woman could cut her throat and discover the rest of the sack's contents. Morgana couldn't risk that. She'd have to sacrifice one of the treasures to protect the other three.

"Please don't hurt me. I'll give you what you want."

"The apple. Where is it?" the woman growled.

Morgana wriggled in her grasp. "I'll get it, but you have to let go of me first."

Much to her surprise, the woman obliged. She released her grip and threw Morgana onto the ground. "You'd better not cross me."

Morgana crawled to the sack. Her pulse throbbed in her ears. She carefully reached in and pulled out the golden apple, trying not to bring any attention to the other items.

"Here." She twisted around, getting her first glimpse of the woman—her face hidden under the hood of a gray cloak.

Dark, slender fingers slithered out of her sleeve. Out of nowhere, they darted toward Morgana and snatched the apple. A blast of sand burst forth from the woman's other hand, sending Morgana flying back into a nearby tree.

In the seconds before the world went black, a whistle as piercing as the fiercest of winds blared. The horse reared up and galloped into the distance. *Nasser, don't leave!* Morgana cried inside as the cloaked woman vanished into a cyclone of sand.

22

Beautiful Mess

Sahara's father had a remarkable way of consoling her. Without judgment or questions, he allowed her emotions to spill out, his calm containing every last one. After she'd collapsed into his arms, he cradled her shaking body while she cried into his chest. When Naima ran downstairs to check on her, he let her know that Sahara would come by when she felt better, continuing to hold her close until her crying subsided.

"What are you doing back so soon?" she sniveled, eyeing the wet trail her tears had made on his shirt. "Where are Fanta and Uncle Gamal?"

"They're still at the ahwa. I left early. How much coffee can one man have?" He smiled, wiping her tears with his thumb. "How about we go for a walk, and you can tell me all about what's got you this upset?"

"It's . . . it's a long story."

"Good, we'll make it a long walk, then." He took hold of her hand.

They strolled along Sittu's street, still bustling with people, even on a Wednesday night at ten. The air was warm but not stifling as it had been during the day. Sahara drew a deep breath and filled her dad in on what had happened. He listened silently, only interrupting once to ask, "You thought your uncle's fiancée broke into the shop?" It sounded even more far-fetched coming out of his mouth.

The whole point of tonight was to prove that it *wasn't* impossible. But the proof hadn't been there, discrediting their entire hypothesis. So why was Sahara not convinced of Magda's innocence? Had El Ghoula somehow outsmarted them? Ugh! It would be much easier if people were more like robots and computers—consistent and predictable.

"I wanna go home," she cried. "We shouldn't have come. We should've gone to Merlin's Crossing." *Then I'd still have Mom's necklace.* She didn't bother telling her dad about the hamsa or its berserk behavior. He'd never have believed it anyway.

"This is quite a mess, but going home won't fix it."

How could he say that? If they went back to Queens, she'd be far away from El Ghoula. "Why not?"

"Because no matter how many miles you put between you or how much time passes, you will still *know* the mess is there. Believe me," he sighed as they passed a shop selling rugs. The owner sat outside smoking a tall glass water pipe, his head jiggling like a bobblehead to the music coming from inside the store. "After your mother died, I told myself that I'd never come back here. How could I return to the place where we'd fallen in love and gotten married?"

As if Sahara weren't feeling lousy enough, guilt came and rained on her already crappy parade. "Is that the reason we've never visited before?"

Her father nodded. "I didn't think I could bear it. But now that I'm here, I realize I was wrong to stay away for so long."

After tonight, Sahara wasn't sure he'd been wrong.

"Being here is . . . it's messy, but it's *also* beautiful," he added. "Life's like that—beautiful and messy. You can't have one without the other."

"You sound like Amitu when she took that philosophy class last semester."

Sahara wished her aunt were here. She'd know what to do. But when she asked if they could call her tonight, her dad said they'd have to wait until tomorrow when the central phone office opened because Sittu's telephone didn't make overseas calls. Great—not only was Amitu not here, but Sahara couldn't even talk to her when she needed to. Apparently, when Amitu had said "call anytime," she meant anytime the central phone office was open.

"Everything in Egypt takes time. But that's not always bad. In New York, people are always in a rush. *I'm* always in a rush." He paused, then pointed to the tall minarets in the distance. "One of the things I love most about being here— the call to prayer echoes throughout the day, as it has done for centuries, and everyone stops what they're doing." He shut his eyes. "Nothing's more important in that moment."

If there were a way to bottle up the adhan, the real one,

not the one that came out of the miniature mosque he owned, she'd find it for him. Sahara wished there weren't things he missed so deeply.

"Dad . . . if you liked living here so much, how come you left?"

He opened his eyes. "No place is perfect. There are things I wish were different about Egypt too." He jerked his head toward a local vendor selling pita. "You see that bread stand? It's been around since I was a little boy, only that man's father ran it back then and his grandfather before him."

"So they've passed down the stand. What's wrong with that?"

"Nothing's wrong with it. There's dignity in earning a living. I told you that the day you met Sittu's maid. It's only *wrong* if that man imagines something different for his life but can't achieve it, and not because he hasn't tried. It's very difficult for a person to change his circumstances here." Her father stopped walking and looked directly at her. "It wasn't easy for me when I first arrived in America. I had to work harder than I care to remember to prove myself. But eventually, opportunities opened up for me that wouldn't have been possible here. And now, *you* have them too."

Sahara nodded, remembering how Mrs. Hoffman had described America as a melting pot of people from all over the world who'd come to America in search of a better life. Until now, she hadn't thought of her dad or Amitu as the people her teacher had referred to. But they *were*. And they'd done it not only for themselves but for *her* too.

"It's just confusing," Sahara said as they began walking again. "Which one's home? Which one are we—American or Egyptian?"

"Both, Susu."

"I wanna be just one. It would be easier to be *one*."

"Easier, maybe. Better, *no*."

"I guess."

"Beautiful and messy, not one or the other," her dad repeated.

"Well, tonight was more messy than beautiful." She snorted as they passed the bread stand again. "Are we walking in circles?"

"Sorry, it's been a while since I've navigated the streets of Shobra. We're here now." He gestured ahead to a cart where a man waved a fan over orange embers.

"Another thing I love about Cairo—dora mashwi." Her father's voice bubbled with excitement as they walked toward it. "Where else can you get grilled corn on the street at ten thirty at night?" He proceeded to pay for two ears of charred corn, which the vendor packed in a paper bag.

Luckily, her dad did a better job navigating their way *back* to Sittu's building. Ten minutes later, they sat on the steps outside and ate their corn. It had been grilled to a sweet and nutty-flavored perfection.

"What do you think of the dora?"

"Mmm. Delish!" A kernel fell out of Sahara's mouth onto her violet galabeya.

Her father picked it off, then smiled at her feet. "I don't think I've ever seen a galabeya worn with sneakers before."

Sahara stared at her white Keds and laughed. "You said it— Egyptian *and* American. Not one but *both*."

"Indeed." He grinned, corn stuck in his teeth.

UPSTAIRS, SITTU WAS waiting for them at the dining table with cups of shay bi laban. Sahara's dad carried his to bed, leaving the two of them to talk.

"I'm . . . I'm sorry I ruined tonight." Sahara took a sip. The tea was the perfect temperature—the milk easing the heat and the sugar balancing the slightly bitter taste.

"You didn't," Sittu reassured her. "Parties in Egypt always end in drama. I'm not sure what you and Naima were up to, but it wasn't all a disaster. We had fun."

Maybe for like three seconds before El Ghoula showed up. "Uh. I guess."

"Tab'an. I got to dance with my granddaughter! Who taught you? Malak?"

Sahara nodded, her chest clenching with missing at the sound of Amitu's name.

"She deserves a million thanks for helping raise you into the beautiful girl before me."

Sahara's throat tightened. "Khalu's fiancée doesn't think so. She thinks I behave badly because I grew up without a mother."

"If anyone misbehaved tonight, it was Magda! And you are *not* without a mother. She's in here." She placed her hand on Sahara's heart. "And all around you."

Sittu intertwined their hands like she'd done when they first met. They sat this way for a few more minutes, silently drinking their tea, the yearning to go home melting away. Tonight may have been a total fiasco, but Sahara wasn't ready to leave Sittu or Naima or the rest of her mother's family. They were finally part of her life, and no one, especially not the wretched El Ghoula, could make her give them up.

All Good Here

Sahara inhaled the cool morning air. Fixing things with her dad always made her breathe easier. She stood on a stool in the balcony holding the pulley's wheel still while he attached a brake caliper that would prevent it from spinning out of control again. *Everything* had spun out of control last night.

The wedding was less than ten hours away, and Sahara still had no idea how to prove Magda was guilty, but at least she could help repair the pulley. It had been her idea to use bicycle brakes. She wasn't the least bit surprised when her dad returned from the shop with a caliper from one of Fanta's old bikes. A store that jam-packed with awesomeness was bound to house nifty odds and ends.

After successfully testing the safety, it was time to head to the central phone office to call Amitu. Her father's navigation skills were way more reliable during the day, landing them in front of the office a little after 9:30.

"Are you sure Amitu won't be asleep? It's two thirty in the morning in New York," Sahara asked her dad as they entered.

"Trust me, she'll be up. Omar is like a brother to her. And the night before my wedding, Malak didn't sleep a wink." Her father chuckled.

Sahara shrugged and followed her dad toward the counter, where a bald clerk listened to a soccer match on a small radio. He instructed her father to write down their telephone number, then charged him ten pounds for fifteen minutes of call time, assigning him a number corresponding to one of the cubicles that filled the office. There wasn't much in the way of privacy, save a thin plexiglass divider between each desk. Fortunately for Sahara, there were only a few patrons this morning. Within minutes, the phone at cubicle #6 rang.

A lump formed in Sahara's throat the second Amitu picked up. *Don't cry,* she told herself, afraid the tears would come when she opened her mouth. Luckily, she didn't have to do much talking. Her father had been right. Amitu was *wide-*awake. And she had a gazillion questions that only required short answers: "How are you liking Egypt?" "What do you think of your cousins?" "Are you sleeping okay?" "Sittu's making sure you're eating, right?" "Are you ready for the wedding?" "Any word on what the bride's dress looks like?" and on and on.

After Amitu was finally done with her line of inquiry, she hesitated, then asked, "Are you sure you're all right, Susu?"

She could always tell when Sahara was upset, sometimes even before she knew it herself.

Sahara wanted to shout, *No, I'm not all right! Mom's necklace is gone, Khalu Omar's marrying an evil witch, and there's nothing I can do about any of it!* But instead, she blurted, "Yeah. All good here. You were right—Cairo's awesome. I'd better go before time runs out. See you soon."

"Sahara," Amitu cried. The line went dead.

She had meant to tell her aunt everything, but after hearing the tinge of concern in her voice, the last thing Sahara wanted was to make her worry more. Besides, what could Amitu possibly do from thousands of miles away? Sahara hung up the phone and headed back to her dad.

"Everything okay?"

"All good here," Sahara responded for the second time in the last minute.

ON THEIR WAY up to Sittu's, Sahara stopped by to see Naima, who was bent over a wooden chest in her room.

"Whoa! It's like a library in there." Sahara marveled at the books overflowing out of the chest.

"I know." Naima smiled. "Most of them belonged to Giddu. I've been keeping your mother's journal in here." She slid it off the top of the stack. "I think she'd have liked seeing it with his books."

Sahara thought so too. She'd let Naima borrow the journal after she asked to read the stories. Knowing how much these old tales meant to her cousin, Sahara happily obliged. Besides, she'd have plenty of time with it back home.

Sahara pointed at the chest. "Khalu Omar said my mom was our grandfather's biggest fan, but it looks like he was wrong. *You* are."

Naima giggled as she took a seat on a leather pouf and opened the journal.

"Anything good in there?" Sahara steered clear of last night's disaster.

"Not good, *amazing.*" Naima scooched over, making room for her to sit. "Giddu may no longer be here with us, but thanks to your mother, his stories *are.*"

Too bad Sahara couldn't read them on her own. When she got back to New York, she was determined to ask Amitu to teach her. *This* time, nothing would stop her from cracking the Arabic code.

Naima flipped through the pages. "There are classic tales in here like 'Ali Baba and the Forty Thieves' and 'Ala el-Din and the Magic Lamp,' but there are even ones from *One Thousand and One Nights* most people haven't heard. My favorite characters, like Peri Banu, are from those."

"That fairy who married a prince?"

Naima nodded. "Fanta thinks marriage would've been impossible since she was a jinniya, and Prince Ahmed, a human. He knows nothing, especially when it comes to love or magic."

Sahara didn't have the heart to tell her she thought her brother was right. Instead, she asked, "What's a jinniya?"

"A female jinn."

"But I thought you said Peri Banu was a fairy, not a wish-granting genie like in the story of Aladdin."

"She *was* a fairy. There are different kinds of jinn, not only the wishes kind like in Ala el-Din's tale. What did you call him?"

"Aladdin."

Naima laughed. "All jinn have powers and were born from fire before Allah made man, but some are good, and others are evil." Her voice dipped at the end to sound scary. "Fairies are the good kind. I'm not sure if Peri granted wishes. She might have." She shrugged. "Have you ever heard of Husnaya or Julnar?"

Sahara shook her head. Even if she had, she knew that wouldn't have stopped her cousin from telling her about them. Her eyes were dancing again.

Naima hopped up. "Sitt Husnaya was the most beautiful princess."

Of course she was. The women in these ancient tales were either gorgeous maidens men fought to marry or ugly ogres they ran from.

"But that's *not* why I like her. When Husnaya was growing

up, she learned sorcery and divination from a servant who worked in the palace. By the time she was old enough to marry, she'd chosen her magic over all the suitors begging for her hand. She became the most powerful sorceress to ever live."

Now *that* was awesome. Sahara listened more closely.

"And then there was Julnar of the Sea." Naima turned to another page and read, "'When an evil witch threatened her kingdom, the mermaid queen summoned a mighty jinn army from the depths of the sea to defeat her.'"

These were Sahara's kind of women. "Too bad they're only characters from old stories. We could use their help with our Magda situation." She blew out a breath. They couldn't avoid talking about her forever.

"Exactly. They'd have known how to handle El Ghoula." Naima knelt in front of Sahara. "I'm sorry about last night. If it makes you feel better, after you left, I told Magda I knew she was behind everything and that she wasn't fooling *us*."

Naima had guts. Not a hint of evidence of Kitmeer's bite, and she *still* had stood up to El Ghoula. Naima was *fierce*. "You're awesome."

"Awesome and in trouble," Naima snorted. "Mama's furious. After the party, she made me tell her what we were up to. You should've heard her." Naima imitated her mother. "'El Ghoula! It's no secret Magda wouldn't have been my first choice for a sister-in-law, but a witch? I've never heard such kalam farigh!'"

Sahara couldn't blame her aunt for thinking it didn't make

sense—it didn't. Speaking of Khaltu Layla, her voice blared through the tiny gap in the doorway like an alarm bell reminding the girls that it was time to pick up the ful for tonight.

"Yeesh, your mom has powerful lungs!"

Naima rolled her eyes. "And she's making Fanta come since there are so many garlands to carry."

"Does he know about the enchanted jasmine?" Sahara whispered. She couldn't believe she'd used the words *enchanted* and *jasmine* in the same sentence.

"No. And he *shouldn't*. Allah knows how fast he'll run and tell Mama. I'm already in enough trouble as it is."

Sahara shook her head. "No more I's. *We* are in this together."

Naima grinned. "So you still want to expose Magda even though we didn't find proof?"

Sahara nodded. "We have to." She flipped the pages in the journal still in Naima's hands, stopping at the hamsa's sketch. "If this drawing had been made by anyone else, if the words underneath had been written by anyone else, I wouldn't believe them. But they're my mom's, and I can't ignore them. If there's still a way to stop the two that mustn't join from becoming one *and* get my necklace back, then I've gotta find it."

"*We've* gotta find it." Naima squeezed her hand.

Sahara smiled. *Gotta* had a special ring to it in a British-Arabic accent.

"She tricked us last night!" Naima huffed. "But how?"

That was the million-dollar question. One Sahara didn't

have an answer to. "Quick! I need a piece of paper." She'd add it to the planet pad later.

Naima ran to the chest and returned with a sketchbook and pencil. Sahara immediately wrote *Ways El Ghoula Concealed Kitmeer's Bite* at the top and scribbled down the first ideas to pop into her head: *high-tech invisible Band-Aid, skin-colored sleeve, bionic arm, special effects makeup.*

Naima peered over her shoulder. "How is it that you don't believe in magic but think bionic arms are real?"

"Because they don't just *poof,* pop out of thin air." Sahara pointed to her list. "These are actually possible. I saw on TV that an engineer in Scotland is working on making a bionic hand right now."

"Fine. But if you're going to include those, then write down: *a spell from her witch's grimoire.*"

Naima had totally missed the point, but *no answers are wrong in a brainstorm.* Mrs. Hoffman's reminder played in her head as she added the zany idea.

When Khaltu yelled their names again, Sahara folded the paper and stuck it in her shorts. They had six hours until the wedding ceremony to figure out how Magda had outwitted them. In the meantime, they'd better head to Umm Zalabya's. Though Sahara wasn't entirely sold on the merits of the enchanted jasmine, what choice did she have? If there was even the slightest chance the ful could safeguard her family from El Ghoula's villainy, she had to take it—for them.

24

Mustafa Fouad

Downstairs, Kitmeer waited for Naima in front of the shop. When she gave him the okay to tag along, his long tail swished so excitedly it nearly hit his face. But Naima made it clear that he'd have to hang back when they reached Umm Zalabya's because of her cat—terms he readily agreed to with a high-pitched *arr-ruff.*

"Yalla." Fanta marched past them. "We don't have all day."

"He always walks like someone's chasing him," Naima griped as they set out.

In the hour since Sahara had returned from the central office, the streets had grown way busier. She glanced at her watch—11:04 a.m.—before they turned a corner, entering a labyrinth of narrow roads. Sahara took hold of her cousin's hand. She could see how Naima had once gotten lost. She'd never be able to find her way back if they got separated. All the streets looked alike, each filled with pedestrians navigating past countless apartment buildings and ground-level shops.

Personal space, Sahara railed in her head when an older

woman busted through her and Naima to get to wherever she was going. But judging by how everyone brushed shoulders as they walked, perhaps there wasn't *enough* space for anyone to have their own.

As the sun climbed higher in the sky, Sahara wiped the sweat off her forehead. She glanced over at Naima, who appeared perfectly comfortable in her long-sleeved shirt and jeans, while Sahara baked in her overall shorts. Sahara slid the scrunchie off her wrist and twisted her hair into a bun, suddenly feeling a bunch of eyes on her.

"Naima, why's everyone staring at me?"

"They don't see many Americans here." Her cousin shot a sharp look at the gawkers. "Don't pay them any attention."

But it was hard not to. Sahara gazed at her feet. *In America, I'm Egyptian, and in Egypt, I'm American. Which is it?* If her father were here, he'd remind her she was both. *Easy for you to say,* her inner voice snapped back as she dodged the local onlookers.

"Oof, Mustafa Fouad!" Naima glared down the street at a boy talking to Fanta outside one of the shops. He crossed his arms, standing a little taller than her brother. A posse of boys loomed behind him, blocking Fanta from getting past. "That stuck-up gazma goes to school with my brother. His family thinks they're the royal family of Shobra. They have money, but nobody knows how they make it. It can't be from owning a barbershop."

As Naima and Kitmeer headed toward the boys, Sahara

followed, inspecting the thick gold chain around Mustafa's neck and the shiny black Reeboks on his feet, likely paid for by his family's shady business.

"We don't have time for this today, Mustafa!" Naima blasted.

"Hello, Na-eee-ma." Mustafa grinned, stretching out her name.

Sahara could see why her cousin disliked this boy. Naima returned his salutation with an impressive eye roll while Kitmeer slunk in front of her, ears pinned back, tail at full attention. He flashed his teeth, and a low but threatening growl escaped from the gaps between them.

Mustafa took a step back. "I see you're still hanging around with that filthy dog."

Naima wrinkled her nose. "And I see you still *smell* like one."

"Watch it," Mustafa hissed, then swiveled toward Sahara. "This must be your cousin from America." He leaned forward to kiss her cheek.

No way. Sahara jumped back, leaving Mustafa's puckered lips hanging in the air.

He scowled at Fanta and Naima. "It seems your cousin's as unrefined as the rest of you."

"Leave her out of this," Fanta barked, straightening his bandana. "This is between you and me. Last time you beat me, but it won't happen again."

"Fanta, we don't have time to settle a score," Naima pressed, then turned to Mustafa. "Tell your thugs to get out of our way."

Mustafa puffed out his chest. "Make me."

"I have to finish this," Fanta told his sister. Naima huffed but stepped aside.

Sahara couldn't believe what was happening. "Isn't there another route we can take to Umm Zalabya's?"

Naima shook her head. "And this fool isn't going to move unless Fanta beats him. He's insulted Sittu didn't invite his crooked family to the wedding."

"Yalla, karate boy." Mustafa threw punches in the air.

Sahara knew how important it was to get the jasmine, but she couldn't believe Naima was going to stand by and watch her brother duke it out with this jerk. As she braced herself to dive into the middle of the teen boys' fists, Mustafa bent down and pressed play on a massive state-of-the-art boom box—quadruple the size of her cousin's. The ensuing explosion of music shook the street. Within seconds, a gaping crowd huddled around the boys.

"What the heck's happening?" Sahara yelled over the music.

"A dance battle." A smirk flickered across Naima's face.

Sahara was speechless. It didn't take long to identify the song blasting from the stereo—Michael Jackson's "Wanna Be Startin' Somethin'" off the *Thriller* album.

"Last time's winner goes first." Mustafa swaggered to the center of the crowd. At the start of the song's first refrain, he broke out a choreographed set of slides, spins, and thrusts.

Sahara hated to admit it, but he was good. He ended by dropping to the ground and spinning his legs like a windmill, a maneuver that made the crowd chant his name.

It was her cousin's turn now. Fanta showed off many of the same moves. Though his passionate but turbulent delivery paled in comparison to his adversary's poised performance, Fanta *did* have one critical advantage. He looked like he was having the time of his life—earning the crowd's praise as he sealed his first round with a spin. Sahara flinched at the sound of a loud whistle, only to find that it had come from Naima.

"Whoa," she mouthed. Naima winked back.

Sahara cheered Fanta on for round two. He had to win. Not just because they needed to get the garlands, but because she knew it would bring him a great deal of satisfaction. Plus, it would put nasty Mustafa in his place.

Fanta jumped high, performing an air-bound split that made the crowd go wild. Right before his feet hit the ground, one of Mustafa's goons stuck his foot out. Fanta stumbled, nearly face-planting, his hands catching his fall at the last second. The crowd gasped. Naima and Kitmeer growled at the smug culprit.

Sahara's cheeks turned hot as Fanta tried to shake off his spill. "Foul!" she yelled at Mustafa. "No fair! You cheated!"

"Fair? Pfft. Look around you. There are no rules here," Mustafa scoffed, then strutted to the middle, bowing and flexing his muscles at the crowd.

Anger seized Sahara. She couldn't let Mustafa win. But first, she had to check on her cousin. She hurried over to his side. "Are you okay?"

"Fine," he seethed as his adversary took his final bow.

Fanta *wasn't* fine. The moment he started his last round, it was clear that the fall had rattled his confidence. The crowd's enthusiasm waned. Sahara couldn't watch anymore. She had to help her cousin clinch the win Mustafa had stolen from him. Plus, there was no way she was letting this bozo and his henchmen keep them from getting to Umm Zalabya's. She stepped forward.

Mustafa got in her face. "Go back to America. You don't belong here." His obnoxious smirk was as bad as Corey Burke's.

Sahara was tired of people telling her she didn't belong. "Prepare to be defeated, Mu-sss-tafa." She pushed past him.

Naima jumped up and down with excitement, releasing another piercing whistle. Sahara's pulse raced as heads spun and necks craned to get a better view of her. She took a deep breath and began to move her feet together and apart. Fanta raised his eyebrows in confusion. "Just keep dancing," she yelled over the music. He nodded. He probably wasn't thrilled she was coming to his aid in front of everyone, though she had a feeling he'd forgive her *if* they won.

Sahara tried to imitate her cousin's moves, but spins and splits weren't exactly her thing. So she let the music lead her— shaking, twisting, popping, stomping, and leaping to its pulsing beat and fiery lyrics. As the song's final bars blared from the boom box, Sahara collapsed onto her knees.

It was eerily quiet, then the sound of cheers and applause. Sahara felt herself being pulled to her feet. She looked up, her eyes locking on Fanta's beaming face. A uniformed officer pushed through the crowd, and for a split second, Sahara worried they'd be busted for disturbing the peace. Instead, he grabbed hold of their hands and launched them into the air, declaring them the winners. There *were* no rules here.

Out of the corner of her eye, Sahara spotted an indignant Mustafa ducking into the barbershop, his squad of flunkies trailing behind him. Ordinarily, his money had afforded him fancy clothes, jewelry, *and* power. But today, the people of Shobra had decided it wasn't enough. Victory belonged to the heartfelt efforts of their karate kid and his American cousin.

25

Jinx

Kitmeer sat tall on his hind legs like a sentinel at the entrance to Umm Zalabya's building while the children retrieved the garlands. Sahara hurried up the stairs. Mustafa's antics had cost them precious time—time she and Naima needed to plan their next move against El Ghoula.

She reached the roof first, where Umm Zalabya was peering at the sky through some kind of gold disc hanging from her finger. Did this woman ever do anything normal like read a book or watch television?

"Right on time, my desert rose," she said as Fanta and Naima joined Sahara's side. Almaz slithered toward them, rubbing her head against their legs and purring.

After embracing each of them, Umm Zalabya loaded their shoulders with rings of jasmine. "You had better be off. I am sure you have a lot to do before the wedding." Her face turned serious for a moment. "Make sure you and every guest wear one."

Seeing the puzzled look on Fanta's face, Naima threw in, "What's a wedding without ful?!"

They gave their word—everyone at the wedding would get a garland. As Sahara turned to leave, Umm Zalabya took hold of her arm.

"One more thing. Tomorrow, the moon and Saturn will align. You must make your way to the highest point of the city before the sun rises."

Sahara scrunched her eyebrows.

"You will understand when it is time." Umm Zalabya smiled, releasing her arm. "Go."

Sahara raced after her cousins. With the wedding looming, she didn't have time for more of Umm Zalabya's cryptic predictions.

"Our desert rose," Fanta teased as she caught up with them on the first floor.

"Shut up," the girls groaned simultaneously. Sahara immediately yelled, "Jinx!"

Naima cocked her head in confusion.

"You say *jinx* when you and someone else say the same thing at the same time."

"Jinx," Naima repeated to herself, stepping outside.

THEY HURRIED HOME—the trample of their feet on the pavement leaving behind clouds of dust infused with sweet jasmine. Sahara grinned, imagining the three of them as a gang of outlaws with floral lassos, but instead of the Wild West, the untamed streets of Shobra were their domain.

When they neared Sittu's building, Naima crossed the street and reached into her pocket. They watched her heave the tennis ball deep into the alley, sending Kitmeer charging after it.

"Even with kilos of ful on her shoulder, she can still throw." Fanta chuckled. "She hates leaving that sorry dog."

"Shh! Duck, guys," Naima whispered from behind a nearby fruit stand.

Sahara did a double take. Naima had managed to get across without either of them noticing. They hurried toward her, crouching behind the stand. Fortunately, it was closed for lunch. Otherwise, they'd have some explaining to do to its owner.

"What?" Sahara mouthed.

"They're standing in front of the building." Naima jerked her head, eyes wide. "It doesn't look good."

Sahara peered around the kiosk. *Magda and Fayrouz*. A chill ran down her spine as El Ghoula glowered at her grandmother's maid. Words spilled violently from her red lips.

"This is ridiculous," Fanta said through gritted teeth. "Why are we even hid—"

They all went silent as Magda grabbed hold of Fayrouz's arm. Sittu's maid yanked it away, sending El Ghoula's purse flying off her shoulder. It hit the ground hard, crashing open, with its contents spilling onto the sidewalk. Magda spun around to retrieve her bag, giving Fayrouz enough time to escape into the building. A passerby offered to help pick up the remaining items, but whatever El Ghoula said sent him running.

Magda thrust everything back into her purse, then took one final look around. Sahara and her cousins ducked. Who knew what she'd do if she spotted them?

After a few minutes of lying low in a hot huddle, Fanta ventured out into the open.

"She's gone," he called out in a casual voice. "We'd better get upstairs. You know how Mama gets when we're late. Today's not the day to test her patience."

Naima and Sahara rose slowly. Once they'd confirmed the coast was indeed clear, they followed him across the street.

"Don't pretend you weren't scared too," Naima ranted at his back.

He spun around. "I wasn't scared, but I couldn't leave the two of you hiding behind Hassan's kushk."

As Sahara neared the building, something small and rectangular stuck out between the sidewalk and the front tire of Uncle Gamal's car. She bent down to take a closer look.

"Guys, I think Magda dropped this," she said, picking up a leather-bound book.

Naima's face went white. "It's Noora's." She took it from Sahara's hands.

"The maid who used to work for Sittu? The one you said our uncle *should've* married?"

Naima nodded and opened the book. "Noora asked me to teach her how to read. She'd never gone to school, but she learned quickly. Last year for her birthday, I gave her *this* copy of *One Thousand and One Nights*." She traced the words on the inside of the cover. "'Kol sana winty tayiba—'" Her voice broke.

"Happy birthday," Sahara repeated.

Fanta read the rest. "'Now you can read all your favorite stories on your own! Love, Naima.'"

Sahara put her arm around Naima, who stared at the ground.

"But why would Magda have her book?" Fanta asked.

Naima's head shot up. "Because she's done something to Noora. I tried to tell you she was evil. What if Noora didn't go back home? What if El Ghoula hurt her or, worse, what if she—" Naima hesitated, her lip quivering.

Sahara's pulse raced.

Fanta's face flashed several emotions, unable to settle on one. He started and stopped a few times, finally managing to mumble, "It can't be . . . We can't talk like this . . . The wedding's starting soon."

"We have to stop it," Naima declared.

"No. No. No!" Fanta shook his head, his voice getting louder with each objection. "We can't ruin our uncle's wedding!"

"But the book." Naima held it in front of his face.

"I see it! There could be a million reasons for it being with Magda. We can't accuse her of murder because Sahara found the lousy thing on the ground." He snatched the book out of his sister's hands, then stomped over to the corner and tossed it furiously.

"Fanta, you're such a buffoon," Naima yelled as he walked past her and into the building. She turned to Sahara. "We have our evidence, right? And now we have to do something before it's too late."

For the first time, Sahara wasn't sure that doing something *was* the right thing. She wanted to protect her family and get her necklace back more than anything, but what could they possibly do against someone capable of the unthinkable?

"Uh, I don't know. Maybe there *is* an explanation for Magda having the book." Preferably one less deadly.

No sooner had she thought this than Kitmeer came bounding back with Noora's book hanging from his mouth. He dropped it at Naima's feet and barked.

"At least *you* believe me." Naima squatted and took the book. She balanced it on her knees, wrapping her arms tightly around her dog. Kitmeer's nose wiggled furiously over the yasmeen garlands.

Sahara looked away, unable to bear the betrayal on her cousin's face as the first afternoon call to prayer echoed around them. She lifted her gaze to one of the mosque's towering minarets, imagining the muezzin standing tall behind its open arches, summoning all who could hear him to worship. Squeezing her eyes shut, she mouthed a prayer, bundled into a single word—"Help."

26

The Magical Trio

985 CE

Morgana blinked her eyes open, regaining consciousness. Wings fluttered above her in the canopy, gleaming in the dappled light. *A bird? A butterfly?* It hurt to think. Her head throbbed. Why was she sprawled out under this tree?

"The apple!" Morgana cried as the memory of the cloaked woman came crashing back. It was gone. Less than a week in her care, and the magical apple was now in the hands of a fiend who'd disappeared into a whirlwind of sand. She'd been a fool to think she could do this on her own. And now she was really on her own. Nasser had been so spooked, she couldn't imagine him coming back. Her heart sank. She should just leave the magical treasures behind and disappear too. They'd be better off here—out in the open—than in her care. Her mawlay would be so disappointed.

"Ihdi." A voice tinkled above her like tiny bells.

Morgana propped herself onto her elbows. "Who . . . who's speaking?"

"You're safe," the voice continued. "The witch is gone."

"Show yourself!" Morgana's eyes searched for the source.

The leaves rustled with movement. "Up here."

Morgana gasped. The golden wings hovering above her belonged to a tiny woman. "Jinniya?" She'd heard stories about the jinn but had never actually seen one.

The fairy looked down at her ruby dress. "Yes, I suppose I am." She giggled. "But you can call me Peri Banu." Her words sang with the high pitch of a child, though the contours of her face were those of a lady.

Morgana rubbed her temples. The light behind the jinniya was too bright for evening. "How long have I been out?"

"Since last night. Your poor head, you hit it quite hard."

She'd been unconscious all night! What if—Morgana's eyes darted to the spot where she'd left the sack, right before she was ambushed. Alhamdulillah. It was still there. She turned back to the fairy. "You . . . you called the woman who did this to me a *witch*."

"She *is*, and a dark one at that. Her evil sorcery sent you crashing into this tree."

Morgana's head pulsed with pain. "Yes, I know. The app—" She stopped herself. Peri may have been remarkable looking, but that didn't mean Morgana could trust her with the enchanted treasures.

Just then, Morgana detected movement down by the water. For the second time this morning, she beheld an unbelievable sight. *Am I dreaming?* she asked herself as a tall silhouette emerged from the stream. It glimmered in the sunlight with the rest of the water's surface, making it hard to tell where the stream left off and the figure began. It wasn't until she stepped out, oddly dry, that Morgana could make out a body, a *woman's* lithe body, adorned in fabric gleaming like the inside of an oyster.

"Who's that?" she asked, unable to look away as the breeze rippled through the woman's cascade of midnight hair. Before today, she'd never imagined being visited by one of the jinn, let alone two.

"*That* is Julnar of the Sea, the mermaid queen." Peri waved excitedly. "She's right on time. Now, where's Husnaya?"

"Someone else is coming?"

The fairy flashed a smile and whirred her wings so fast it made Morgana dizzy.

"Not just *someone else,* but Sitt Husnaya—the greatest seer of our time." Peri aimed a tiny finger to the east.

Morgana followed it, shielding her eyes from the sun. The sound of pounding hooves swelled as she made out the nearing shape of a woman on horseback—garbed in linen and leather like a Bedouin warrior. A sudden gust blew the ivory scarf wrapped around the rider's hair. The rider shut her eyes and leaned into the wind, instinctively guiding her horse to the mermaid queen's side. Once there, she hopped down, and together, the two women strode toward Morgana and the fairy.

Peri zipped around excitedly as they arrived. "We're all here!" She swooped down toward the horse, which had a pale gray coat with glints of silver in the mane. "And this beautiful creature is Almaz."

Husnaya didn't speak. She joined her sun-beaten hands—dark brown leather cuffs buckled around her wrists—in prayer at the tip of the silver widow's peak sticking out of her scarf and bowed her head.

Julnar glided forward, her eyes shimmering the colors of the ocean, her voice silky. "My dear Morgana. I take it you've had an exhausting couple of days."

That was an understatement if Morgana had ever heard one. "How do you know who I am?"

"Because we've been looking for you," Peri said matter-of-factly.

"You have?" Morgana's hands trembled. What if these women had been sent by the emir too? Morgana blasted herself for not running the minute she'd regained consciousness. Were these her final moments of freedom? "I'm . . . I'm innocent," she stammered.

"There's no need to worry," Julnar assured her. "We know you aren't responsible for what happened in Baghdad."

Husnaya's face darkened. "It was the sorcerer."

"That blasted fiend!" Peri huffed.

After the officers' vicious allegations, Morgana couldn't imagine there was anyone left who'd presume her innocent.

Relief swept over her, and she breathed in deeply. "You believe me?"

Peri fluttered over her shoulder, Julnar reached for her hand, and Husnaya nodded slowly. "Of course," they answered in unison.

27

Witness

Omar and Magda's wedding wouldn't only be the first *Egyptian* one Sahara had attended, but her first *ever*. Sure, she'd seen people get married on television and in the movies, but something told her this wedding would be different. And not only because of the cultural rituals, but because the bride was El Ghoula.

After Sahara had gotten dressed for the ceremony, her father entered Sittu's bedroom carrying a white headscarf. Amitu had mentioned she should cover her hair as a sign of respect for the imam officiating the wedding.

"Layla just brought it up. It's one of Naima's." Sahara's heart sank as he draped the scarf over her head. Naima not delivering it herself could only mean one thing—she was still hurt.

"I know Amitu said I should wear one because of the imam, but Sittu says covering your hair is a choice."

"And it is," her dad answered. "As is showing respect to an honorable religious figure. Do you want to be respectful of the imam?" His tone heavily suggested that there was only one way to answer the question.

"Yes, I want to be respectful of the imam," she repeated.

"Did you know that when Amitu visited the Vatican a few summers ago, she had to cover her shoulders and make sure her skirt went past her knees? Wearing modest clothing in a religious institution isn't unique to Islam," he explained as he arranged the silk tarha over her arms and the sides of her navy-and-white dress. Red stitching lined the frock's nautical-inspired collar and capped sleeves.

"But the ceremony is taking place here, not the mosque," Sahara pointed out.

"When the imam comes to your house, he may as well be bringing the mosque with him." Her father chuckled. "It's the same thing."

"I guess," Sahara said. She hadn't thought of it that way before, but it kind of made sense. Even though Amitu didn't pray at home every day like Sahara's dad, when she did, she always covered her hair. She wasn't at the mosque either. Maybe this was like that.

Her father took a step back. "You look beautiful, my hijabed sailor."

Sahara cracked up, giving his joke more credit than it deserved. She hadn't told her dad about the argument they'd witnessed between Magda and Fayrouz or the discovery of Noora's book. In part to avoid a long-winded lecture on how she and Naima had once again let their imaginations get the best of them, but mainly because she didn't want to think about it. His ignorance was *her* bliss.

"So, what should I expect today? What was your *big day* like?" She poked him playfully with her elbow.

"Well, some things about my 'big day' were the same as you'd see at an American wedding."

He told her how he'd worn a suit and her mother a white gown, but Sahara already knew that from the photos she'd seen. She wanted to know if her mother had walked down the aisle.

Her father shook his head. "That part's different here. The bride doesn't do that. But after our ceremony, your mother and I danced together through the streets of Shobra. Our guests strolled behind us, along with a band of musicians pounding on their tablas and shaking their riqs. What a night!"

Little did he know *Sahara* had just danced in the middle of Shobra, she thought, continuing to ask more questions. "Will the imam pronounce Khalu Omar and Magda husband and wife after they say the whole 'till death do us part' stuff?" Her stomach lurched at the latter part.

"Not quite. They'll vow to love each other, but the most important part of the ceremony will be the signing of the nikah—the wedding contract—by the couple and their chosen witnesses."

It sounded more like a trial than a wedding, which wasn't that off base in Magda's case. "Do you swear to tell the truth and nothing but the truth, so help you God?" Sahara quipped.

"Susu, you kid, but committing to marry another is serious business. It's one of life's greatest blessings and responsibilities. Not only does it bind the couple to each other, but it unites their families too. Marriage should be entered into with the utmost honesty and purest of intentions."

"Okay, I get it." She raised her hands in surrender. Too bad there was nothing honest or pure about El Ghoula.

Her father glanced at his watch. "Only a few minutes until the ceremony. I'll be next door. See you there, all right?"

Sahara nodded as he left the room. But it wasn't all right. *Nothing* was all right. She balled her fists, recalling how excited she'd been to wear her necklace tonight and tell everyone how she'd gotten it. Curse Magda for taking that moment away and being so wicked it made Sahara tremble. For the first time, she found herself in a situation she couldn't—was too afraid to—plan her way out of.

IN A MATTER of hours, the Room of Photos had been transformed into the ceremony hall. All the chairs from Sittu's dining table, plus a few from the Saeeds' apartment, had been moved inside and arranged in neat lines facing the sofa. The marble table was draped in ivory silk organza, and a few of the jasmine garlands had been scattered around the gold wedding bands overlapping in a small ceramic dish at the center. The soft light of late afternoon passed through the window's sheer curtains, surrounding the room with a warm glow.

Sahara sat beside her father, waiting for the ceremony to begin. She spotted Naima a few chairs away—her hard stare set on Magda, perched on the sofa with Khalu Omar. The imam sat between them, dressed in a long white robe and donning a domed cap Sahara thought was called a taqiyah. The deep lines on his face and the gray and white hairs in his beard suggested he might be older than Sittu. He unrolled an ivory parchment on the coffee table, which Sahara's father confirmed was the nikah.

Seated by the door, beaming at the bride and groom, was Fayrouz, of all people. Although Sahara didn't know what had passed between Magda and Fayrouz, she *had* seen El Ghoula viciously grab Fayrouz's arm. She couldn't fathom how the maid could be looking at her now with anything short of contempt.

Speaking of disdain, Sahara glared at the white patent leather shoes squeezing the life out of her feet. She reached down to loosen the buckles, relieving the throbbing in one foot, before her dad nudged her to sit up for the start of the ceremony. *Please don't do anything you'll regret,* she begged in her head as she shot one more glance in Naima's direction.

The imam led the room in a recitation of the first verse of the Koran, the *Fatiha,* followed by a sermon on the sacred bond of marriage. Khalu Omar's face gleamed with joy and affection for his bride. Sahara wanted so badly to be happy for him, but as hard as she tried, she couldn't ignore the dark cloud of suspicion that hovered over Magda, especially when

Naima sat a few seats away, looking so distraught. X-ray vision would've really come in handy now so that she could see inside El Ghoula—beyond her pretentious facade—and discover the truth. *Are you evil enough to kill someone?*

"Allah is our witness." The imam's voice penetrated the room. "We are all witnesses." He stretched his arms out wide, his eyes making contact with each of them.

Sahara felt like she'd been punched in the stomach. Could she stand by and *witness* her uncle, on what was probably the biggest day of his life, marry this woman while she did nothing?

Just then, her cousin rose from her seat.

"Naima, what are you doing?" Khaltu tried to get her to sit.

"I can't, Mama . . . I have to say something." She moved toward Omar and Magda, Noora's book in her hand.

Fanta leaped up, practically unrecognizable without his bandana—though he'd managed to sneak it into his dress shirt pocket as a makeshift handkerchief.

"She wants to say how happy we all are for you both, right, Naima?" he pressed, trying to undo what his sister had set into motion. But it was too late.

"Ahmed, sit."

It was the first time Sahara had ever heard Naima call her brother by his real name. Fanta huffed but took a seat nonetheless. His face twitched with worry.

Naima addressed her uncle. "I'm . . . I'm sorry." Her voice shook.

"Omar, please. Are you going to let *her* interrupt our wedding?" Magda turned to the imam and bowed her head. "Please forgive the insolent child."

Khaltu Layla sprang up. "How dare you call binti insolent!"

Uncle Gamal pulled on her hand, trying to defuse the situation with humor. "Tab'an, my wife. We're the only ones who can call her that."

The imam cleared his throat. "The girl has been called to speak. Let's hear what she has to say."

Naima looked to Sittu, who nodded for her to continue.

"Do you recognize this?" Naima held out Noora's book.

Khalu Omar hesitated, then took it from her hand. "It's . . . it's a copy of *Alf Leila wi Lelia*." He softly traced the title on the cover.

Sahara thought she glimpsed a hint of recognition in his eyes. Could Magda's hold on him be wavering?

"Open it," Naima requested softly.

He scanned the inside cover, reading her inscription, his voice tinged with sadness. "It's Noora's . . . How did you get it?"

Naima turned on Magda. "It fell out of *her* purse."

Sahara expected El Ghoula to retaliate with something scathing, but she just stared at the book with a dazed expression.

Omar turned to his bride. "Is that true?"

"I . . . I don't know," El Ghoula answered, her shoulders slumped.

Magda was acting so weird. Was this some kind of trick? Whatever it was, Naima wasn't buying it.

"Don't play innocent now. You're lying! Sahara found it on the ground right after you grabbed Fayrouz and your purse went flying."

"What's going on here?" Sahara's father muttered.

Sahara didn't answer. What was she supposed to say? Where would she even begin? The only thing she knew for sure was that Naima was the bravest person she'd ever met, and she couldn't let her do this alone. Everyone's heads twisted in her direction as she rose from her chair and plodded over to her cousin's side. Naima's eyes twinkled with gratitude.

Sahara stared directly at Magda. "We . . . we saw you," she started, willing her fear to take a hike until she'd said what she needed to. Luckily, El Ghoula's gaze was still on the book. "Naima was right. She's been right all along." Sahara reached for her cousin's hand.

"What is the significance of this book, girls?" the imam demanded.

"It belonged to Sittu's old—" Naima hesitated. "It belonged to my friend Noora," she continued, explaining how she'd disappeared. "Something had to have happened to her. She'd never just leave like that!"

"What are you saying?" Khaltu asked. "Do you think Magda had something to do with Noora's disappearance?"

"Yes!" the girls answered in unison. Despite the seriousness of the current situation, Naima mouthed a quick "jinx." Sahara smiled back, proud to be standing with her cousin.

A whimper came from the back of the room. It was Fayrouz.

"I'm afraid there's been a terrible misunderstanding, Madame Zainab. Magda didn't drop the book . . . I did."

"What?!" Sahara wasn't sure if the word had flown out of her mouth, Naima's, or the two of theirs together.

El Ghoula finally looked up, her fiery gaze returning to the room.

"Remember when you asked me to pack up Noora's belongings and send them to her family?" Fayrouz reminded Sittu. "I . . . I did as you asked. I put them all in a box. But the book was at the top. It must have fallen out as I loaded it into the van headed to Ismalaya. It's *my* fault," she cried.

Fayrouz headed over to Khalu Omar, her head down. "Please forgive me, ustaz."

"You see, my love. I told you I'd never seen it before." Magda caressed Omar's shoulder and sneered at her accusers.

"Of course, habibti." He peered into her eyes—back under her spell—then put the book in Fayrouz's hand, asking her to make sure it got to the right place this time.

Fayrouz gave her word and hurried to her seat.

Khalu Omar turned to the girls. "Naima and Sahara, sit," he half asked, half ordered.

Sahara couldn't move. Her eyes darted to her dad's confused face.

"But she still hasn't explained why she and Fayrouz were argu—" Naima started.

"Sit down *now*." There was no mistaking their uncle's tone this time.

Khaltu Layla rushed forward, ushering the girls to their chairs.

"Imam, we apologize for wasting your time with this childish business." *Ouch.* Omar bowed his head. "Please proceed."

28

A Gift

Fortunately for Sahara, her father was too busy helping with preparations for tonight's reception to ask for an explanation of her actions at the ceremony. But he *did* manage to shoot a few gut-wrenching looks of disappointment her way. And so, Sahara decided it would be best to get out of Dodge and dressed for *Cursed Wedding Part Two* at Naima's. She cringed as she stuffed her dress for the reception into her backpack. With only twenty-four hours' notice, she hadn't had time to shop for dresses. Amitu had rushed out to buy them, returning with the mediocre sailor dress and a bubble-gum-pink puffball Sahara hadn't had the heart to admit she hated.

She slipped past the dining table, where Sittu and Khaltu were busy reviewing a list of items they needed for the reception while Fayrouz poured a pink drink into glass pitchers.

"What's this sharbat Fayrouz has been making for the last few days?" Sahara asked as she chucked her dress onto Naima's bed.

Naima, who'd barely said a word since the ceremony,

half-heartedly explained that it was a drink made by crushing roses into water and adding sugar—*lots* of sugar.

Sahara wrinkled her nose at the idea of drinking flowers.

"It's not bad." Naima shrugged. "The taste doesn't matter anyway. It's all about the bride and groom sharing some—she from his cup and he from hers—as a symbol of their marriage. All the guests then have their own in honor of the couple." She rolled her eyes. "It's a silly tradition."

"Sounds silly." Though if the bride were anybody other than El Ghoula, it might be kind of cute.

"I refuse to have any." Naima lifted her chin. "There's *nothing* for me to celebrate."

"I won't either. Yuck!" Sahara pretended to retch.

Despite her attempt to stifle it, a giggle escaped from Naima's mouth. She plopped down onto her bed. "I messed things up."

"No, you didn't." Sahara sat beside her. "I was too afraid to say something, but *you* did."

"I tried not to, but then all of a sudden, I was holding Noora's book in front of our uncle."

Sahara winced, thinking about how distraught Khalu Omar had looked, the usual light gone from his face. She could've lived with causing him pain if it had stopped him from marrying El Ghoula. But it had been for nothing. And worst of all, she had no idea if she'd ever see her necklace again.

"I was sure I was right. Then Fayrouz started blubbering, and everything went wrong. I don't know what to think. If Fayrouz dropped the book, then Noora *did* just leave. After all these years, she left and never looked back." Tears fell down Naima's cheeks. "Fanta and Mama say this El Ghoula stuff's all in my head. Do you think they're right?"

Sahara shook her head. "My money's on you, Naima Saeed."

Even though Sahara hadn't collected any valid data incriminating Magda, she could fill her planet pad with irrefutable reasons to believe in Naima.

There was a knock at the door, followed by Uncle Gamal's muffled voice. "Girls, are you dressed yet?"

"Not yet, Baba."

"Enough chitter-chatter, Miss Cairo and Miss New York. Twenty minutes until we leave for the funeral . . . I mean the reception." He howled through the door.

Naima huffed at her father's bad joke, but Sahara had to laugh. How did he even know the term *chitter-chatter*? A few days ago, she would've balked at Uncle Gamal's ill-timed humor, but now she appreciated how it made her feel—that all was not lost if you could find something worthy of a laugh or a smile.

"Before we get dressed, I have something for you." Sahara unclipped the neon-green rabbit's foot from her backpack and held it out.

Naima looked wary.

"It's a rabbit's foot. Don't you have those here?"

"We have rabbits, and they have feet, but we don't put them on key chains. And they're not bright green."

"In America, they're good luck charms. And they don't

start off green. They're dyed that color. My best friend gave it to me on our last day of school."

Naima took hold of the rabbit's foot. Her eyebrows lifted as she stared at it dangling from her finger.

"You're supposed to rub it and make a wish."

"It's soft." Naima stroked the fur.

"See, I knew you'd like it."

"I do, but I can't take it. It was a gift for you. Won't your friend be mad that you gave it away?"

"I *want* you to have it." Sahara closed Naima's hand around the key chain. "And Vicky would too. Wait till I tell her the rabbit's foot she bought in Queens now lives here. She's gonna die. Besides, she'd love you as much as I do."

A wide smile spread across Naima's face, one she didn't attempt to hide this time. "I love it." She closed her eyes. Sahara didn't have to guess her cousin's wish. She had made the same one.

"What do you think will happen now that the two that must not join *have* become one?" Naima whispered. "I hope Umm Zalabya's ful can protect us."

Unlocking what has been hidden in the dark. The ominous words twisted into a knot in Sahara's stomach. She wasn't sure anything could protect them against El Ghoula, but she was certain of one thing. She took hold of her cousin's hand, the warm fur of the rabbit's foot between their palms. "Whatever it is, we'll deal with it together."

29

The Spyglass

985 CE

Morgana stared at the magical trio, the sunlit canyons behind them. Hope grew in her heart. They believed she was innocent. If they did, maybe Deena did too. Everyone always talked about the sacred vows of marriage, but what about the promises of friendship? Could they withstand calamity too?

"So you're not here to apprehend me on the emir's behalf?"

Peri shook her tiny head. "We're here on *your* behalf."

"I only wish I had been able to foresee your location before the witch got to you and stole the apple." Husnaya gestured to the sack.

Morgana's breathing quickened. "What do you know about those?"

Julnar waved her fingers, urging her to calm down. "I know this is all hard to understand, but listen first. You see, Peri was once married to Prince Ahmed of India. He and his two brothers were the ones to discover the enchanted apple, spyglass, and carpet."

Morgana crossed her arms. Ali Baba had told her all about his visit with the *two* Indian princes, Ali and Hussain. "My mawlay never mentioned a third brother named Ahmed."

"Those no-good sons of—" Peri mumbled a few choice words. "They didn't mention him because of *me*. They never forgave him for the sin of marrying a jinniya," she blasted, flying in circles.

While Peri continued her rant, Morgana wondered if the trio knew about the lamp. As if reading her mind, Julnar spoke. "Husnaya was a trusted adviser to Ala el-Din and Badr."

Morgana's hands trembled at the word *was*. For days, she'd tried to shake the image of their lifeless bodies sprawled out on the reception room floor, the princess's dazzling crown hanging clumsily off her head. It wouldn't leave Morgana. Nothing that had happened that night would *ever* leave her. But at least *she* was alive. Regret wormed its way around her heart and squeezed. *You survived, but* they *didn't.*

"The prince and princess looked to me for guidance. I couldn't protect—" Husnaya's voice caught in her throat.

It turned out Morgana wasn't the only one suffering from guilt or who wished she could've done things differently. Why had she served that cursed tea? "Is it true that it was the tea that killed them?"

"Soaked in poison," Peri whispered in her ear.

"Poison!" Morgana threw her hands up to her mouth.

"It's not your fault, my dear," Julnar consoled. "You couldn't have known."

"Of course not. It was a deadly toxin created by a sorcerer who succumbed to the darkness long ago. He was obsessed with power. The prince and princess were constantly looking over their shoulders. Now, at least they can be at peace . . . even if it is in death." Husnaya hesitated, clearing her throat. "But it was meant to be this way. That's why I counseled them to bring the lamp to you for guarding."

"You mean to my mawlay."

"No, to *you*," the seer repeated. "Ali Baba played an honorable role in protecting the enchanted treasures. But his part is over, and yours is just beginning."

"I . . . I don't know if I can do my part. I've already lost the apple. I've lost everything."

"Not everything." Peri flew over with a large—well, large for her—ivory tube.

The spyglass!

The fairy hovered with it in front of Morgana.

"I'm not supposed to. I promised my mawlay I wouldn't use any of the magic."

"It's all right, dear. Surely, he would understand after everything that's happened," Julnar assured her.

So much *had* happened. It seemed like a lifetime had passed since her mawlay had brought home the enchanted treasures. Morgana prayed he'd forgive her, then peered into the glass.

"Think of what you desire to see," Husnaya instructed.

Morgana closed her eyes for a second, gasping at what—
whom—she saw when she opened them.

"Deena."

Forget the Scrunchie!

Just as it was time to leave for the reception, Sahara remembered her scrunchie. She had been in such a hurry, trying to avoid her dad's wrath, that she'd forgotten it in Sittu's room—*tonight* of all nights. Already dressed like a massive tuft of cotton candy, the last thing she needed was extra fluff on top of her head.

She rushed upstairs, stopping at the partially open bedroom door. Her grandmother's and aunt's voices came from inside. What were they still doing upstairs?

"Are you sure we shouldn't tell the girls?" Sittu asked. "It may be the right time with Sahara here."

Sahara's pulse quickened. The "girls" had to be her and Naima. What did Sittu have to tell them?

"Mama, after their outburst at the ceremony, I'm not sure they're ready for such a big responsibility," Khaltu Layla asserted. "There's no rush. You didn't show me the chamber until I was eighteen."

"Perhaps you're right. Guarding the treasures may be too

much for them when they're still young and impulsive. And after what nearly happened to the shop, I suppose it's best to wait."

Treasures, chamber—what on earth? Sahara's mind rushed back to the words in her mother's journal. What if *unlocking what has been hidden in the dark* wasn't about El Ghoula casting some horrible spell but about *this* secret chamber?

"We'd better head downstairs," Khaltu said.

Sahara sprinted to the front door. Her scrunchie would have to wait. But this news couldn't. She had to tell Naima.

31

I See You

Scrunched in the back seat between Khaltu Layla and Naima, Sahara chided herself for not coming up with a secret language only she and her cousin could understand. They hadn't had a moment alone since she'd hurried downstairs. Within minutes, they were ushered into a taxi to take them to the Ramses Hilton for the reception while Fanta and Uncle Gamal drove over in the Fiat with Sittu, Fayrouz, and her sharbat. Before they'd left, the maid had begged Uncle Gamal to transfer the wooden crates of rose-water he'd just loaded in the trunk to the back seat, where she thought they'd be safer. Needless to say, he wasn't thrilled.

That left Sahara and her dad to ride over with Naima and Khaltu, who conveniently used the twenty-minute trip to let the girls know, in no uncertain terms, that their plotting and scheming had better have come to an end. Although she wasn't Magda's biggest fan, she wanted tonight to be wonderful for her brother.

"No more hissa," Khaltu warned against any more drama.

Even in the dark car, it was impossible to miss the steely look in her eyes.

Sahara's father threw in his own parental mandates as the taxi pulled into the hotel's circular driveway. "Enough talk of stolen books and witches. Let's try to enjoy tonight."

"Maybe if she stopped acting like El Ghoula, we'd stop calling her that," Naima said under her breath as she slid out the cab.

Sahara scooched toward the open door, which was no easy feat in her poofy dress.

As Sahara hurried into the hotel after her cousin, a glorious bubble of cold air enveloped her. "Air-conditioning," Sahara sighed in relief, momentarily forgetting about getting to Naima. That is until her father circled back and pulled her along.

Eventually, they came to a halt in front of the two towering wooden doors that led to the Ramses Ballroom. "Let's have a look inside." Khaltu Layla reached for the brass handle and opened the door.

Sahara didn't know where to look first. Bouquets of red roses sat in the centers of the round tables that filled the hall. She'd never seen such long stems before. Each table was outfitted with gold silk tablecloths, red fanned napkins, pearl-white dishes, gleaming silverware, and the most crystal-clear glasses she'd ever seen. Sahara carefully inched around the chairs, covered in matching gold-and-red fabric. Deep in the ballroom, in front of the stage, sat two throne-like chairs surrounded by a canopy of red roses. They were probably for the bride and groom. "Her Majesty, El Ghoula," Sahara grumbled before spotting the intricate Persian rug covering the floor. It was ginormous. But the pièce de résistance, as Amitu would say, was the sparkling crystal chandelier that hung from the center of the high ceiling.

Everything about the Ramses Ballroom was grand. Sahara turned to her dad. "Was your wedding like *this*?"

"Definitely not. But then again, I didn't need all this sparkle. I had the greatest jewel of all—your mother."

"Yeah, sure. But this is amazing!" She gazed back at the empty seats. "Where are all the guests?"

"They're getting ready for the zaffa."

"What's that again?"

"You'll see." Her father grinned.

AFTER SEVERAL MINUTES of trotting alongside Khaltu and Sittu like a show pony for all to meet "Amani's famous American daughter," Sahara helped her cousins distribute the yasmeen garlands. The girls made sure everyone in the family received one of Umm Zalabya's enchanted ful first. Since their ceremony antics, Fanta hadn't spoken to either of them, though he watched them closely as they passed out the ful.

When there were no more garlands left, Sahara searched for a private spot to talk to Naima. Just as she eyed a quiet nook next to the elevators, her dad showed up, insisting the zaffa—whatever that might be—was about to start. A wedding was *the* worst place to have to tell someone a secret, not to mention one this major. Sahara huffed, following him to the foot of the marble staircase leading down from the mezzanine.

The air buzzed with conversation, and necks craned, trying to catch a glimpse of the bride and groom before they made their grand entrance down the red carpet. Fanta cruised along the steps, mingling and joking freely with the guests. He seemed to sense Sahara's gaze, flashing a curt glance in her direction. *If looks could kill!*

With the warning of a single drum tap, an outburst of music made Sahara jump. She lurched her head up to the mezzanine, where a band of percussionists, clad in matching gold vests, pounded their goblet-shaped drums and tambourines.

Doom! Tek! Pah! Sahara's heart swelled with every smack, shake, and slap, recognizing the thundering beat as its own. The music reached inside, shaking all her sleeping parts awake.

"This is awesome!" she yelled to her father over the drumming.

"Zaffas always are."

Naima tapped her shoulder, jolting Sahara out of her ecstasy. She pointed upstairs to the arrival of the bride and groom.

Hand in hand, Khalu Omar and Magda eased their way down the first few steps as the band followed closely behind. El Ghoula had traded in her toned-down ceremony dress for a strapless lace ball gown decked out with hundreds of tiny crystals that sparkled as she moved. There was nothing low-key about this dress. A veil topped with a crown of silk white roses adorned her hair while a diamond choker glimmered around her neck, and of course, the infamous gold cuff was clasped to her wrist. Witch or not, she was a sight to behold.

They continued down the staircase. Omar waved at the guests, and El Ghoula blew kisses. Sahara couldn't look away as Magda approached the landing on her uncle's arm. Her father congratulated the bride and kissed his brother-in-law's cheeks. Magda's amber eyes blazed at the girls. She whispered something before making her way into the ballroom. It was hard to decipher over the drums, but Sahara thought she heard, "I see you."

"Did you get what—" Just as Sahara started to ask Naima what she'd made out, they were swept into the ballroom on the current of the crowd behind them. Judging by the distressed look on her cousin's face, she'd heard the same thing. A threat.

It Feels Like Love

After the zaffa had led the bride and groom to their distinguished seats in the ballroom, Sahara sat with her family at a nearby table—El Ghoula's smoldering eyes and icy whisper playing in a loop in her head. She and Naima were trying so hard to get through tonight without further confrontation. The last thing they needed was another one of Magda's obscure threats. *I see you*—what did that even mean?

Sahara didn't snap out of her El Ghoula trance until the waitstaff shuffled by, rushing to fill the glasses around the room with sharbat. Just then, Uncle Gamal stood and let out a blaring whistle that silenced the room. Naima had clearly inherited that skill from him.

"Assalamu alaikum." He welcomed everyone with the traditional greeting of peace and thanked them for coming to celebrate Omar and his "beautiful aroosa."

"Beautiful bride, pfft," Sahara grumbled under her breath as Uncle Gamal continued his hosting duties.

"Omar and Magda, please raise your glass before your

beloved and take your first of many drinks together. Allah willing, may you always be one as you are tonight."

The entire ballroom froze as Khalu and El Ghoula lifted their glasses to each other's lips and stared dreamily into each other's eyes. Magda deserved an Oscar for her part as the doting bride. Sahara could feel Naima's eyes rolling from across the table.

The moment the bride and groom placed their glasses down, the guests erupted into cheers and applause. Many women, including Sittu, placed their fingers over their mouths and produced a high-pitched trill. *Lolololololoeee!*

Sahara startled. Though the celebratory sound wasn't new to her—Amitu sometimes made it in honor of good news, like the time her dad had received a raise—she'd never heard it like this. The combined power of the women's zaghrata shook the ballroom.

"Whoa! Wasn't expecting that." Sahara giggled nervously.

Uncle Gamal tugged off his suit jacket and wiped the beads of sweat from his forehead. "To Omar and Magda." He lifted his glass high for everyone to see. The guests raised theirs at once, following Uncle Gamal's lead like an orchestra follows its conductor. And when he took a swig of his sharbat, without missing a beat, they did too.

Sahara's eyes flitted around the table. Her father gulped down his glass while Sittu and Khaltu slowly sipped theirs. Fayrouz twisted in her seat, proudly checking how the table next to theirs was enjoying the sharbat. Naima crossed her arms, doubling down on her refusal to celebrate the couple's union. Meanwhile, Fanta brought the glass to his mouth, looked over his shoulder, then poured it into a nearby planter. He was too busy pretending he'd guzzled it to notice Sahara watching. *Gotcha!* Fanta might have wanted them to think he was Team Magda tonight, but his actions—much to Sahara's satisfaction—said otherwise.

"Susu, you have to take a sip. It's rude not to," her dad muttered.

Though Sahara was hoping her father wouldn't notice her part in tonight's sharbat resistance, she had come prepared. Without missing a beat, she held her belly and grimaced. "My stomach's acting weird. I feel like I'm gonna be sick." She crossed her fingers behind her back so the lie wouldn't count.

It worked. He suggested she have water instead, sliding a glass in front of her.

"I think that's a good idea," she moaned. Maybe she should say she had to use the bathroom, somehow signaling Naima to join her so they could talk.

"And now we have a wonderful surprise," Uncle Gamal declared, making Sahara jump. She hadn't seen him head over to her father. "My brother-in-law has come all the way from America with his beautiful daughter to celebrate Omar and Magda's wedding."

Sahara's cheeks grew hot as the room's attention shifted to them. There was no way she could leave the table now. She pulled her hair back, forgetting she didn't have her scrunchie. *Crap!*

"Those of you who knew Kareem when he lived in Cairo may remember his beautiful voice."

Kareem's beautiful voice? Sahara cocked an eyebrow. He just sounded like her dad when he sang.

Uncle Gamal thrust his arm toward the stage. "Kareem bey, please take your place with the band."

As her dad made his way onstage, Sahara's jaw nearly hit the fancy Persian rug. What the heck was happening?

Naima slid into his vacant seat. It would've been the perfect time to tell her what Sahara had overheard, but she couldn't think straight as her father stepped in front of the microphone.

"I've been told this is one of Omar's favorite Abdel Halim songs. It . . . it was one of my wife's too." His voice trembled. Sahara's heart lurched. She had never heard her father refer to her mom as anything other than her mother. But she'd been much more than that to him.

" 'Zay el Hawa,' 'It Feels Like Love,' " her dad said softly into the mic before the band started to play.

The tempo of the music began slow, picking up as a raqasa danced onto the stage. Her legs peeked out of the long slits on the sides of her red silk skirt when she dropped and lifted her hips. Amitu had told Sahara that the belly dancer was one of the best parts of an Egyptian wedding. But as the woman approached Sahara's father—gold coins dangling from her bra and jingling over her stomach as she shook—Sahara couldn't help but think it was the most *awkward* part.

It wasn't until the raqasa had stepped down from the stage and danced toward the bride and groom that Sahara released her breath. She could appreciate her artistry now that the dancer was far enough from her dad. The dancer's movements were completely in sync with the music. It was impossible to tell whether she responded to the beat or it responded to her.

"Zay el hawa, ya habibi." The words flowed out of her father's mouth, spreading adoration and longing across the ballroom.

"'And when you were with me, the world was in our hands,'" Naima translated a lyric to the rhythm, whispering it in her ear.

Sahara's eyes filled with tears. *Not now.* The last thing she wanted was to cry in a room full of strangers, especially El Ghoula.

When the song ended, Sahara stood up and applauded with all the guests. Naima and Uncle Gamal sounded their signature whistles as her dad made his way to the table.

"You were wonderful," Naima praised, giving him back his seat.

Shoot! Sahara had missed her chance to talk to her cousin.

"What about you, Susu? Tell me the truth. Did you like my singing?"

She'd *more* than liked it—she'd loved it. She leaned in close and whispered, "It was a beautiful mess."

And it was. For Kareem Rashad had once loved a girl named Amani Abdel Aziz, long before either of them was a father or mother. Though their love had been whole and separate from Sahara, she'd been born out of it, entangling their hearts forever.

I Knew It!

The wedding reception continued deep into the night with the band playing another sappy love song—after the tenth one, they all began to sound the same. Sahara shook her head, willing away any sleepiness. She had to talk to Naima.

Luckily, opportunity struck a few minutes later when the music sped up to announce the belly dancer's next set. Sahara tiptoed around the back of the chairs to her cousin even though there was no need for stealth. Her family was so entranced by the raqasa spinning onto the stage that she could've leaped across the table and no one would've noticed. "Meet me in the bathroom."

By the time they'd made it inside the women's WC—her dad had explained those letters stood for *water closet* when she'd had trouble finding the bathroom earlier—Naima's eyes were wild with excitement. "What happened?" Her dress shoes clicked on the marble floor as she rocked back and forth.

Sahara peeked under the stalls and made sure they were alone. But just as she opened her mouth to speak, the door swung open. Two young women, draped in silk and doused in perfume, strolled in. Unlike Khaltu's light floral fragrance, their scent blanketed the room with a heavy and stifling intensity, making Sahara cough.

Naima introduced them as sisters Rabya and Ranya, who lived across the street. They resembled each other so much that they had to be twins. The duo descended on the girls, squeezing their cheeks and saying how cute they looked dressed up. Sahara hated being called cute. She wanted to rip off her hideous pink poodle dress. Thankfully, the cheek-pinching only lasted a few seconds, the sisters turning to the giant bronze mirror to reapply their lipstick. They were too preoccupied with their precious, nearly identical reflections to notice the daggers Naima shot at them as they gushed over Magda's gown.

Sahara let out a sigh of relief when they finally left, then spilled what she'd overheard Khaltu Layla and Sittu talking about. Naima listened carefully, her grin growing wider with every word and her eyes flashing at the mention of the chamber and the treasures.

The moment Sahara stopped talking, her cousin clapped her hands together. "I knew it! I told you they were hiding something. This must be what Umm Zalabya meant when she said a dark presence was after what our family held dear."

Sahara nodded. "And why El Ghoula tried to break into the shop."

"Young and impulsive!" Naima huffed. "I can't believe Mama said that . . . Well, I can, but it's not true!"

"Of course not." Sahara squeezed her cousin's shoulder, trying to keep her on track. "If what you said before about your mother and Sittu disappearing in the shop happened—"

"Tab'an, it happened! You still think I made that up?"

"No, not anymore."

While Naima harped on nobody ever believing her, Sahara scanned her memory of the shop: the crowded shelves of choc-olate and candy, the freezer of ice cream. *Focus.* And there was that old—"The refrigerator!"

Naima's brows rose, skimming the edge of her headscarf. "The broken talaga? It's been there forever." She froze, a light bulb turning on in her head, illuminating her face. "Ya Allah! It's been there forever because it *is* the secret chamber."

That's not quite what Sahara was getting at, since the fridge wasn't big enough to be technically considered a chamber. "Or it could *lead* to the chamber."

"Like the wardrobe in *The Chronicles of Narnia*." Naima gasped, taking in so much air Sahara was surprised she hadn't burst. "The old talaga is a portal to a world of magical treasures!"

"Slow your roll, C. S. Lewis. I'm not saying that. But one thing's for sure. The treasures are valuable enough to require guarding." Sahara was thinking more along the lines of

mounds of sparkling gems and gold coins that some villainous one-eyed pirate had stolen hundreds of years ago—but
that might be because she and Vicky had watched *The Goonies*
a gazillion times.

Naima's eyes glimmered in the warm light of the surrounding glass sconces. "What if your enchanted necklace is one of
the treasures?"

"Except my mom didn't find it in the chamber. The fortune teller gave it to her, remember?" But Naima was getting
at something. Maybe the hamsa was more than just a magical
alarm. Sahara's fingers tingled. If the reason Magda stole her
necklace was connected to this secret chamber, then discovering what was inside could be the key to getting it back. The
key to finally finding out why it was important enough for a
mysterious woman to insist it was meant for her long before
she'd been born.

"We've gotta get to the shop now!" Sahara spat out. "There's
just one problem—the shop *and* the fridge are locked."

"We'll take Mama's keys. There's no way she brought them
tonight. Did you see her tiny shanta? They have to be in her
usual purse back home."

Sahara didn't like the idea of going through Khaltu's bag,
but they had to get inside before El Ghoula did. How could
they leave the wedding early without arousing suspicion? "I
can say my stomach's hurting again. But even if my dad buys
it, there's no way he'll let us hop in a taxi alone."

"We won't be *alone*." Naima took Sahara's hand, leading her out the door.

Sahara had no clue what her cousin was up to, but where there was a will—and there most certainly was one with Naima Saeed—there was a way.

34

Through the Talaga

As much as Naima wished Kitmeer could live upstairs, sneaking out to feed him late at night did have one critical perk—she saw and heard things others wished she hadn't. Like the bathed-in-perfume twins, whose eyes nearly popped out of their heads as Naima looked toward an older couple sitting across the table and warned, "Get us out of here, or I swear I'll tell your parents you snuck out of your apartment last Thursday *after* the lights went out."

It was no surprise the sisters insisted they drive Sahara home when she staggered over to her dad grimacing and holding her stomach. Naima would tag along to take care of her cousin, of course.

A little after midnight, the girls arrived in front of Sittu's. Sahara had never seen her grandmother's block this quiet. But then again, half of Shobra might still be at the wedding. After a quick outfit change—there was no way Sahara was hunting for a chamber in a pink frilly dress and strappy shoes—she grabbed her scrunchie and met back up with Naima, who was busily rummaging through Khaltu Layla's purse.

Back downstairs, Naima removed her mom's keys from her pocket. They jingled, piercing through the dark, empty streets. Fear twisted in Sahara's stomach, along with the longing to recover her mother's hamsa. It was the reason she'd lied to her father. The reason she was standing out here in the middle of the night waiting for her cousin to unlock the gate. *Click.*

"We'd better keep the lights off," Naima warned as she stepped inside.

Sahara inhaled deeply and followed, then tripped over the bottom step. *So much for stealth,* she thought as she crashed into a rack of potato chip bags. Luckily, Naima caught it before it toppled over. With the overhead bulbs off, Sahara could scarcely make out the old refrigerator, let alone the small lock dangling off its handle.

"Any flashlights lying around?" she asked.

"No, but Baba always keeps batteries in some of the lanterns in case the electricity goes out." Naima grabbed one from a shelf behind the counter and switched it on. "Better?"

Before Sahara could answer, the whir of spinning tires came from outside. She froze. What if it was Sittu? Or her dad? Sahara peeked outside, then scurried behind the counter. "Just a passing car, but we'd better hurry."

Immediately, Naima bent down in front of the refrigerator

while Sahara held up the lantern. Within seconds, her cousin was shaking her head.

"What's happening? Not enough light?"

"It's not the kind of lock that opens with one of *these*." Naima shook the keys. "It's a combination lock." *And I've got no clue what the code is,* the frown on her face seemed to say.

Sahara crouched beside her cousin. They hadn't come this far to give up now.

"Wahid, itnin, talata, arba'ah, khamsa," Naima counted, pointing to the barrel-shaped lock's five dials, each engraved with a series of Arabic letters. "It could be anything."

She was right. There were countless combinations the letters could form. They had to narrow them down. The lock Sahara used for gym opened with numbers, but Vicky's unlocked with letters—her dog's name. "Whose name in our family has five letters?" It definitely wasn't hers because she always thought it was weird that it took six letters to spell in English but only four in Arabic.

Naima slapped her head. "Tab'an! We'll start with mine." She lined up the dials to form her name. It didn't budge.

Sahara spewed more family members' names. Except for Fanta's, none were spelled with five letters. Naima swore it couldn't be her brother's, but Sahara made her try both his nickname and real name. They didn't work either.

Who else could it be? A warm breeze floated in, blowing the loose curls out of her face. With it came the answer.

"Try my mom's name." Even though her voice shook, a certainty filled Sahara.

Naima nodded gently. She turned the lock's dials, then slid over. "You should be the one to open it."

Sahara hadn't realized her hands were shaking until she took hold of the lock. She steadied them enough to pull up on the latch. In an instant, it gave way. Naima squeezed her hand. "I'm so glad you came this summer."

Sahara smiled. Never in a million years could she have imagined any of the stuff that had happened this week, but there was no one else she'd rather be outing witches and searching for hidden chambers with than her cousin.

She grabbed hold of the refrigerator handle. "On three, we open it."

Naima placed her hand over Sahara's as they counted, "One . . . two . . . three."

The door's suction gave way with a *thwpt*. Sahara lifted the lantern.

"There's nothing in it!" Naima blasted.

Sahara thrust the light farther inside. The girls gasped in unison—and not because of what they saw, but what they *didn't*. Not a single shelf or drawer sat inside, and the back panel was missing, revealing a large, dark hole in the wall. Except it didn't lead to another room or the outside, but underground. *A tunnel to the chamber.*

"Yalla." Naima signaled for Sahara to follow her, then crept inside.

"Wait." Sahara yanked the back of her sweatshirt. "Take this." She handed Naima the lantern, then grabbed another one for herself. They'd each need their own wherever it was they were headed.

Not until Sahara had crawled halfway into the fridge did she realize there was no handle on the inside. And she wasn't about to leave the door to a secret chamber open. She'd have to push it with her foot with enough momentum to get it to swing back and shut. *Please work,* she pleaded as she kicked the door all the way open, then hurried deeper inside before it caught her legs.

Thwpt. She'd done it. Phew! She crept in farther, entering the dark, downward-sloping tunnel. A shiver ran down her back. She shook her head, trying to shake away the fear. She had to do this if she had any hopes of finding her necklace.

Gloves would've made crawling along the rocky ground much easier, but luckily, she'd changed into leggings. Otherwise, her knees would be taking a beating too. The good news was the deeper she went, the softer the dirt underneath her became. The bad news was the deeper she went, the tighter the tunnel became. She wasn't claustrophobic—at least she'd never been before—but she struggled to breathe as the walls of the passage narrowed. How had Sittu or Khaltu done this? Was there an express elevator she and Naima had missed?

Sahara sucked in air. The woodsy smell reminded her of the thicket of trees and shrubs behind her building back home on a spring day. *Home*—never had it seemed so far away.

"Do you . . . do you see anything yet?" Sahara called out.

"Not yet. But it's getting wider . . . Wait, there's something up ahead . . . an opening, I think." Naima crawled faster.

Sahara picked up the pace too, then sighed in relief as the ceiling rose and the sides opened up.

"Oh no," Naima said. "Come look. The ground ends here."

Sahara caught up to her cousin. A dark pit, who knows how deep, loomed below.

"Can you see what's down there?" Sahara gripped the rough edge of the opening with her fingers.

Naima shifted from all fours to sitting. "It's too hard to see anything from here. But it's the chamber. I can feel it." Her voice fluttered with excitement.

Sahara's pulse quickened. She felt it too. Pulling her onward, the way the adhan had the night she'd met Sittu. Before she could figure out how far down they needed to go, her cousin leaped.

"Naima!" Sahara yelled way louder than she should've on a covert mission.

"I'm all right. It's not too far. Trust me," Naima called back a second later, though it had felt like an eternity.

Sahara rolled her eyes, but the truth was she did trust her cousin *and* the voice that traveled from her heart to her ears. *It is time, Sahara.*

She slowly twisted onto her bottom, loosened her grip, and pushed off. For a quick moment, she was airborne, then gravity set in. *Help!* Sahara swallowed back a scream. After the

longest second of her life, her feet hit the ground. She stumbled forward, her hands meeting with something cushy but
coarse. The lantern rolled out of her grip, but it didn't break.
She grabbed the light and rose to her feet.

Her legs wobbled as she moved closer to Naima. Never
had she been anywhere this still. The out-of-print section at
the back of the library was quiet, but down here, there was
silence—the kind where secrets live.

"We made it." Sahara let out a nervous giggle that echoed
around the chamber.

"Of course we did." Naima circled her lantern. It was no
match for the pitch-black that surrounded them.

Sahara didn't bother looking for a light switch. There was
no way there was power down here. "Weren't you even a teeny
bit nervous? How did you know we wouldn't be leaping to our
deaths?"

"I was too excited to be nervous. And I didn't *know*, I
believed."

"What's the difference?"

"One depends on facts, the other on hope. I always go with
hope—much more reliable."

Sahara couldn't help but smile. *The eighth wonder of the
world, Naima,* Sahara thought, waving the lantern by her feet.

"A carpet," Naima remarked, then both of them dragged
their twin light beams over its maroon and gold fibers. Some
sort of large rosette had been woven into the center.

How on earth had anyone gotten a carpet down *here*?

Sahara had once calculated in science class that the average length of her steps equaled 1.2 feet. Judging by how many she'd taken in each direction before the rug ended, it measured somewhere around four feet wide by six feet long. There was no way Sittu could've lugged a carpet that size through the tunnel. Unless the chamber was older than her grand—

Sahara froze. A quick wave rippled through the rug, momentarily lifting them a few inches off the ground.

"Did you feel that?" Naima cried. "The carpet's alive!"

Sahara was thinking more along the lines of an earthquake, but either way, it was freaky.

And then, the echo of voices came from above.

"Girls, we know you're down there."

Sahara didn't have to see their faces to know she and Naima were goners.

SAHARA WIPED HER sweaty palms on her leggings as Sittu and Khaltu Layla descended the rope ladder they'd dropped seconds earlier. She blasted herself for not taking the time to look for one before leaping after Naima. She'd let her judgment lapse. And for what? To face the uncertain wrath of her aunt and grandmother!

"How in Allah's name did you get down here without the ladder?" Khaltu asked, her voice tight. "Don't tell me you jumped. You could've gotten hurt. I have never seen such recklessness! What do you have to say for yourselves?"

"We were looking for—" Naima began.

"Of all the foolish things you've done, Naima," Khaltu railed, "*this* is the most fool—"

"It's not her fault." Sahara couldn't let her cousin take the fall for their paired mischief. "It's mine. I overheard you and Sittu talking about the chamber and the treasures. It was my idea to leave the wedding early so we could come here."

"Is that true, Naima?" Khaltu asked.

"It is, but it's *your* fault for hiding this place from us."

"Kifaya." Sittu's declaration bounced off the walls of the chamber. "Enough casting blame. I should've trusted my instincts."

"But, Mama, they weren't . . . they're not ready."

"Layla, whether they are or not doesn't matter now. They are *here*. We must trust Allah's plan."

Sittu struck a match, lighting a torch above her head. Once ablaze, its flame lit a series of other torches around the chamber, one by one like dominoes. She inhaled deeply, and with her exhale came the words:

"It's time for the truth . . . the truth about our family."

PART FOUR
The Chamber

35

Why Me?

985 CE

Morgana's pulse raced as she stared into the spyglass. She'd thought of what she desired to see, and it showed her Deena—standing in front of the city gates back home, holding something tightly in her hand. Heading toward her was the emir's cavalry, her husband leading the charge.

"If Morgana says she did not do this, then she didn't!"

My letter.

Deena clutched the parchment to her chest and locked her eyes on the men. Her gaze hard, like when she was planning her next move in a game of backgammon. Only the cost of losing was much higher now.

"If any more of you dare go after her, you will have to strike me down first! Return to your wives and children." The tremble in Deena's voice lingered in the air.

After a few seconds of silence, her husband twisted around and gave a curt nod to his officers. One by one, they retreated.

Morgana looked away. She'd seen what she needed to see.

She pressed the necklace to her heart as Peri returned the spyglass to the sack.

"You see, she never lost her faith in you." Julnar smiled. "Nor should you."

Morgana nodded, wishing she could believe in herself the way Deena believed in her.

"You *can* protect the treasures," the mermaid queen continued. "Do not blame yourself for the apple. It was stolen by an evil ghoula with sand magic the likes of which we've never seen."

Morgana winced, remembering the way the blast of sand from the witch's palm had forced her into the tree. First a dark sorcerer and now a witch! Who else would come after the enchanted items? How was *she* supposed to protect the treasures against such powerful forces?

Husnaya kicked the ground, sending a cloud of dust into the air. "Not one prophecy mentioned El Ghoula's arrival! Where did she come from?"

Prophecy? When Morgana was little and helped Cook handpick tiny stones out of the rice he'd brought from the market, he liked to tell her about the seers who touted prophecies of incredible men with extraordinary futures. Her favorite foretold a faraway time when man would soar past the earth and set foot on the moon. But Husnaya wasn't talking about some improbable event that might take place thousands of years from now—she was talking about yesterday's apple-stealing witch.

"If none of the prophecies predicted El Ghoula's appearance, whose did they foretell?"

Julnar's eyes sparkled with the answer. "Yours, my dear. The prophecy led us to you."

Morgana shook her head. Prophecies were supposed to be about great men, *not* young servant girls. "It can't be." But try as she might, she couldn't deny what she'd just heard. The truth, even the most unbelievable, rings at a frequency all its own—one the whole of nature, from the sparrow to the lion, immediately recognizes.

Peri zipped toward the seer. "Show her."

"I have seen it in the wind." Husnaya pointed to the sky.

Morgana must have been missing something, for all she saw were a few random clouds scattered among the blue sky.

The seer waved her finger, sending the clouds floating toward each other. They swirled around before joining together. "Look again."

Morgana lifted her head to the sky. The clouds formed a face—*her* face.

"Morgana Salem, you and those who will descend from you are the only hopes we have of keeping our world from succumbing to the darkness that would prevail if the lamp fell into the wrong hands," Husnaya proclaimed.

"But why me? What about your magical powers? Surely, the lamp would be better off with you."

"Why not *you*?" Julnar took hold of Morgana's hand. "Didn't *you* help Ali Baba guard the chamber and keep its location secret? Didn't *you* leave everything behind out of duty to your mawlay?"

"But in the end, I couldn't save him."

"Not for want of trying," Husnaya insisted. "Do you forget you have blood on your hands? You killed a man defending yourself and Ali Baba."

Morgana hadn't forgotten. How could she?

Peri perched on her shoulder. Her little wings flickered with sparks of light, sending a tingle down to Morgana's feet. "If not for you, the sorcerer would've escaped with the lamp. *We* didn't stop him—*you* did."

Julnar raised Morgana's chin. "Despite all that has happened, here you are. Who else but you could have done this all? We may have magical abilities, but don't underestimate the power of your courage."

Morgana had been called many things in her life—loyal, faithful, dutiful, and recently, murderous—but never courageous. She liked the sound of it.

"Everything is unfolding as it was written in the beginning by Allah," Husnaya told her. "We may never know why, but we must trust there is a reason bigger than you, or me, or any of us."

Peri zoomed up and examined the floating image. "It's definitely you!" Her words rang through the canyons.

It was, down to the beauty mark on her right cheek.

Morgana drew in a deep breath and held it. When she was ready, she blew out an audible exhale, letting go of the uncertainty and fear clenched in her muscles since the awful night back home.

"That's it, my dear." Julnar smiled with approval. "Now, before it gets any later, *we* must do our part to safeguard the lamp."

Morgana didn't dare guess what the enchanted trio intended. Whatever it was, was sure to be spectacular. But the words that came out of Husnaya's mouth as she pointed to Morgana's chest were the last she expected to hear.

"Your hamsa—we must have it. It is the key to locking the lamp."

36

Ancient Secrets

All secrets have expiration dates. Whether it be ones whispered in the ears of close friends or passed down over generations, all eventually meet their end.

"Whoa," Sahara said quietly as the flickering flames brought the chamber to life. They were in some sort of underground cave. Hanging along the rocky walls, below the torches, was a collection of portraits. There had to have been at least twenty. All of them of women—some smiling, others more serious—but it was the determination in their set jaws that drew Sahara in. Her gaze lingered on one of the silver-framed paintings. Like the rest of the women, the woman in this painting had dark hair and eyes, but something about her face seemed strangely familiar. Sahara couldn't pinpoint what it was.

Beside this portrait stood a wooden curio. The floral and scroll patterns engraved on its door reminded Sahara of the henna artists' designs. Too bad its doors weren't transparent.

Anything hidden down here in an ancient-looking cabinet was bound to be good.

She couldn't confirm it without a tape measure, but Sahara was confident she'd been right about the size of the carpet. It was slightly larger than the three-by-five area rug at the foot of her bed back home. The next size up would be four by six feet—if a carpet in a secret chamber even conformed to standard sizes.

"What is this place?" Naima's eyes scanned the room like the beam of a lighthouse.

"*This* is Morgana's chamber," her mother answered.

Sahara had heard that name before, but where?

"Morgana, as in the one from Ali Baba's story?" Naima asked excitedly.

Right, she was Ali Baba's servant. But obviously, Khaltu wasn't talking about *that* Morgana.

Sittu sat on the edge of a boulder in the corner and gestured for the girls to join her. They squeezed in next to their grandmother, her soft arms and the sweetness of the yasmeen still around her neck wrapping them in a tender embrace.

"Morgana Salem lived over a thousand years ago in the city of Baghdad . . ."

FOR THE NEXT ten minutes, Sittu recounted her ancestor's life. It sounded like a tale out of Sahara's mom's journal, not history. But their grandmother insisted that Morgana's story was fact, *not* fiction.

"All tales, even the most fictitious, grow out of a seed of truth. Ali Baba and Morgana were once as alive as we are today."

Sahara rubbed her head, trying to make sense of it all. "So we're in the thieves' underground chamber . . . No, that was in Baghdad . . . Where are we, then?"

"Morgana eventually reached Cairo. You're standing in the chamber where she hid the lamp and the other enchanted treasures," Sittu told her. "When she had daughters, she passed on its location and the promise to protect its magic. And they passed it on to their daughters. For a thousand years, the women of our family have continued Morgana's mission—to keep the chamber's magic out of the hands of those who would misuse it."

The light of all the torches combined was no match for the smile that spread across Sittu's face. Sahara couldn't help but smile back. But she did wonder whose hands they were keeping the magic out of. "If Morgana killed the sorcerer in self-defense, then who was she afraid would misuse the magic?"

"Even though the sorcerer died, his descendants sought to reclaim the lamp they believed was rightfully his, just as Morgana's sought to protect it," Sittu explained.

"We're . . . *I'm* related to this Morgana?" Naima asked in disbelief.

"Yes, and all the women who came after her." Khaltu circled her finger around the chamber. "*These* are your ancestors."

Adrenaline rushed through Sahara. How could any of this be true? She was related to a superhero! And now, she and Naima were part of her crew. Morgana might not have been able to fly or see through walls, but she *was* super. She'd only been one year older than them when she'd risked everything to keep the treasures safe.

Sahara walked over to the portrait that had captivated her earlier.

Sittu joined her side. "It all began with her."

Morgana. Her eyes traced the violet scarf that hung loosely over her ancestor's raven hair. In Morgana's steady gaze, Sahara recognized a spark. It was the same one she'd seen in Naima's right before she did something brave. "Who painted these?"

"It's a mystery," Sittu answered. "Every time a Salem woman passes, fulfilling her commitment to guard the chamber, her portrait mysteriously appears on the wall. Nobody knows how it gets here or by whose hand it was made."

Just as Sahara was about to ask about the lamp, Naima blurted, "Ali's—our shop was named after Ali Baba! I knew it was more than a regular store!"

"It might've been named after Morgana's mawlay, but it *is* only a shop," her mother maintained. "Our ancestors had to make a living somehow."

"But why did they need to work if they had an enchanted

jinni lamp? Couldn't they have wished for anything they wanted? Could we wish for anything we want?" Naima paced around the chamber, her head presumably whirling with zany wishes.

"Tab'an, la," Khaltu answered firmly. "It's our duty to guard the treasures. Under no circumstances should we use them for profit. Our ancestors built the store around the tunnel, leaving a hole in the wall to access it. That way, they could guard the chamber *and* work. But since a large cavity in the wall would've aroused suspicion, over the years, they placed different items in front to conceal it. When the old refrigerator broke, Mama decided it would be a good cover."

"All those times Baba offered to take away that broken talaga, and you said, 'No, Gamal. My father worked hard to buy that refrigerator. We can't get rid of it,'" Naima scoffed. "Does Baba even know about this place? Did Giddu?"

Sittu shook her head. "Neither your father nor grandfather knew. It wasn't easy keeping it from them, but it's what the women in our family have always done. After Ali Baba's death, Morgana didn't share the secrets of this room with any other man, even after she married."

Did that mean Sahara would have to keep the chamber a secret from her dad? Sure, she'd lied to him before and had plenty of little secrets, like chewing bubble gum after she'd brushed her teeth, but never about anything as big as this. Never about anything she'd have to keep from him *forever.* She pointed at the curio. "Is the lamp in there?"

"It was for many years," Sittu answered. "But before you arrived, I had the same dream night after night—little wings flapping above me and a voice warning that someone was coming for the lamp, beckoning me to remove it from the chamber."

Amitu had also mentioned wings flying above her. Except that voice had said, "Ma tinseesh," reminding her to give Sahara the jewelry box. Could whatever this fluttering thing was have visited Sittu too?

Naima approached her grandmother. "Don't you see? Your dream was warning you that Magda was after the lamp. That's what Sahara and I have been trying—"

"Not again with this nonsense," Khaltu Layla huffed. "Magda is many things, but she's *not* a thief. Naima, you must think before you speak, especially now that you know about the chamber."

"*You're* the one not thinking!" Naima shouted. Sahara's eyes bore into Naima's, pleading with her to back off. But Naima was too far gone. "How do you explain Sittu's dream? If not El Ghoula, then—"

"You forget yourself, my granddaughter. That is no way to speak to your mother!"

Naima dropped her head. This was exactly what Sahara had been afraid of. Her dad and Amitu always made such a fuss about respecting your elders. Even though Sahara agreed with her cousin, she knew neither of these grown-ups would tolerate Naima's tone.

Sittu lifted Naima's chin, her voice softening. "I applaud your passion for protecting the chamber and its treasures. I expect no less from a Salem woman." Naima smiled faintly as her grandmother continued.

"Though we've managed to protect the lamp from the wicked sorcerer's descendants for centuries, they have never stopped looking for it. If my dream was a warning against any-one, it was them, *not* Omar's wife. I pray it never happens, but even if they managed to get ahold of the lamp, they wouldn't be able to use it. It's locked and has been since Morgana brought it to Cairo."

"All that matters now," Khaltu added, "is the lamp is safe, and your uncle is happily married. No more talk about Magda being El Ghoula, all right?"

Naima nodded, defeated.

Clearly, it was time to get off the subject of the witchy bride. Sahara twisted toward her grandmother. "If the lamp isn't down here anymore, where is it?"

"Inside the bottom step in the shop."

"The loose step," Sahara murmured to herself.

"Mama, I told you that might not be the best place to hide it," Khaltu said. "Maybe we should bring it back here?"

"But what's *here*? You haven't shown us anything. I just see pictures of our relatives and this sigada." Naima pointed to the wool carpet.

"It's not *just* a rug." Khaltu Layla snapped her fingers. She and Sittu hurried off the carpet, which instantly rose three feet off the ground, taking Naima with it.

For the first time, Naima was speechless, her mouth hanging open. She wobbled as the carpet waved back and forth midair but quickly found her balance.

The hairs on the back of Sahara's neck stood up. She circled the rug, searching for hidden strings, but there weren't any. The carpet was floating *on its own.*

With another snap of Khaltu's fingers, the rug touched down. Sahara ran over. "You were flying!"

"I know." Naima laughed a low chuckle that quickly built to a hysterical howl. She turned to her mother. "Again!"

Khaltu shook her head. "That's enough for now. I was just showing you that there are indeed objects worth protecting down here."

Sittu had said Morgana fled with the lamp and three other enchanted items. The flying carpet had to be one, leaving two more they hadn't seen yet. "Are the other treasures down here too?"

"The rest can wait until tomorrow," Sittu responded. "We must head back before the men return."

As Khaltu climbed the ladder, Sahara had one last question for her grandmother—one that couldn't wait. "Did my mom know?"

"No." Sittu cupped Sahara's face with her hands. "By the time Amani was old enough, she and your father had already decided to move to America. I didn't dare burden her with an obligation she couldn't honor from far away."

But Sahara found that hard to believe. The whole time she was in the chamber, it was like she'd remembered a truth she had let slip away. It was back in her grasp, and she felt more tied not only to her mother but to the deepest caverns within her own heart.

911

Although Sittu had returned, Sahara still spent the night at Naima's. As far as her father knew, she'd been there since the twins had dropped them off. Veering off course from their original plan would only lead to more questions—ones she was too spent to talk her way out of tonight.

Even in her exhaustion, Sahara couldn't help but think about her mother and the chamber. What if Sittu was right and her mom *hadn't* known about it? After all, her painting wasn't among those of the Salem women who had passed. But despite this evidence to the contrary, Sahara still had her doubts. It couldn't be a mere coincidence that she discovered the chamber the same week she'd received her mother's necklace and journal *and* started having dreams of her.

A few more rounds of connect the cryptic dots, and she drifted off to sleep.

"Sahara." Her mom's voice shrouded her with tenderness.

When Sahara turned around, Amani raised her hand, pressing the hamsa dangling from her daughter's neck to her heart. A wave of warmth coursed through Sahara. She wished they could remain connected here indefinitely, wherever *here* was.

After some time—if there was such a thing as time in dreams—her mom's index finger began to glow. She lifted it above her head, and within seconds a torch was ablaze, followed by another and then another, illuminating the stone walls of the chamber.

"You've always known where, Sahara." Amani smiled, Morgana's portrait behind her.

"You've been here before, haven't you?"

Her mom nodded, then reached to open the curio. Everything inside was blurry, except for a small vial. The glass tube and its bronze cap, in the shape of a lion's head, glimmered inside the otherwise dark cabinet. Before Sahara could ask about it, a distant whooshing sounded. She didn't know where it was coming from, but she was certain from the growing noise that it was moving in one direction—hers.

"The winds of fate are coming," her mother shouted over the roar.

The invisible storm raged, whipping Sahara's hair in her face and driving her back.

"Don't resist. Let go and use the key." Her mom pointed to Sahara's chest, and Sahara immediately felt the hamsa pulse.

The wind blasted again. "Mom, I can't . . . I'm scared."

Grains of sand hit her face, stinging her eyes and flooding

her mouth. Something was pulling her away from the chamber, from her mom. She groped for her mother's hand, but it was too late.

"Let go," her mom called as Sahara hurtled farther away. "It's the only way."

SAHARA'S EYES FLUTTERED open in the dark. Her mom's words lingered in the space between sleep and wakefulness. *Let go and use the key.*

The purpose of a key was to keep something important safe. Like the magic lamp, which had been locked and hidden in the secret chamber for ages. What if the journal's warning that what was hidden in the dark would be unlocked was about the *lamp?* That would mean that the key that had kept the jinni under wraps all these years had been compromised. Sahara brought her hand to her heart, the truth materializing. *My necklace is the key.*

It made perfect sense. *The two that must not join become one* had never been about Magda and Omar, but the lamp and necklace. That's why El Ghoula had stolen the hamsa. Now the girls just had to make sure she didn't get her perfectly manicured hands on the lamp too. She had to wake Naima and tell—

Barking exploded through the window. *Kitmeer!* Sahara sprang out of bed, bumping into her cousin.

Naima's eyes were wide. "Kitmeer . . . the shop. We have to go!"

Sahara's throat went dry. She couldn't speak. A half-asleep Fanta staggered into the room. "Why is that stinky dog—"

"Ahmed, go wake everyone," Naima ordered, but her brother froze. "Now!" she shouted.

Sahara raced past them, bounding down the steps in her bare feet. Having only slept an hour, she was so exhausted she could barely remember her name, let alone to throw on shoes. When she reached the ground floor, she waited for her cousin, not daring to go out alone. It was quiet, *too* quiet. *Why's Kitmeer not barking anymore?* Sahara worried as Naima shot out of the building.

"Kitmeer!" her cousin howled.

Sahara rushed out into the dark to find Naima slumped on the sidewalk, her long nightgown billowing in the breeze. The dog's still body was sprawled out underneath her.

Sahara needed to get help. Her eyes darted toward Sittu's terrace. Why hadn't anyone else come downstairs? She should call 911. Was there even a 911? Someone—her grandmother, her father—should've told her what to do in case of an emergency. *Why didn't anyone tell me what to do?* her mind screamed.

Rage flooded her body, driving her toward the shop. The gate was up, its lock lying broken on the ground. Sahara stepped down.

Instantly, someone seized her arm and wrenched her

inside, pressing a cold and sharp object against her neck. There was no mistaking the porcelain skin of the hand wielding the knife or the gold cuff around it. And the icy voice.

"Move again, darling, and I will cut your throat."

The Lamp

Sahara trembled in El Ghoula's grip, her mind doing what her body couldn't—escaping. She searched for a place to hide, slipping into one of her favorite memories. It was the snowy eve of her twelfth birthday, when her father had staggered into the living room, cradling Omni's box in his arms. She could see herself jumping up and down as the robot came to life, vrooming and beeping around the apartment.

She'd be safe hidden here. *But what about Naima?* As much as Sahara yearned for refuge, she couldn't stay. Helping her cousin, who she could still hear wailing over Kitmeer's body, called her back to the present.

"No, Magda," Sahara said, her voice steady and defiant. "I won't be still *or* quiet."

"You *stupid* girl," El Ghoula hissed.

Sahara winced, the sting of the blade digging into her neck.

"Now that you understand this is not a game, girl, get me what I came for. The lamp!"

If there was any doubt left in Sahara's head about who Magda was and what she was after, it was gone now. *There's no way I'm turning over—*

"Stop! I'll give it to you." The words came from Naima, who stood at the foot of the shop's steps, her cheeks still wet.

"You too?" There was a hint of surprise in Magda's voice.

Sahara was relieved to see her cousin, but she couldn't risk her safety. "Run, Naima! Go get help!"

"Help," El Ghoula scoffed, her confidence returning. "There's no one who can help you." She clenched her arm tighter around Sahara's neck, making it hard to breathe.

"I won't leave you," Naima cried.

Sahara struggled to get the next words out. "Kitmeer? . . . Is . . . he . . . de—"

"No! He's breathing." Naima turned toward Magda and seethed, "You hurt him."

"If you're referring to your nasty pet, he's sleeping off a blow to the head. But don't worry, darling. He'll be up soon. Too bad the same can't be said for your family."

"What did you do to them, El Ghoula?" These words hadn't come from Naima but her *brother*. "Why aren't they waking up?"

Sahara's heart pounded in her ears. No one had come downstairs before because they hadn't been able to.

"Moi? *I* didn't do anything. It was all the sharbat's doing."

Sahara hadn't liked the idea of the sharbat to begin with, but now she loathed it.

"Though its spell appears to have missed the three of you, buzzing all over the place like annoying gnats. Enough with the small talk, children. The lamp!" Magda demanded.

"Lamp? What lamp—" Fanta started.

Naima pressed her hand over his mouth. "I told you I'd get it," she answered as Fanta's face alternated between confusion and betrayal.

Sahara had never hit anyone in her life, but she'd have knocked Magda out if it weren't for the inconvenient dagger at her throat. The image of Sittu beaming with pride as she'd described how generations of Salem women had guarded the chamber's treasures rushed back. Knife or no knife, Sahara couldn't let El Ghoula destroy their family's legacy. God knows what she was planning on doing with the lamp. Sahara couldn't let her hurt anyone with the magic Morgana had risked everything to protect.

"You can't give it to her! She can unlo—" Sahara felt the angry bite of the blade. Her cousins screamed. She couldn't look down if she tried because of the way El Ghoula's arm was wrenched under her chin. But she didn't have to—she knew she was bleeding. Her knees started to buckle. *Stay standing.*

"Now look what you've done." Magda's voice quivered. "Why couldn't you do as you were told?"

"Ihdi, Magda." Naima urged El Ghoula to stay calm. "Let me get what you came here for." She backed up and knelt in front of the bottom step, gesturing for her brother to come over. "Lift the top."

Fanta pried the brick up, even though he had no clue what was happening.

"This better not be a trick." Magda tightened her grip. Sahara's neck burned fiercely. She squished her lips together to keep from crying. She wouldn't give El Ghoula the satisfaction.

Naima promised they weren't deceiving her as she stuck her hand inside the step. Within seconds, she pulled out the shiny brass lamp, her eyes flashing with awe for a split second before they darted to Magda. "Let go of Sahara, and I'll give you the lamp."

"Hand it to me first," El Ghoula ordered.

Naima held it out with her shaking hand. Magda grabbed the lamp, throwing Sahara onto the ground and pushing Naima out of her way. Sahara sucked in air as Fanta ran over with a towel and pressed it against her neck.

It was then that Sahara caught her first glimpse of El Ghoula since she'd pulled Sahara into the shop. She still wore her wedding dress, its crystals shimmering, the lamp in one hand and the knife in the other. Sahara's stomach flipped at the sight of her blood on the blade.

Magda stroked her gown like it was a kitten. "It really was the most beautiful wedding."

Sahara felt like she was going to be sick, but she had to know. "What about Khalu Omar? Did you hurt him?"

"Like you hurt Noora?" Naima cried.

"Noora? I'm . . . I'm not sure what happened to . . ." El

Ghoula hesitated. Her eyes dimmed. When she spoke again, it was with a softness Sahara didn't think her capable of. "But I would never hurt Omar. I love him."

Her admission lingered in the dark stillness. Maybe they could get her to stop for their uncle's sake?

"Magda, you can end this. Just tell us how to wake everyone up and give us back the lamp and my necklace." Sahara crossed her fingers behind her back, tighter than tight. "Then everything can go back to the way it was." That was the worst lie she'd ever told. Nothing would ever be the same.

"It's too late for that." Magda's amber eyes blazed in the darkness, her villainy reawakening. "Your necklace—you'll never see it or the lamp ever again!" El Ghoula twisted toward the steps.

"No—" Sahara started to yell, but the words caught in her throat.

Magda glanced back to blow a kiss. "Au revoir, darlings."

And just like that, she was gone, taking the lamp and any bit of hope left inside Sahara with her.

"ONLY BROKEN SKIN. I'm okay," Sahara assured Naima, who sat next to her on the floor anxiously eyeing the bloody towel at Sahara's neck while Fanta chased after El Ghoula. But she *wasn't* okay. Not only had Magda threatened her life, but she'd fled with the lamp. Sahara hated feeling this . . . this powerless. Wasn't it enough that her mother wasn't here because of her? Now the lamp was gone too. Too much had been lost so that she could live.

"How could you give her the lamp?" She lashed out at her cousin. "My necklace is the key that unlocks it. I didn't get a chance to tell you before . . . before this bloody night happened. Now El Ghoula has both. She has both!"

"That's why there was a hamsa etched on the lamp's lid," Naima muttered, shock overtaking her face. "I didn't know, but even if I did, what was I supposed to do? I was scared. She was holding a sikeena to your throat."

Sahara's stomach twisted at the tremble in her cousin's voice. It couldn't have been easy handing over the lamp, especially for Naima, who revered all things magic. She had been faced with an impossible choice. And if she'd chosen differently, Sahara wouldn't be here to criticize her for it.

She rested her head on Naima's shoulder. "Thank you for not running away after I told you to."

"Would you have left if it had been me?"

Sahara nestled deeper into her cousin. They both knew the answer to that.

"How did you figure out your necklace was the key?" Naima asked.

"By trusting what my mom said in my latest dream and connecting it with what we already knew. Belief and reason are a good team."

"Yes, they are." Naima squeezed her hand.

Fanta returned out of breath. "She's gone . . . probably flown away . . . on her broomstick."

"What about Kitmeer?" Naima cried. "Is he up yet?"

"Not yet." He took a seat next to them. His eyes darted from Sahara's neck to his sister. "We should get her to a hospital."

The last thing Sahara wanted to do tonight was go to a hospital. Besides, how would they explain to a doctor what had happened? *Khalu Omar's bride broke into our family's shop to steal an ancient jinni lamp, and we're here alone because all the grown-ups are under a sleep spell* wasn't going to fly.

Sahara shook her head. "It's already stopped bleeding." She removed the towel. "See? No need for stitches."

Her neck burned as Naima moved her thumb across the cut, insisting that they had to at least clean and bandage it. Immediately, Fanta was at her side with a bottle of antiseptic, gauze, and surgical tape he'd pulled off a high shelf. Was there anything the shop didn't sell?

"This might hurt," he warned, applying it to her neck.

Sahara braced herself for the worst, and it came. She yelped in pain and squeezed her eyes, tears spilling out as Fanta disinfected the wound and secured the gauze. All the while, Naima held her hand and prayed.

When Sahara could no longer feel Fanta's fingers working, she blinked her eyes open. "Done?"

He nodded. "I should've listened to you both about El

Ghoula." His voice broke. "Maybe if I had, none of this would've happened. And Baba and Mama would still be awake."

A glimmer of hope flickered in Sahara's heart. "Wait, does that mean my dad isn't under the sharbat's spell?"

Fanta shook his head. "I'm sorry, Sahara. I tried to wake him too, but I couldn't."

Sahara's lip quivered. She glanced at Fanta, who wiped his wet cheeks with the back of his hand. They *all* had lost a lot tonight. How could she blame him for having doubts about El Ghoula when up until ten minutes ago, she'd had them herself? "It's not your fault."

"Tab'an it is." Naima pointed a finger at her brother. "You never listen to anything I say. You always accuse me of making up stories. Well, I didn't make this one up, did I? And how come *you're* awake? I saw you raise your glass to the bride and groom."

"That's because I didn't drink the sharbat. I might not have believed Magda was a witch, but that doesn't mean I wanted to toast her marriage to Khalu."

A covert smile slipped across Fanta's face and passed to his sister like a note bearing the message *I believed you all along.*

Before Naima could reward his loyalty with affection, Fanta quickly changed the subject. "Is one of you going to tell me why our family had an oil lamp hidden inside the step? The step I tripped over a million times the past few weeks."

Sahara shot Naima a nervous look. The men weren't supposed to know about the chamber or the treasures. But after tonight, how could they *not* tell Fanta?

"I'll explain everything after we help Kitmeer. We can't just leave him lying in the street." Naima's voice cracked.

Fanta nodded, appeased for now. "We could move him in here."

"No, it's not safe. El Ghoula could come back," Naima asserted.

Sahara leaped up, wobbling on her still-shaky legs. "I've got a plan."

Hope

Once, in the fifth grade, Sahara had returned from school livid after Corey Burke threw a paper airplane at her head. When her aunt demanded to know why she hadn't said anything to the teacher, Sahara explained that her class was in the library, where there was a strict rule against talking. A dismayed Amitu pointed out, "If no one ever challenged the rules or laws, some of your classmates wouldn't be allowed to attend the same school as you because of their skin color. We must question the rules, even the most established."

Sahara smiled, thinking of Amitu's words as she pointed to her cousins' balcony. "I know your parents don't think Kitmeer should go upstairs, but I'm sure they'd understand."

Fanta snorted.

"They *would*," Naima insisted to her brother. "Doesn't Sittu always say he's one of Allah's creatures? We can't leave him like this."

"I know," he groaned. "But how do you expect to *get* him

upstairs? Even with all my karate training, there's no way I can carry him up three flights."

"We can do it together, then."

Sahara shook her head. "Fanta's right—we can't. But we don't have to." Despite everything that had happened tonight, her hands still tingled with excitement at her budding plan. "We'll *pull* him up!"

Her cousins stared blankly back at her. She'd have to spell it out. "The pulley. We'll use it to hoist him up to your balcony, but first, we need something big enough for him to fit inside."

Fanta ran upstairs. Seconds later, he lowered Khaltu's large laundry basket while Naima knelt and caressed Kitmeer. Her tears dripped onto his head. It was Sahara's turn to hold out hope—to believe—for the both of them.

"He'll wake up. I know it. And don't worry about the pulley. No more crashing, I promise. My dad and I installed a brake. It's super safe." Sahara would bet on anything she and her father had fixed together. Her throat tightened. Would they ever have a chance to be a team again? she wondered as Fanta returned.

Carefully, each of them wrapped their arms around a different part of Kitmeer's body and lifted him into the basket. Wisps of his fur floated around them as Naima gently curled his legs into his belly, and Sahara checked that the basket was securely clipped. Not wasting a second, they raced up the steps to the third floor.

Using every ounce of strength left in their tired bodies, they pulled Kitmeer up, collapsing on the balcony floor once he was safely inside. Sahara was anxious to check on her father and Sittu but would need a few minutes to catch her breath.

"Are you going to tell me about the lamp now?"

Naima deflected again. "Yes, but we should go see if Khalu Omar's okay first."

Sahara was worried about their uncle too, but she wasn't sure Fanta's curiosity could be diverted this time.

"And what about poor Fayrouz?" Naima added. "She spent the night there to help the awful bride settle into her new home. Allah knows what El Ghoula has done to her."

Poor Fayrouz was right. She'd been so proud of her homemade sharbat. If she only knew what Magda had done to it.

Fanta narrowed his eyes. "Why do I get the feeling that you're hiding something about this lamp? Don't tell me—it belonged to Ala el-Din?"

Bingo. Sahara pressed her lips together, afraid the truth might slip out.

He stared at them, waiting for an answer. When neither of them said anything, realization flashed in his eyes. "It *is* Ala el-Din's lamp. Ya Allah!" Fanta rubbed his bandana. "First, our uncle marries a witch, and now our family's been hiding a jinni lamp!"

"Who said anything about a jinni lamp?" Naima feigned ignorance, but not well. "And even if it is, we can't tell you. Mama and Sittu said so."

Stop talking, Sahara yelled in her head, watching her cousin dig them into a hole deeper than the chamber.

"Even *Baba* doesn't know. None of the men in our family have *ever* known."

Fanta looked to Sahara. She wanted to tell him about Morgana and the chamber so badly but didn't know if it was her place. Where would she even begin?

The betrayal that had flashed across Fanta's face earlier returned, only now it settled into the hard lines on his face.

"Fine. Don't tell me!" He jumped up. "You two have it all figured out." His voice grew louder. "You think I don't know what I'm doing." He was shouting now. "That I can't be trusted with your precious secrets!"

"Just because you're older doesn't mean you always get to be in charge," his sister yelled back. "Well, this time, you're not!"

"And how's that going for you? Our family's under El Ghoula's spell, she attacked Sahara, and the lamp's gone!" He tore off his bandana and threw it at them. "Here. You take it now, heroes."

"Fanta, where are you going?" Sahara cried as he bolted off the balcony. With the grown-ups unable to help, they needed to stay together.

"To check on Khalu," he yelled before the door to the apartment slammed.

"Oof. He can be such an oaf sometimes." Naima picked up her brother's bandana.

"Don't even think about putting that on. I know he threw

it, but he'll be *so* mad if he comes back and sees you wearing it. And we *need* him. Sittu, our parents, and half of Shobra are asleep. We need all the help we can get figuring out how to reverse the spell and get the lamp and my necklace back before El Ghoula unlocks it." *If she hasn't already.*

"What makes you think *he* can help us? He knows nothing about magic."

"Neither do I. And besides what you've read in your books, do you know anything about reversing spells?"

"No, but I know someone who does."

Sahara crossed her arms. "Please tell me you're not thinking of telling *her*. Besides, you can't just knock on people's doors in the middle of the night."

"It's Umm Zalabya. She's not like other people," Naima pressed.

Sahara couldn't argue with that.

"I'm sure she already knows I'm coming, just like she knew our family was in danger. That's why she gave us the enchanted ful."

"Some enchantment," Sahara snorted. "It didn't stop El Ghoula's spell. What was the point of it?"

"That's what I'm going to find out."

SAHARA'S DAD MAY have been a skilled engineer, but he was a disaster in the kitchen. She never understood how he could put together intricate blueprints that would one day become magnificent buildings but not be able to reheat dinner without burning it. Despite all his cooking missteps, her father insisted on making lissan asfoor—a chicken soup loaded with lemon and orzo—for Sahara when she was sick. It was the only time Amitu let him near the stove. Although illness didn't make Sahara the best judge of taste, no matter how awful she felt, she always felt *less* awful after a bowl of his soup.

Now seated by her father's side, Sahara would have given him all the lissan asfoor in the world if it meant he'd wake up. She rested her head on his chest and tuned into his steady heartbeat as the Fajr adhan sounded. Amid all the chaos of the last few days, the familiar sound of the call to prayer had become a source of comfort. This was the first time she'd been awake for the dawn adhan. Outside, the sky was navy, with only the faintest sliver of pale blue light on the horizon foretelling a future sunrise.

"Can you hear it, Dad?" Sahara whispered. The words *hayya ala salah* echoed through the open terrace, beckoning those listening to come to prayer. It had been a few years since Sahara had prayed with her father, but she felt compelled to do just that, particularly since he and Sittu couldn't.

She slid off the bed and headed to her grandmother's bedroom, where Sittu was sound asleep, the fan rustling her hair. Her garland lay on the nightstand, the jasmine petals opening in the twilight. Sahara walked over and squeezed her hand. "I'm sorry we gave her the lamp. We let you down." Her voice shook. "But we'll fix it, I promise. I've just gotta figure out how."

She slipped a silver headscarf out of the armoire and tied it around her neck, returning to her father's room. As she'd seen him do multiple times since they'd arrived, she retrieved the prayer rug from behind the door and unrolled it toward the corner of the balcony—toward Mecca.

Quietly, she removed her sneakers, then planted her feet on the soft rug, lifting her hands to her ears. The old sacred motions and words rushed back, never having left in the first place. She needed only to show up, her heart broken open, ready to receive. With every utterance and movement hope bloomed inside her like the yasmeen she prayed were as magical as Umm Zalabya had claimed. She would find a way to get back her necklace and the lamp. And if it took a hundred planet pads of brainstorming to come up with a plan to wake her family, then so be it. She wouldn't stop until she did.

Tell me where to begin, she prayed, lowering her head to the velvet rug.

In the stillness of dawn, her mother's voice sounded in her ears—*You've always known where.*

The Amulet of the Four

Morgana clutched the hamsa closer to her chest. She was past the point of wondering how the trio knew about it since they seemed to know everything, but how could they use it to lock the lamp?

"My necklace? It's not magical. It . . . it was a gift from my mawlay's daughter."

"That's precisely *why* we need it," Julnar said. "The spirit of love and friendship with which it was given to you resides in it. And if we are to create an amulet capable of locking the enchanted lamp, we must harness that benevolent energy."

"If the lamp's so dangerous, why not destroy it?"

Husnaya's eyes flashed to the steel hammer protruding from her leather belt. "As much as I'd like to smash it to pieces, I cannot. Only the dark magic that made it can destroy it. And the possibility of that died with the sorcerer."

Whom I killed. Would she ever forgive herself?

"Though he no longer poses a threat," Husnaya continued,

"his descendants will seek to reclaim the lamp, just as yours will be bound by a duty to protect it. We cannot change these fated paths, but we *can* confine the powerful sorcery inside the lamp. And nothing is better suited for this task than your hand of Fatima."

"That and a stone from the depths of the sea," Peri added.

The mermaid queen smiled, holding out her hand. In seconds, a sparkling indigo gem crystallized from the center of her palm.

"Gorgeous," Peri squealed.

She was right. Morgana had never seen a more brilliant gem.

"Your best work yet," Husnaya praised her, then shifted her kohl-lined eyes to Morgana. "Now that we have the stone, all we need is the necklace and the lamp."

"Are you ready, my dear?" Julnar asked.

Morgana *wasn't* ready, but she'd promised her mawlay she would protect the treasures. And forever etched in her mind would be Princess Badr's eyes imploring her to keep the lamp safe. She couldn't let them down.

"Will I get it back after the lamp is locked?"

Husnaya shook her head. "Once the Amulet of the Four is forged from our combined energy, it will reside in the earth until the time comes for it to surface again."

Morgana began to see red. "You're going to bury it! Why?" She'd already said goodbye to so much. Now she had to give up her necklace.

"Once the amulet seals the lamp's power, the two must be kept apart. For the hamsa that locks it can also be used to *unlock* it."

"Have you seen that in the wind too?" Peri asked.

Husnaya nodded, removing a scroll from her belt. She unrolled it and read, " 'When the moon and Saturn align, the two that must not join become one, unlocking what has been hidden in the dark.' "

"If you know that will happen, then stop it. Use your magic to stop it!"

"We cannot—" Husnaya started.

"What good is your magic if you can't use it to stop bad things from happening?"

"We cannot interfere with what has been written from the beginning," the seer maintained. "The effects of using our magic that way could be catastrophic."

"Then bury the lamp. Let the earth have that instead." Morgana shook her head fervently. "I can't give you the necklace! I won't! Deena had it made for me. No one has ever had anything made for me before."

Julnar stepped closer. "Nothing can diminish the affection with which the necklace originated. Nothing can take away the love with which it was cherished. Without them, an amulet powerful enough to lock the lamp couldn't be created." She took hold of Morgana's hand. "You have sacrificed so much out of duty for those you love. Your faithfulness will live on in the necklace. But now you must let it go so it may find its way through time to its next rightful recipient.'"

Wasn't *she* its rightful recipient? "Why should I believe you? Why should I believe any of this?" In all her life, Morgana had never raised her voice to anyone, but her indignation boiled over like water left on the fire for too long. "I'm to let go of the *one* thing I have left of my closest friend, of my home, because it must find its way to someone *else*!"

Peri darted past her. "I knew you had fire in you—"

"Pfft!" Morgana wasn't in the mood for one of the fairy's quips. "Who has decided that I must give it up? You?" She pointed a shaking finger at the trio. "*You*, who have magic but are afraid to use it."

"Not us, but the winds of fate." Husnaya waved her hand in the air, and a soft breeze swept past Morgana, loosening her resistance with a reminder.

When the winds of fate blow, let them carry you.

"I'm not sure I can, Mama."

Julnar rubbed her back. "My dear one, no one *else* can. But first, a vow—she who receives the necklace next will treasure it as much as you do. She *must* if she's to harness the promise of love within it to keep the lamp's power at bay when wickedness threatens again. But there is hope." She turned to the scroll in the seer's hands.

"'Take heart, for all is not lost in the light of love's promise,'" Husnaya read. She returned the scroll to her belt, joining her hands in prayer at her chest. "It will not be easy for her as it has not been for you, but she *will* be worthy of it. There is a curious strength in those who surrender to the wind and allow it to lead them home, even if it is not where they expected to find it."

Morgana pressed the hamsa to her heart one last time. She pulled the chain over her head and kissed it. "Forgive me, Deena," she whispered before holding it out to Husnaya.

The seer shook her head. "Not yet."

When Morgana retrieved the lamp from the sack and pushed it toward Husnaya, she shook her head again.

The lamp too? "Why?"

"You'll see." Peri fluttered her wings excitedly.

Her beloved necklace clenched in one hand, the jinni lamp dangling from the other—Morgana couldn't believe what had become of her life.

Smiling, the mermaid queen glided forward and took hold of her right fist. A wave of warmth coursed through Morgana as Julnar unfurled her fingers. Morgana gasped at her open palm. The hamsa pendant was still there, only now the sapphire stone from the depths of the sea sat at its center.

"Ya Allah!" Morgana cried as the trio formed a circle around her. Husnaya's voice reverberated through the surrounding canyons.

"We stand before you as the Four—Julnar the Water, Peri the Fire, and I the Wind around Morgana of Baghdad, the Earth. We ask all that is good in Allah's realm to protect the lamp and to keep its power out of the hands of those who would misuse it."

In seconds, the sun yielded its glow to the hidden moon and stars. Silver rays of light burst forth from each of the trio's chests toward the pendant. Morgana braced herself as it began to shake wildly in her hands. A bright indigo light flashed from the center of the sapphire, joining the silver beams to create a brilliant shield around the Four.

Morgana fell to her knees as the engraved hamsa broke away from the pendant with a loud crack. It floated toward the lamp and pressed itself onto the lid, leaving behind an identical hamsa-shaped indent. Sparks flew as it fused back with the necklace.

In those flickers, girls' faces flashed one after another—their eyes glimmering with the promise to carry on what she'd started. The last one bowed her head of wild curls. Was that the hamsa around her neck? Before Morgana could be sure, the girl disappeared, and the amulet dove down just as the earth opened to catch it.

Scared and Ready

There wasn't a second to waste. Sahara had to find her cousins and head to the chamber. Though her life had been turned upside down since the day she'd opened the jewelry box, she wouldn't be here if she hadn't. Her heart beat with the truth her mother had come to tell her before she'd left for Cairo. It was *time* for her to learn the truth about her family because the day would come when she'd be called to defend their legacy. *That* day was here, and *that* legacy was worth protecting.

The most powerful magic in the chamber had never been the treasures themselves but the promise Morgana had made to protect the world from the perils of their misuse. The promise reflected in the faces of the women in the chamber. That ancient promise coursed through Sahara now.

She raced downstairs, nearly colliding with Naima somewhere in the middle of the third and fourth floors. Every muscle in her body relaxed when she saw who was standing next to her.

"Kitmeer!" Sahara threw her arms around him, letting go of the breath she'd been holding since El Ghoula had seized her.

"When I got back from Umm Zalabya's, he was awake," Naima cried. "Can you believe it?"

"I never had a doubt." Sahara smiled. Now that Kitmeer was okay, they could focus on helping the grown-ups and stopping El Ghoula. "So what did Umm Zalabya say about the ful?"

"She was relieved that everyone had been wearing their garlands when they drank the cursed sharbat. Her magic yasmeen might not have stopped the spell, but if it wasn't for them, there would be no way to reverse the curse."

"And our family and two hundred wedding guests would be asleep forever."

Naima nodded. "Alhamdulillah for the ful!"

Sahara thanked every lucky star in the universe that they'd passed out the garlands. There was a way to fix this! "Did Umm Zalabaya say *how* to reverse it?"

Naima shook her head. "She said *you* would know where to find what we needed."

Sahara gripped Naima's hand and pulled her downstairs. Kitmeer bounded after them.

"Where are we going?"

"To the chamber, of course."

"Yes! I knew you'd say that!"

"First, we've gotta get my mom's journal."

Swiftly, Naima fetched it from her room and handed it to

Sahara to secure in her backpack. As they reached the first floor, the sound of footsteps came from outside.

Sahara stiffened. "Don't come any closer," she ordered as Kitmeer let out a low, warning growl.

Fanta lurched back, holding his hands up in surrender. "It's only me."

"We thought you were El Ghoula," Naima railed.

He slipped off his headphones. "Why? Has she been back?" His head twisted around the first floor.

"No, she hasn't," Sahara assured him. "But how's Khalu Omar?"

"Under the sleep spell too." He groaned.

"And Fayrouz?" Naima asked.

Fanta shook his head. "No sign of her anywhere. Maybe she ran away."

"Or maybe El Ghoula *did* something to her," Naima cried.

Sahara's pulse raced. First Noora and now Fayrouz. What was El Ghoula's beef with Sittu's maids?

"Why are you two down here and not with Sittu and our parents?"

Naima began to concoct some harebrained excuse, but Sahara insisted on telling Fanta the truth. They didn't have time for lies. She pulled out the journal and flipped to the page with the amulet. As quickly as she could, she filled him in on everything, ending with how her hamsa was the key that connected this whole twisted mess.

After, Fanta threw karate chops in the air and muttered

to himself. Sahara knew this was all hard to believe. It wasn't logical, but it *was* the truth. "I know none of this makes sense. We'll have plenty of time to talk about that later. But we've gotta get to the chamber. Are you with us?"

"Pfft. I thought you said that for generations only the *women* in our family—"

"It's time to let that go," Sahara told him. "This all may have begun with Morgana, but it's up to us now. And *we* need your help."

"And what about you?" Fanta looked to his sister.

Naima didn't answer. Instead, she removed something from her pocket and held it out.

"My hachimaki!" He took it from her hands.

Naima smiled. "You'll need it for whatever comes next."

"In or out, Fanta?" Sahara asked again.

He tied the bandana around his head. "I'm in."

OUTSIDE, THE SUN slowly gained on the horizon, preparing to overtake the darkness. Sittu's street remained as quiet as the night before. Sahara would've given anything to hear its music again. They had to wake Shobra up.

As she'd done countless times before, Naima flung the tennis ball deep into the alley, but Kitmeer didn't budge. After a few attempts, she returned to the shop, where Sahara was helping Fanta lift the gate.

"It's like he knows we're up to something," Naima huffed,

marching into the shop, Kitmeer trailing her closer than was usual, even for him.

"Ready?" Fanta asked.

Sahara pulled her hair back. "I . . . I thought I was."

"Of course you are. Who else could've helped me beat Mustafa?"

Fanta had chosen a heck of a time to finally give her credit for their dance battle win.

"You know, not everyone's *ready* has to look like Naima's *ready*," he continued. "She's like Baba. They dive headfirst into everything."

"And you don't?"

"Remember when you asked how long I've been practicing karate?"

Sahara nodded, though she wasn't sure why he was bringing it up now.

"I *did* miss one day—last year when the boys' team from a karate school in Alexandria came to Shobra to compete against ours. It was a big deal. Even Baba would be there. But the morning of the competition, I couldn't go. What if I lost in front of my father, the army hero? So I lied to my parents and said the match was delayed because a pipe had burst at the studio."

"Did they believe you?"

"Yes, but my teacher stopped by the shop later to find out why I hadn't shown. Luckily, Sittu was the only one there, and not Mama or Baba, or worse—Naima."

"Was she angry that you lied?"

Fanta shook his head. "She could see I was disappointed, so she promised to keep my lie between us as long as I told her the real reason I hadn't gone. When I said that I didn't think I was ready for the competition, especially since Baba would be watching, she told me that I *was* ready but *also* nervous, and there was nothing wrong with feeling both at the same time. Sittu said, 'Sometimes ready is nervous *and* ready, but it's still ready.'"

Sahara smiled. Her cousin was full of surprises. "Don't worry. Your secret's safe with me, Mr. Miyagi," referring to him as the wise sensei from *The Karate Kid*.

He puffed out his chest. "Are you ready, Sahara Rashad?"

Sahara stared at the fiery orange-and-red promise of the sun. She drew in a deep breath. "Scared and ready."

The words smoldered between them as she stepped inside, blazing past him.

The Curio

This is unreal, Sahara thought as she wriggled through the tunnel behind Naima and Kitmeer. Despite Fanta's many pleas to leave the dog behind, it was clear that he wasn't letting Naima out of his sight. As the tunnel narrowed, Sahara's backpack grazed the top. It would be filthy in the end, but there was *no way* she was ever getting a new one. Vicky would think it was beyond cool that Sahara had brought it to the magic chamber once she'd found a way to tell her about it. That's if she could even tell her, since generations of men in the family hadn't known.

When Sahara reached the opening, she climbed down the ladder—way easier *and* safer than plummeting into the chamber. She breathed in the cavern's cool air as Naima pulled a matchbook from her pocket. Within seconds, the entire room lit up, the smell of the blown-out match lingering. Kitmeer circled the chamber, his nose wiggling over every inch. Sahara's eyes darted around. Where should they begin?

"How could this have been down here all this time?" Fanta marveled as he climbed down. "Are all those women related to us? What's in that cabinet? Is that the flying sigada?"

Sahara knew how he felt. She'd been here before and was *still* amazed. She walked around the infamous carpet—not yet ready to step on it—toward the curio. "Should we start with this?"

"Yes, I can't wait to see what's inside!" Naima hurried over.

"Shhh, someone might hear you," Fanta warned.

"Who could hear us down here?"

"El Ghoula," he whispered, looking over his shoulder.

Naima was bold but not naive. She heeded her brother's advice. Gently, Sahara pulled the curio door, but it didn't budge. A firmer tug did the trick. As it creaked open, something small rolled out and toward her. She caught it before it hit the floor. It was an ivory tube, the length of a ruler. On each end were two round lenses enclosed in brass.

"What's that?" Fanta asked as his sister inspected the cabinet.

"A telescope." Sahara held the smaller glass lens to her eye and aimed the other end across the chamber at Morgana's portrait.

"Ah, a minzar. I've never seen one that small."

"That's because it's more like a spyglass," she explained, moving it around and studying the intricate strokes of paint that gave her ancestor's face such character. "Sailors used them on their voyages." Sahara was no stranger to these hand-held telescopes. Her father had helped her make a collapsible one for last year's science fair.

"Amazing. Can I see it?"

Sahara handed it to him, then walked around the portraits, pondering the absence of her mother's. Maybe her painting didn't hang in the chamber because her job wasn't done. The dreams, the necklace, the journal—she'd been helping them all along.

She turned to Naima, whose eyes darted between the flying carpet and the ivory tube in her brother's hand.

"The carpet and the spyglass—they're both from Prince Ahmed's story, but the part *before* he met Peri Banu. I'd forgotten about it until I saw it in your mother's journal."

Sahara removed the journal from her backpack and passed it to her.

Naima flipped through. "Here." She tapped a page and began reading. "'The Tale of a Prince Named Ahmed and His Two Brothers: The three princes of India had all fallen in love with Princess Noor al Nihar. Their father, the sultan, couldn't decide which of his sons should wed her, thus creating a challenge to help him choose. Each of them would go on an expedition in search of the rarest and most wondrous item he could find. The sultan would then judge these objects after they returned and reward the son who brought back the most remarkable treasure with the princess's hand in marriage.'"

Wouldn't it have been a lot easier if he'd just asked the princess whom she wanted to marry? *Ridiculous!*

"'The brothers traveled together,'" Naima continued, "'until they reached a road that branched off in three different directions. Prince Hussain went one way, eventually reaching the land of Bishangahr. There, he visited a marketplace where he found a merchant selling a one-of-a-kind carpet that could transport whoever sat atop it to anyplace they wished, no matter how far.'"

Sahara pointed to the rug in the chamber.

Naima nodded. "'Prince Ali headed in a different direction, arriving in Persia, where he purchased a rare ivory tube with a piece of glass at either end.'"

"The spyglass," Sahara whispered as her cousin read.

"'When raised to the eye, it allowed the viewer to see whatever he de—'"

"Magda!" Fanta cried. "I . . . I can see her! And she's got Fayrouz!"

43

One Amazing Ride

anta's words echoed through the chamber—the spyglass still pressed to his eye. In a flash, Sahara and Naima were by his side. Even Kitmeer ran over, his tail and ears at attention.

"Tell us everything you see," his sister implored.

"Magda . . . she's still wearing her wedding dress and holding something. The lamp, I think. Fayrouz is there too. She . . . she looks upset."

"Can you tell where they are?" Naima asked.

"It's hard to see. They're outside? I . . . I don't know. You look." Fanta thrust the telescope at his sister.

Sahara held her breath as she watched Naima raise it to her eye. "I don't see anything but the torches."

"Fanta, what were you doing when you saw Magda?" Sahara asked.

The last few minutes had taken their toll on her cousin, fear stealing the color from his warm brown skin. "I was just playing with it, looking around the chamber."

There had to be a reason he could see El Ghoula and his sister couldn't. "Were you thinking about anything?"

He shook his head. "Well, not at first. But then I wondered where the lamp had been hidden when it was down here."

"That's it!" Sahara turned to Naima. "You have to *think* about what you wanna see. Remember the story. 'When raised to the eye, it allowed the viewer to see whatever he desired.' You were gonna say *desired*."

"I see Magda!" Naima cried out a second later. Kitmeer jumped up in response to the urgency in her voice. "She's outside. It's windy. Her veil's blowing." She tilted the spyglass. "You were right, Fanta! I see Fayrouz. She's standing in front of a metal railing. The whole city's below." Naima lowered the scope, but her eyes remained wide open.

"What are you doing? Why did you stop?" Sahara shouted.

"Because I know where they are—el Borg."

Sahara had heard that name before, but where? She racked her brain until a memory from her first night rushed back— the cylindrical tower hovering over Cairo. *The highest point!*

Sahara grabbed the spyglass from Naima's hand, asking it to show her what she needed to see. Before her, a tattered scroll unraveled, revealing a string of words. Though they were written in Arabic, she had no trouble reading them in the glass. *When the moon and Saturn align, the two that must not join become one, unlocking what has been hidden in the dark. But take heart, for all is not lost in the light of love's promise.*

"All is not lost!" Sahara cried, lowering the tube. "We have to stop El Ghoula. We *can* stop her. Yesterday, Umm Zalabya said something about the moon and Saturn and how I'd have to make my way to the highest point before sunrise. I thought it was more of her gibberish. But she was trying to tell me what we have to do now. I know there's something down here that's gonna help us wake everyone up. But first, we've gotta get to the tower so we can keep Magda from releasing the jinni." Sahara's eyes darted to her watch—5:30 a.m. "How much time do we have till the sun rises?"

"Thirty minutes until the morning adhan," Fanta said. "It'll take us almost that long to get there by car. And we still have to climb out of here and grab Baba's car keys."

"We're *not* going to drive. Baba would kill you for taking his Fiat! We'll use the sigada." Naima's eyes flashed to the carpet underneath their feet.

Sahara's breath grew shallow. She'd rushed over so quickly to Fanta's side she hadn't realized she was standing on it. She resisted the urge to lunge off. Nothing bad had happened so far, and besides, now wasn't the time for running away. "I'm not sure how this thing works, but maybe it's been down here all these years for a reason."

"I thought you said we're not supposed to use any of the magic," Fanta pointed out.

"I know." Sahara bit her lip. "But sometimes rules, even ones that have been around forever, are meant to be broken. We can't let El Ghoula open the lamp. We can't let her hurt Fayrouz."

Naima squeezed her shoulder, her eyes gleaming brighter than ever. "We'd better sit, though." She took a seat, instructing Kitmeer to lie down at her side. "I could barely stay standing when it just floated in the same spot for ten seconds."

Sahara lowered herself next to Fanta. Crossing her legs, she gripped the edge of the carpet with one hand and a wool tuft from its center with the other.

Think of it like a ride at the fair. Hopefully, no one would throw up or worse—

"Ready?" Naima asked from the front. That's if this thing had a front.

Sahara turned to Fanta. He nodded, looking as nervous and ready as she felt.

"Ready," they called together.

Naima snapped her fingers as her mother had done earlier.

The carpet came to life with a jerk, rising off the ground. Sahara held on tighter.

"Whoa!" Fanta blurted out. "Okay, what do we do now?"

A one-of-a-kind carpet that could transport whoever sat atop it to any place they wished. "We make a wish," Sahara said.

Naima nodded. "I wish for you to take us to el Borg!"

Those were the last words Sahara heard before the carpet took off. Whatever sorcery the rug possessed allowed it to shrink its passengers and itself to a size tiny enough to fit through the curves of the tunnel. Sahara squeezed her eyes closed, expecting to crash into the refrigerator, but to her great surprise, its door swung open. They flew into the shop and toward the locked gate, which also submitted to the carpet's power, instantly lifting before them. Zooming through, they careened up into the twilight sky.

As they whizzed past the pillars of the mosque, Sahara felt a jolt course through her body, returning her to normal size. She didn't dare look down until the carpet reached its desired altitude, slowing slightly and beginning to fly straight. The warm wind whipped her hair in front of her eyes. No scrunchie could withstand its power. She squinted through her curly tendrils, spotting the lights of the buildings and the cars below. They appeared like miniature versions of themselves, as they had from the airplane.

Fanta lifted his hands in the air. "This is amazing!"

It *was* amazing—terrifying too—but unbelievably amazing! Sahara unwrapped her fingers from the carpet and held up one hand. She felt a sudden urge for more freedom, letting go with the other and placing it on Naima's shoulder. "Woohoo!" she yelled into the sky.

Naima glanced back and beamed, entirely in her glory, then raised her head. "Ya Allah, your world's beautiful!"

Kitmeer followed suit, lifting his snout and delivering his own skyward jubilation. *Ow-oooooooooh!* His howl traveled deep into the universe, touching the heavens, then falling back to earth. The stars seemed to join the reverie, relishing their final twinkles before the sun seized the celestial throne. Sahara had never felt so alive.

The carpet flew over the glistening waters of the Nile, extending like tree branches through the city. Before Sahara left for Cairo, Amitu had told her all about the river, referring to it as "the heart of Egypt." It was hard to believe that was only last week, and now she was zooming high above a world as spellbinding as the dark magic she was trying to protect it against.

"We're almost there." Naima pointed to the illuminated tower ahead.

The rug tilted down, forcing Sahara to grab hold once more.

"How do we stop this thing?" Fanta shrieked.

"I don't know!" Naima shouted. They were headed straight for the tower.

Sahara shut her eyes, bracing for a collision. Instead, her body lurched forward then back as the carpet came to an abrupt halt.

She slowly opened her eyes. *Thank God!* They were hovering a few feet above the observation deck of el Borg.

"Naima, if you're going to sit in front, you better control this thing," Fanta hissed. "I thought we were going to die."

"Ma'lish," Naima shot back an insincere apology. "Magic carpet of ancient times and infinite power, be sure to stop more smoothly next time for my *dear* brother."

Sahara scanned the round deck. There was no sign of Magda, Fayrouz, or anyone else, but she didn't want to take any chances. She brought her finger to her lips and nodded toward the tower. "Shh."

Naima was the first on her feet, holding her arms out to maintain balance as the carpet swayed in the air. Kitmeer watched her closely. "They're here. I can feel it," she said, then jumped toward the deck.

Sahara threw her hands over her mouth, stifling a scream as her cousin leaped through the small stretch of air between the carpet and the tower. Sure, the metal rail around the deck would prevent her from falling to her death, but still, they were *hundreds* of feet above the ground.

When Naima safely landed, she gestured for Kitmeer to join her. He scooted back, folding his ears down. It was the first time Sahara had seen the dog hesitate where her cousin was concerned.

"*Now* you choose not to follow her." Fanta stood up and wobbled to the front of the rug. "Ta'ala," he ordered Kitmeer to come as he hopped down next to Naima, but the dog didn't budge.

Sahara carefully rose and walked toward Kitmeer. *Don't look down.* "It's okay, boy. I know you're scared. I am too. But we've gotta do this."

Just then, a piercing scream came from inside the tower. El Ghoula *was* here.

El Borg

There was no time to wait for Kitmeer. After throwing one final glance at the brightening sky, Sahara leaped to the tower. She raced after Naima and Fanta, losing sight of them as they circled the observation deck. The wind blew fiercely, making it hard to keep her eyes open. She pushed through it, stopping short of hurling into her cousins' crouched bodies. They'd come to a halt in front of a set of wooden doors leading into the tower. She knelt beside them and caught her breath.

Their eyes were wide, mirroring the fear that flooded her. But they had to keep going—Fayrouz's life was on the line. Sahara reached for the knob and turned it, opening one of the doors enough to peek inside. Ceiling lights illuminated a small tiled hallway with steps leading downstairs. The murmur of voices traveled up, but it was impossible to make them out over the wind.

She needed to get closer. Sahara slid through the gap

between the doors. Her cousins quickly followed. She tried to eavesdrop from the top of the steps, but it was still too hard to hear. They'd have to head downstairs. *Light as a feather,* Sahara told herself as she crept. As she reached the landing where the staircase made a quarter turn, there was no mistaking Magda's icy timbre, though Sahara picked up a slight tremble in it.

"I'll . . . I'll give it to you." The lamp shook in her gold-cuffed hand. "Then will you leave me alone?"

Only the lower half of her wedding gown was visible from the steps. Behind her, wooden chairs encircled tables covered with white linens and set with dishes and silverware. *A restaurant?* Sahara froze as a figure wearing a gray cloak came into view.

"After you hand me the lamp, I'll have no need for you."

Sahara turned to her cousins. They were just as confused. Who was talking to Magda?

"I have what I came for," the mystery woman continued. "And thanks to your precious wedding, Zainab Salem and her family can't get in my way when I finally unlock the lamp."

"I'm done helping you!" El Ghoula yelled. "I should never have agreed to any of this."

"Why? Didn't you get what you wanted?"

"I wanted him to love me, but I loathe what I've become." Magda's voice was full of sorrow. "Here. Take it and be gone."

Sahara listened in disbelief, her heart racing. *What's happening?*

El Ghoula turned over the lamp to the cloaked hand, then fell to the ground with a thud.

"Naima!" Fanta cried as his sister sprinted down the steps. Sahara reached for her arm but missed.

The next voice was her cousin's. "The lamp belongs to my family! We are its protect—" She let out a scream.

Sahara and Fanta bolted downstairs. When they reached Naima's side, Sahara gasped, understanding her cousin's distress. It took a moment for her stunned brain to register that the cloaked woman with the lamp in her hands was none other than—

"Fayrouz," Sahara muttered as her grandmother's maid, once so unassuming, boldly loomed over a slumped Magda— her wedding dress spread in a messy heap and the tiara of flowers askew on her head. "It's been *you* this whole time?"

"Of course it's been me." Fayrouz flashed a sinister smile. "You were too busy watching the wretched El Ghoula. You never saw me coming." Her words thundered through the restaurant.

Sahara caught a flicker of silver around her neck. *Could it be?*

Fayrouz turned on Magda, who was struggling to get up. "How dare you not tell me they were awake? Have you gone soft?"

"We're awake because we didn't drink your gross sharbat!" Naima blasted.

"What a shame. I heard it was unforgettable," Fayrouz scoffed. "Just ask your parents. Oh, that's right—you *can't*."

Fanta pointed a shaking finger at her and shouted, "Shaytana!"

"Devil—definitely not. Witch, sorceress—why not?" Fayrouz shrugged. "And now"—she held up the lamp—"this is back where it belongs before that fool Ala el-Din stole it from my family."

Perhaps it was shock, but Sahara felt the floor underneath her move.

"Finally, the prophecy will be realized. The power in the lamp will be mine!" She reached under her cloak.

"My necklace!" Sahara cried.

Naima headed straight for Fayrouz. "Give it back!"

Murmuring words Sahara couldn't understand, Fayrouz thrust her hand at Naima. A gust of sand burst out of her palm.

"Nooooo!" Magda jumped in front of Naima, intercepting whatever dark magic Fayrouz had unleashed. The blow hit El Ghoula straight on. She flew back into one of the tables, sending the dishes crashing. Though she'd absorbed most of the blast with her body, the rest of it diffused, knocking everyone else off their feet.

Sahara struggled to stand as Fayrouz's cloak swept past her toward Magda. Fayrouz snatched the gold cuff from Magda's wrist and stepped on it, smashing it into pieces. "I told you love would be your downfall," she sneered, heading up the steps and out of sight.

Fanta crawled toward his sister, who wept over Magda. As Naima lifted her head, Sahara could see that she wasn't moving—only it *wasn't* El Ghoula anymore.

45

Good Catch

N oora," Naima cried, removing the off-kilter tiara from her friend's brown hair, which up until a few minutes ago had been Magda's golden tresses. Tan skin, bearing life's marks and scars, had also taken the place of El Ghoula's unmarred porcelain.

Blood trickled down where the gold cuff had been. Fanta took off his bandana and tied it around Noora's wrist. Within seconds, a deep red stain spread through his white hachimaki.

Sahara couldn't look. She jerked her head toward the floor-to-ceiling windows that surrounded the room. She was already feeling off-kilter, but the glimmering lights of the city and the boats on the Nile made her dizzier. She fell to her knees.

Fanta pointed to the carpeted floor, then circled his finger.

Shock wasn't the only reason for her light-headedness— the floor *was* moving. Her gaze flitted to the lavish tables. This had to be the spinning restaurant her father had told her about. When Sahara could finally speak, she turned to Naima. "How?"

"I . . . I don't know." Her cousin twisted her head, searching for an answer. Not finding one, she looked back at an unconscious Noora. "All along, I thought *she* was El Ghoula, but it was Fayrouz. How could I've been so wrong?"

"*We* were wrong," Sahara said, finally managing to stand.

"Fayrouz had us all fooled. It's not your fault." Fanta touched his sister's shoulder.

Just then, Noora began to stir. Naima squeezed her hand. "We're here," she assured her as a small bird flew past the windows.

Sahara's eyes darted to her watch—five minutes until sunrise.

"Sahara!" Naima cried.

But she was already on her feet, running toward the steps.

Sahara flew up the stairs. *Operation Stop the Real El Ghoula* would have to be driven by instinct—Naima would be so proud—because there was no time to outline a plan. She had to stop Fayrouz now. And not just because generations of Salem women had sworn to guard the lamp, but because Fayrouz had taken too much—Sahara's hamsa and her family—from *her*. *No more,* Sahara vowed.

As she reached the doors to the observation deck, Fanta jumped in front. "I can't let you do this." He stopped to catch his breath.

"Get out of my way, Fanta. I have to."

"I know . . . I can't let you do this *alone*."

"Okay, but we've gotta hurry."

Together they pushed the heavy doors open, meeting resistance from the wind.

"I don't see her," Fanta shouted over its roar.

Sahara gestured to keep circling the deck. Where could Fayrouz be?

The answer came in the form of a swift burst of sand from above. *Whoosh!* It hit Fanta straight in the chest. He collapsed onto the ground.

"Fanta!"

Sahara jerked her head up. The witch stood balanced like a tightrope walker on a cable extending from one of the tower's communication antennae, the ascending sun blazing behind her. Her cloak blew furiously in the wind.

"You're too late," she bellowed.

Sahara's eyes darted toward her cousin. His chest moved up and down. He was breathing. *Thank God.*

"Fayrouz!" Sahara yelled her name over the wind. "You have to stop before anyone else gets hurt."

"Stop? You can't stop me. You couldn't stop me from stealing your precious necklace right from under you." The flashes of silver around Fayrouz's neck made Sahara burn with anger. "Did you stop me when I ordered Magda to seize the lamp from your family's riffraff shop? My only regret is that she was too weak to cut your throat. Who are *you* to stop *me*? Go back to where you came from. This isn't your home, and this isn't your fight." Her face contorted into a menacing smile as she lifted her outstretched palm.

Unlike before, the twister of sand that emerged from it started slow, growing in intensity as it spun in Sahara's direction. It propelled her backward. She bore down, but she was no match for its strength. Fayrouz had been right. She couldn't stop her. As the morning adhan broke through the howling wind, Sahara's stomach lurched. It was too late.

"Time to claim my destiny!" The witch reached into her cloak with one hand, withdrawing the lamp. She wrenched the necklace over her head with the other and thrust it into the air, jabbing it into the lamp's lid. Sparks flew as the hamsa rotated a half turn. A loud click echoed through the air. An indigo light brighter than Sahara had ever seen exploded out of the sapphire. Within seconds, the lid popped open with a giant boom, shaking the tower. *The jinni.*

There was a second of eerie silence. Then, smoke burst out of the lamp like steam from Amitu's pressure cooker, releasing what it had held back for centuries.

"It's happening!" Fayrouz yelled, her eyes wild as she shot sand out of her palm.

It smacked Sahara's face, making it hard to breathe. Shutting her stinging eyes, she fell to her knees. But then the blackness behind her lids was replaced with the familiar blue glow of the amulet. She felt herself spinning like she was riding the Round-Up at the fair, only faster this time, pulling her away. After the spiraling stopped, an unexpected quiet followed.

She opened her eyes. *Our living room in Queens?* A very pregnant Amani, draped in a sheer white scarf, sat on the couch. A radiant smile illuminated her face.

Mom.

"Sahara," she spoke softly to her stomach. "Don't forget who you are, *all* of who you are. I know it won't always be easy having one foot in America and the other in Egypt. But they are both *your* lands. If you can hold the two of them in your heart, you will be as wondrous as the desert I named you after. The Sahara wouldn't be what it is without the individual grains of sand." She kissed her hand and placed it on her stomach. "My daughter, you are as vast and powerful as the great desert. And so is my love for you—always. Ma tinseesh."

Tears fell down Sahara's cheeks at the certainty in her mother's expression and the promise of her words. She *had* forgotten. She'd spent so much time worrying that the only way to belong was to choose *one* country, *one* culture, *one* way of being over the other. However, no matter how hard she'd tried, neither felt right on its own because she wasn't only one. She didn't need to choose. She just needed to be brave enough to allow herself to be both—to be *more*—and open her heart to her mother's love. She'd always held it at a distance, afraid that if she allowed herself to get too close to it, the guilt would swallow her whole. But now, as she fully let it in, the guilt *didn't* destroy her. It released its grip on her heart, letting the light through.

The moment Sahara reached out to her mom, the spinning returned, whirling her away. She squeezed her eyes shut to keep from getting dizzy. Quickly, the twisting stopped, and a ferocious gust knocked her off her feet. She was back at the tower.

Let go and use the key. Her mom's words echoed over the roar. Sahara unfurled her tight fingers and stood up, leaning into the wind. For once, giving up all the plans and lists—all the control and guilt.

When she dared to open her eyes, there was no jinni in sight. Instead, the radiant silver rays emerged from her fingers. The more Sahara surrendered to the fullness of her being and her mother's steadfast love, the bigger and brighter they became. They pulsed through the glowing lines of her palm, gathering at the center until a dazzling beam burst forth. It joined the sapphire's light, slamming the lamp's lid shut with a *boom*, followed by the loudest *click* Sahara had ever heard.

Fayrouz stared dumbfounded at her hand. "Come on, lamp. Show me what's inside you!" She shook it vigorously.

"It won't work. *I* locked it. Because this *is* my home, and this *is* my fight." The words glided out of Sahara's mouth.

"It has to work. The . . . the prophecy." Fayrouz fiddled with the amulet, positioning it differently and jamming it against the lamp. Fireworks shot out as they made contact, forcing her to yank them apart. She tried again and again, gnashing her teeth, the veins in her face bulging and contorting. Each time the lamp and amulet resisting more until raging flames engulfed her hands.

Sahara's conviction grew with every failed attempt. "It's hurting because they're not meant for you. The amulet and the lamp belong with my family. *We* are their guardians."

Fayrouz growled in pain. A whirlwind rushed out of her mouth, blowing out the fire. An odd look came over her face. She stared at Sahara as if she were seeing her for the first time. Fayrouz let out a piercing whistle, summoning a cyclone of sand that enveloped her own body. "If I can't have them, no one can!" Fayrouz yelled from inside it, heaving the necklace and the lamp into the air before disappearing into a cloud of dust.

"Nooooo!"

Sahara jumped onto the railing as gravity took hold, sending the lamp and amulet careening down toward the Nile. Out of nowhere, something whizzed after them. It moved so fast Sahara couldn't be sure what it was. Had Fayrouz changed her mind and decided to make a last-minute dash for them?

Whatever it was zoomed back up, heading right for her. Sahara shielded her face, expecting a crash, but it didn't come. She slowly brought down her hands. Floating in front of her was the enchanted carpet, with none other than Kitmeer at its helm—the lamp's handle dangling from his mouth and the amulet around his neck.

"Good catch, Kitmeer!" Sahara cried, bursting with joy.

The dog reveled in her praise, his tail wagging wildly.

"Ow-oooh." A weak howl came from behind.

Sahara twisted around. Her cousin held his chest, trying to sit up. "I'm so glad my sister taught him how to catch."

"Fanta!" Sahara ran to his side. "Are you okay?"

His lips curled into a faint smile. "Tab'an."

"Of course." Sahara giggled as she threw her arms around him.

"Oof. Easy, please."

Sahara quickly let go. "Sorry. I'm just so happy you're all right."

"Faan-taaa, Saa-haa-raaa!"

Sahara turned in the direction of their yelled names. They'd come from Naima. She slowly approached, a weary Noora leaning on her for support.

"We're okay!" Sahara shouted back.

Once she'd reached them, Naima helped Noora to the railing and hurried to her brother. "What happened?"

"Fayrouz happened. But thanks to Sahara, she's gone."

Naima looked to her cousin, the worry in her face dissolving. "You did it."

"I had help." Sahara stepped out of the way to reveal the hovering carpet and its pilot.

"Kitmeer!" Naima screeched.

The dog jumped off the rug and ran to her, dropping the lamp at her feet.

"Good boy!" Naima inspected the lamp closely, her eyes

glimmering with the wonder she'd held at bay when she was forced to hand it over to El Ghoula. "All these years of reading about you," she told the gleaming lamp before shifting her attention to Kitmeer. She rubbed his head. "You saved us again." A loud gasp escaped her mouth when she spotted the amulet around his neck. "The necklace too!"

"I was waiting to see how long it would take you to notice," Sahara teased.

Naima removed the silver chain from his neck. "I believe this belongs to you." She placed it over Sahara's head.

It was a first. In the brief time the amulet had been in her possession, Sahara had never actually put it on. "How does it look?"

"Meant to be." Naima winked.

Kitmeer circled Noora, his tail wagging.

"He recognizes you," Naima said.

But as Kitmeer sniffed the bloody bandana around her wrist, he whined.

"Ma'lish." Noora assured him it was all right. "I'm sure I gave you good reason to bite me. I'm sorry . . . I'm sorry to you all. Let me try to explain."

Sahara looked around uneasily. The top of the tower, where Fayrouz had recently disappeared into dust, wasn't exactly the best place for explanations. Besides, she was anxious to get back to the chamber and find a way to reverse the sleep spell. "What do you say we get out of here before Fayrouz decides to return?"

Everyone nodded at once. Kitmeer barked at the rug, which descended to the deck's floor in response. He lowered himself onto the front as Sahara and Naima helped Noora and Fanta aboard.

Naima turned to her cousin. "Ready?"

"Magic carpet, take us home," Sahara declared into the early-morning sky.

PART FIVE
Home

To Cairo

985 CE

For the rest of her life, Morgana would never forget the horrors of her last night in Baghdad, but after today, she'd never forget the magic that followed either.

"It's done." A light wind carried Husnaya's words through the valley.

Morgana kept her eyes shut a little longer, holding on to the vision of the girls who would come after her, united by what *she* had started.

"Morgana . . . Morgana, can you hear us?"

She nodded, looking up from her crouching position to find the trio still surrounding her. The silver-blue shield had disappeared, leaving the sky darker than she remembered. Her eyes drifted to her outstretched palm. The necklace was gone.

"Take heart, my dear," Julnar said. "Thanks to you, the Circle of the Four was complete, instilling the amulet with enough energy to lock the lamp."

Morgana threw a glance at her other hand. Without *her*, the infamous lamp wouldn't be locked. Not bad for a silly servant girl. Despite being torn between love and duty, between a past she yearned to hold on to and a future she didn't yet know, the corners of her mouth curled. She couldn't remember the last time she'd smiled. Her eyes flashed from the lamp to the sack. For once, the duty to protect the treasures felt like *her* duty— not just a promise she'd made her mawlay.

Morgana stared at the inky sky. There would always be darkness, but the stars would glimmer nonetheless. The light was worth protecting. She had no idea what the winds of fate had in store, but she trusted they'd carry her to where she needed to be.

She stood tall and asked, "What now?"

"Now you and the treasures journey to your new home," the mermaid queen answered.

Home.

Julnar fixed the violet scarf that had slid down Morgana's shoulders. "Home and family await you on the other side. If you ever need us, look to the moon. We will find you."

The mermaid queen beamed, mirroring the hope blooming within Morgana. She wasn't alone, and if she'd had the courage to leave one home, surely she'd have the courage to create another.

Morgana walked over to the sack and slid the lamp back inside. When she turned around, Peri floated in front of her, holding a glass vial as big as her fairy body.

"One more treasure for your journey. This should replace the stolen apple."

Morgana reached for the vial, eyeing the clear liquid inside.

"Healing water from the enchanted spring guarded by the four lions," Peri explained. "And though it may appear like a tiny amount, its supply is as endless as its miraculous source."

"Shokrun." Morgana thanked her, then carefully placed the vial inside the sack. She looked up at the dark sky. It was too late to go anywhere tonight. "I'll have to set out for Jericho in the morning to secure another horse." Her heart wrenched thinking of poor Nasser out there on his own. "It's at least an hour on foot."

"There is not enough time for that," Husnaya insisted. "You must get the lamp and the rest of the treasures away from here before the dark witch realizes you were in possession of *more* than an enchanted apple."

"Almaz?" Morgana nodded her head toward the seer's horse.

"No, of course not. Almaz stays with me. But I *can* think of something else." If Morgana didn't know better, she'd have sworn a grin flashed across the solemn seer's face.

Husnaya snapped her fingers, and in an instant, the carpet flew out of the sack, unraveling itself with a few pops. Peri whizzed around it.

"I already told you my duty is to keep the treasures safe, not use them. First, the spyglass, now the rug."

Ignoring Morgana's objections, the carpet floated toward

her and descended at her feet. If she were to use it—just this once—it *would* be the fastest way to get the treasures to safety.

"I think we can make another exception." Julnar winked as Husnaya set the sack down in the middle of the rug, then tapped on the space beside it.

It was now or never. Morgana stepped aboard, her legs wobbling.

"Might I suggest sitting?" Husnaya took hold of Morgana's hand and helped her lower herself down.

"Picture where you wish to go," Julnar instructed.

Morgana closed her eyes, envisioning her aunt in the land of the Great Pyramids. "To Cairo. I wish to go to Cairo!"

"Then, tarta'ay." Peri snapped her little fingers. In a flash, the carpet lurched back and shot up, twisting past the canyons and zooming through the night sky.

47

Noora's Story

The carpet came to a stop in front of Sittu's balcony. Sahara had hoped it would drop them off in the chamber so they could start looking for an antidote, but she was relieved not to have to shrink again. It had been like having her insides mixed up in a blender, then spat out.

Having regained his balance, Fanta helped a still unsteady Noora onto the terrace. It seemed the blow he'd received from Fayrouz's hand hadn't been as debilitating as the one Noora had taken for his sister.

Passenger free, the rug hinged forward as if taking a bow, then swiftly headed back to the shop. Sahara stretched over the rail, trying to catch a glimpse of it shrinking, but it zipped in too fast for her to see anything more than a flash of light.

Fanta hurried inside, returning with a shawl to cover a trembling Noora.

"Do you remember anything from when you were Magda?" Naima asked as Kitmeer lay down at her feet.

"A little, but it's all jumbled up." Noora rubbed her forehead.

"I remember things like you holding the kitab you gave me for my birthday, Fayrouz threatening to expose me in front of the building, my wrist bleeding at Sittu's table, and Sahara asking me if I hurt Omar." Her voice broke. "I didn't hurt Omar, did I?"

Naima shook her head. "You would never hurt him. Even under Fayrouz's curse."

"I hope you're right. I should never have gotten involved with Fayrouz." Noora's eyes grew distant like Amitu's did before a long story. *Crap!* They had to get to the chamber.

Noora went on to explain how she'd met Fayrouz at the bakery in town where she was posing as a local family's maid. "She made me believe she wanted to be my friend. She had this way of getting me to tell her things." Her cheeks flushed. "Even how I felt about your khalu Omar."

"Told you," Naima whispered to her brother.

"That's when she began working me." Noora's voice hardened with anger. "Promising me there *was* a way to get Omar to love me . . . to marry me. And Allah forgive me, I listened to her dark plans."

"Noora, he *already* loved you," Naima said.

"He did? I hoped, but I didn't know. And it was more complicated than love. A doctor and an uneducated maid—your grandmother would never have approved."

Sahara wasn't sure how these things worked, but she couldn't imagine Sittu standing in the way of Khalu Omar's happiness. After all, she'd accepted the despicable Magda because she believed he loved her.

"Can we get off all this love business and back to how Fayrouz turned you into Magda?" Fanta asked.

Noora rubbed her wrist, still covered with his stained bandana. "The bracelet."

A shiver ran down Sahara's spine as she recalled how Fayrouz had smashed the cuff into tiny pieces. Removing the bracelet from Magda's wrist at the henna night had not been enough. It needed to be destroyed to undo whatever weird transformation witchcraft it possessed. "Where did it come from?"

"From the shaytan himself. Fayrouz can wield the blackest of magic. One night, she played on my weakness, persuading me to give her a strand of my hair," Noora cried, running her fingers through her tresses. "She set it on fire with incense, tossing them both into a boiling pot of water and whispering words I couldn't understand. After a few minutes, she stuck her hand into the pot and pulled out the bracelet, clasping it on my wrist before I could change my mind."

"It all makes sense now. That's why Magda turned up when you disappeared." Naima's voice shook. "I was so worried."

"I'm sorry for making you worry . . . for everything. I should never have trusted El Ghoula."

Hearing Noora refer to Fayrouz with the same vile nickname they'd used for *her* when she was Magda caught Sahara and her cousins off guard, to say the least. They exchanged nervous glances while Noora wiped her tears with the shawl and asked, "How did you know where to find us?"

"There's so much to tell you," Naima answered.

Sahara thought about stopping her cousin from divulging the family's secret, but what was the point? Noora already knew so much.

Naima pulled the journal out of Sahara's backpack. "Not only are the lamp and carpet enchanted, but there's also a spyglass, just like in the tale of Prince Ahmed and his brothers." She flipped to the story.

Naima had never gotten to what the last brother discovered because of what Fanta had seen in the glass. "What did the third brother find?" Sahara asked as Naima held the page in front of Noora.

"'Prince Ahmed headed in a different direction,'" Noora read, "'arriving in Samarkand, where he purchased a magical golden apple.'"

"That's the problem," Naima huffed. "The apple was the *one* item from the story not in the chamber. I checked the curio."

"What's so special about this apple, anyway?" Fanta asked.

Noora looked up from the journal. "Its scent can heal any illness."

"Even a sleeping spell," Naima added.

Sahara's body suddenly felt very heavy. She lowered herself

to the ground. The chamber was missing the one thing that could help them wake everyone up.

Noora scanned the story, stopping at one page. "What about the vial? It appears in the second part when Ahmed meets the jinniya. She guides him to the enchanted spring guarded by the four ferocious lions—"

"And thanks to Peri," Naima interjected, "he *does* get past the lions, giving him enough time to fill a vial with its magical water."

Hearing the words *lion* and *vial* in the same sentence jogged Sahara's memory. She'd seen a vial with a lion's cap in her last dream. Sahara sprang up. "Come on!" She grabbed her cousins and sprinted to the chamber.

48

Wake Up

Are you sure about this?" Fanta asked as Sahara twisted the vial's cap.

"I'm nervous too, but I know it'll work." Her mom would never steer her wrong.

"Me too," Naima said, but that was no surprise. She'd always believed.

Sahara bent down beside her dad. Her hands shook as she concentrated on tilting the vial to release only a few drops. So many still needed the curing elixir. *Please don't spill, please don't spill.* A few beads fell onto her father's lips.

The effect of the enchanted water was instantaneous. Her dad's eyes fluttered open. He stretched his arms and legs.

"It's working!" her cousins yelled.

"Dad," Sahara cried as her father let out a big yawn.

He smiled, but his face turned to worry as he spotted tears running down her cheeks. He propped himself up onto his elbows. "What's the matter? Is everything okay?"

"*More* than okay." She hugged him tightly.

He peered over Sahara's shoulder at the others surveying him.

"Hello, Fanta, Naima, and Naima's dog." He hesitated. "Does your grandmother know this dog is here?"

Sahara had never been so grateful to see her father's eyes bulge. She started to stand when he noticed Noora. He hastily straightened his pajamas and hair, then cleared his throat. "And you are?"

"I'm Noora. I can't tell you how happy I am to see you awake, Ustaz Kareem."

"Noora, as in Sittu's maid who disappeared?"

"Aywa." She nodded, smiling.

"How long have I been asleep?"

Sahara jumped up. "We'll explain everything later. We're not done yet!"

The enchanted water continued to work its magic, a few drops to the lips immediately breaking the spells on Sittu, Khaltu Layla, and Uncle Gamal. Even though the vial seemed to replenish itself after every drop, Sahara and her cousins still poured it sparingly, not risking it running out. Noora insisted she be the one to wake Omar, slipping out before Sittu had time to ask where she'd been for the last few months. That left Sahara and her cousins to field the ambush of questions from their family, now gathered at Sittu's dining table.

"Maybe we should have left them asleep?" Fanta joked nervously.

But it was time for the truth. And Sahara wasn't the only

one who thought so. Sittu stood up and took hold of the girls' hands. For the next thirty minutes, they wove together the threads of their family's story: Morgana's promise, the chamber's treasures, Amani's journal, Sahara's necklace, Naima's sacrifice, and the lamp's return.

Afterward, there were a few awkward moments of silence before chaos erupted.

"Now what?" Sahara asked.

Naima shrugged. "We run?"

But then, Sittu yelled, "Khalas!" and no one moved.

"I know it's hard to believe. I know you have lots of questions. Trust me, I'm as shocked as any of you. *More* actually. *I* let Fayrouz into our home. *I* allowed her to conspire against us. But what's done is done." Sittu took hold of Sahara's and Naima's hands. "Fanta, ta'ala," she urged her grandson to come over. When he reached his sister's side, Sittu continued. "If it weren't for the bravery and cleverness of these three children and this dog, we'd still be asleep. We must thank Allah for watching over them when we couldn't and for blessing them with the strength they needed to protect our family's legacy."

Pride swelled in Sahara's heart. They had defended it. And after today, *their* story would be part of that legacy.

Sittu bent down and rubbed Kitmeer's head. "Thank you for being loyal and courageous." The dog spread his body onto the floor, offering up his belly for a rub. "One step at a time." Sittu chuckled. She moved toward Naima and Fanta, opening her arms wide enough to embrace them both and whispering words that made them beam.

Then Sittu turned to Sahara. "And you. All these years apart." She sighed. "Then here you are, when we needed you most."

Sahara's lip quivered. She placed her head on Sittu's shoulder, spotting Omar and Noora in the doorway.

"Omar!" Khaltu Layla ran over to her brother. "You're all right?"

"I am now." He smiled at Noora.

Naima walked over. "Have you told him?"

Noora nodded. "Everything."

Sahara watched as her uncle reached for Noora's hand and tenderly squeezed it. Perhaps he'd held on to her all along. While Noora had been lost to everyone else beneath Magda's ugliness, she had not been to him. He'd managed to see her when no one else could.

"Ladies and gentlemen," Omar announced. "I'd like to introduce you to my bride, Noora Abdullah."

Still dressed in the tattered remnants of Magda's wedding gown, Noora turned to him. "Omar, what are you doing?"

"What I should have done a long time ago. Don't you see? Spell or no spell, I've always loved you. I should've told you that. I should've told everyone that."

"Izay? After everything that's happened?" Noora asked.

Sahara froze as Sittu headed toward her former maid, eyeing her for a few *long* seconds. "You were wrong to trust

Fayrouz," she finally said. "But so was I. You are *not* responsible for her wicked spell or what it made you do." Sittu kissed her cheeks. "Welcome, my daughter. You have always been a part of our family. I can't think of anyone more worthy of my son."

Phew!

Noora brought her hands to her heart and bowed her head in gratitude. "Shokrun, Madame Zainab."

"Does this mean we have to get dressed up for another wedding?" Fanta groaned.

"Tab'an. *This* is the wedding we should've had all along!" his mother said.

"Yes. And it'll be here in Shobra," Sittu added.

"But without the sharbat!" Uncle Gamal bellowed.

Everyone laughed, even Sahara. The returned sound of her family's rowdy banter was music to her ears, though her stomach clenched at the mention of the sharbat.

"What about Fayrouz?" Sahara whispered to her grandmother. She had seen the mania in the witch's eyes when she'd momentarily unlocked the lamp. She couldn't imagine her giving up the hunt for it. "What if she comes back?"

"We'll be ready," Sittu answered firmly. "But now we have the rest of Shobra to wake up."

Wedding: Take Two

Sahara's next week in Cairo was tame compared to the first, though still memorable. Omar and Noora wed once more in the Room of Photos. Their second ceremony may have lacked the drama of the first, but it more than made up for it in sincerity. Nobody had trouble witnessing their virtuous union.

Afterward, a boisterous zaffa of local musicians and neighbors accompanied the couple from Sittu's building to the rooftop of Umm Zalabya's garden for the reception. There was no shortage of yasmeen, and thanks to Ismail's fool and tameya stand, guests enjoyed fava bean and falafel sandwiches all night long. The girls had helped Sittu and Khaltu Layla make two heaping platters of wara ainab. Sahara smiled, eyeing a few lumpy ones at the top.

DJ Fanta grooved to a mix of Arabic and American tunes he played on a gleaming boom box, which he and Sahara had won in a bet after Mustafa Fouad insisted on a rematch and lost *again*. Sahara danced the night away in a silver dress she'd bought with Sittu yesterday—the hamsa tucked securely underneath. She hadn't taken the necklace off since they'd reclaimed it from Fayrouz, vowing to never let it out of her sight again. She pressed it to her chest now before taking her first sip of orange Fanta.

Her cousin watched closely. "What do you think? The best, right?"

"Mmm. Tangy and sweet—just like you. I love the new bandana, by the way."

Fanta sported a new karate hachimaki, featuring two dragons facing each other and the Japanese character for the mythical creatures.

"It was a gift from Baba." Fanta beamed with pride. "He gave it to me last night along with the best news. In two years, the International Junior Karate Tournament is coming to Cairo. I can be crowned champion in my own city!"

Naima strode over, rolling her eyes. "Just when we thought you'd become humble."

Kitmeer hurried over but not before giving Umm Zalabya's cat another growl.

"I almost forgot." Fanta reached into his pocket and removed three white bandanas. "You might not be karate masters, but you're still the toughest girls I know."

This was *huge* coming from Fanta. Sahara bowed her head. "Thank you, Mr. Miyagi."

He smiled, then turned to Naima, handing her two. "One's for you and the other is for Kitmeer, the brave."

Naima flung her arms around her brother. Sahara couldn't be sure because it had happened so fast, but he might've hugged her back. Fanta rushed to his boom box station, escaping further mushiness.

Naima knelt and wrapped Kitmeer's bandana around his neck. After his heroism at el Borg, her parents were hard-pressed to find a reason not to keep him. She may have kicked Fanta out of her room, but she'd happily cleared space for her canine roommate.

A wave of warmth traveled through Sahara as she watched Kitmeer sitting by Naima's side, his new silver tag glinting in the moonlight. Naima had always been his home, and he, hers.

"Sahara." Her cousin said her name softly.

Over the last two weeks, they'd become as close as sisters. Sahara reached for her hand. "I know. I'm gonna miss you too."

"I'm sure you want to go back to New York, but promise you'll visit again next summer. We make a good team."

"Just like logic and magic." Sahara winked. Lately, she'd started thinking of them less like polar opposites but more like partners that made each other better. M&M'S and popcorn on their own were great, but M&M'S corn—whoa!

"And of course I'll come back. I promise." Sahara placed her other hand on her heart, torn between the desire to return to one home and the wish to stay in another. But she wasn't going back to Queens empty-handed. She'd be returning with her *own* special suitcase of stories and memories.

As for the bride and groom, Omar's eyes never left Noora,

who sparkled in a wedding dress handed down from Khaltu Layla. The tiara she'd worn at the first wedding sat on top of her veil. She'd asked Sittu to help her salvage it. They replaced the torn fabric flowers with some of Umm Zalabya's yasmeen. "I might not remember much of my past as Magda, but it's still a part of me. I must respect it for what it was."

Noora was right. The past—all its triumphs and failures, joys and sorrows—should be honored. For the beautifully messy present stands on its shoulders.

50

The Sahara

On the eve of Sahara's last day in Cairo, Sittu surprised her with tickets for the Sound and Light show at the Pyramids. Sahara sat next to her father, gazing at the Sphinx, perched regally atop the desert, the three Great Pyramids behind it.

"I can't believe I'm finally here!" She pointed a finger at the illuminated monuments. "I've seen so many pictures and heard so much about them. And now they're right over there."

"Sahara, *you* are in the Sahara." Her dad beamed, then stared into the far reaches of the desert. "How I wish your mother were here," he said quietly.

Sahara drew a deep breath, quieting the familiar voice of guilt in her head. It had gotten way less noisy these days, drowned out by the resounding certainty of her mother's love. She twisted in her seat and smiled at her newfound family. "She *is* here."

The Pyramids suddenly went dark while the voice of the

show's narrator boomed from the direction of the Sphinx. The half lion, half pharaoh's eyes began to glow.

"For five thousand years, I have seen all the suns men can remember come up in the sky—"

As the evening desert wind blew on her face, Sahara's father whispered in her ear, "What do you think?"

"A-maz-ing."

"More amazing than Merlin's Crossing?"

Even though Sahara hadn't been, she couldn't imagine anything topping tonight. Still, there was no chance her dad was getting out of taking her. "We're still going," she whispered back. When she returned to New York, maybe she'd write to Merlin's people about getting a MAGIC FIVE pin sooner rather than later. After all the Mystery, Adventure, Gallantry, Imagination, and Curiosity of the last two weeks, surely she deserved an honorary one.

For now, Sahara basked in being *in* the Sahara. At twelve, she was a fraction of the desert's age. But like each of its countless grains of sand, she held the power of the vast desert within her. And though from time to time she might forget, she would always be wondrous.

◇─○─◇

Acknowledgments

Scared and ready. Like Sahara, that is how I felt when I undertook the daunting task of writing a novel. For so long, I'd kept the seeds of its story and characters close to my heart. Here are the people who helped me tend them so that one day they might bloom onto the page:

The South Bay Writers Workshop, who listened and gave gentle feedback to the first passes of *Daughters of the Lamp*, graciously allowing me to read first so I wouldn't be late for picking my daughters up from school.

Cara Stevens and Marie Campbell, whose friendship and inspiration over warm mugs of coffee all over the South Bay bolstered me through my first draft.

The MGPies, who are the best writing family in all the land. I am blessed to count myself among you.

Maeeda Khan, my AMM mentor, who recognized that there might be something in the pages of my story and generously helped me figure out how to develop it.

My fellow AMM R8 MG mentees, who were the most

incredible travel companions on the journey of taking apart our manuscripts and putting them back together.

My agent, Kelly Dyksterhouse, who encourages me to write the stories I am called to tell, how I need to tell them, no matter how hard or complicated it gets.

My editor, Polo Orozco, whose editorial instincts are killer. Thank you for laughing at all the right places and asking the tough questions when needed.

The Putnam and Penguin Young Readers teams, who have been wonderful collaborators and made my debut experience stellar.

Bethany Bryan and Cindy Howle, whose ninja copyediting skills are fierce.

Yuta Onoda, whose gorgeous art brought Sahara and Morgana to life on the cover.

My husband, Scott, whose belief never wavered. Thank you for giving me the space to get lost in Sahara's world and holding down the fort until I returned.

Lucy and Violet, who are my greatest treasures and the inspiration for all things magical.

Mom and Dad, who showed me that where I come from is as important as where I'm going.

My big bro, childhood's ultimate mischief partner and adventure copilot, I can't imagine the trouble we would've gotten into with a flying carpet!

My grandmothers, Fatma and Mahassin, whose arms I felt

around me every time I sat down to write. My precious life stands on your shoulders.

Mamalou and Papalou, who are life's most amazing cheerleaders. Hooray, it's finally here!

Randy Walden, who has always encouraged me to embrace all my parts. My world is so much bigger because of you.

My former teachers: Mrs. Taylor, who showed me it was possible to create my very own book. Though, I daresay the process has gotten more complicated than the third-grade days of pencil, scrap paper, and cardboard. Mrs. Tiffany, whose eyes glimmered when she read my twelve-year-old stories, making me believe I just might be good at this writing thing.

My former students, who have kept my feet grounded in the beautifully messy parts of childhood.

Finally, although I spent many solitary hours writing the words on the previous pages, I was not alone. For art is a co-creation between the individual and the infinite well of creativity, sourced by the ingenuity of all those who came before and the promise of those who will come after. My readers, I can't wait to see the wondrous blooms of your artistic seeds.